Penelope Gilbert

and the Children of Azure

Emily A. Steward

Clean Reads
www.cleanreads.com

PENELOPE GILBERT AND THE CHILDREN OF AZURE
Copyright © 2016 EMILY A. STEWARD
ISBN 978-1-62135-585-4
Cover Art and Illustrations Designed by CHAD STEWARD

I dedicate this book to my parents who always encouraged me to be myself and follow my passion, to my awesome husband Chad who continues to support and accompany me on this crazy journey, and to our daughters Addison, Coraline, and Aria who inspire me each and every day.

Chapter One

In her short lifetime, Penelope Gilbert had been left behind at various places a total of twenty-seven times. The first time was on a trip to the science museum on her third birthday. She'd been quite frightened then, but now at the age of thirteen, she'd grown accustomed to it.

Penny's parents were both scientists and were so absorbed in their experiments, they hardly knew they had a daughter. Her family was quite wealthy, but you'd never know it from looking at their small, shabby, brown house. Theirs was the only shabby house on the block. Luxurious homes of all shapes and sizes lined the streets of the upper-class neighborhood.

The only concern they had was for their latest project. They'd lock themselves in the basement and work long into the night, much to the disapproval of the neighbors who were often kept awake by the sounds of banging and tiny explosions.

Boom!

Penny clung to the ladder she'd propped against the house as another explosion shook the rickety

building. Yesterday she'd noticed the blinds on the small basement window had an almost imperceptible bend that was just big enough to see through. That morning, she would find out once and for all what they were working on. Closing one eye, she stood on her toes, looked through the blinds, then sighed. Thick smoke cloaked the room in obscurity.

She liked to imagine her parents were working on something important. Maybe they were trying to cure cancer or perhaps they were working on a top secret government experiment, training rats to be intelligent undercover agents. If she believed their work was crucial, it made her feel better about being ignored.

Startled, she nearly toppled from her perch as the window banged open. She stifled a cough as the smoke puffed out the window into her face.

"I told you we used too much," her mom said.

Penny ventured another peek through the blinds. The smoky room glowed with an eerie blue light making everything look like something out of a science fiction novel. She half-expected there to be an alien lying on the table. Instead she just saw some rather ordinary tools and beakers containing different colored liquids. A tin of opened cat food lay among the various items. Hopefully they were using the cat food in some sort of experiment and not eating it for lunch.

Her father, a tall slender man with dark brown hair and flecks of gray around his temples, stood on a chair near the window, fanning the smoke outside. "It wasn't too much. We simply didn't add enough!"

"If you say so dear..." her mom replied, pushing up her black, thick-rimmed glasses as she picked up several broken test tubes that littered the floor.

Penny's mother was a short and slightly plump woman with striking red hair, which she usually kept pinned back in a clip. Today she wore a pea-green blouse with turtles in top hats printed all over it. Her skirt was black with yellow stripes going around and around. It made her look somewhat like a bumblebee. She held back a giggle as she imagined her mother buzzing around the garden collecting pollen. The poor flowers would probably collapse.

As the smoke cleared, a wooden door became visible. It stood upright in the center of the room. An elaborate series of gears and tubes surrounded it. The blue light seemed to be coming from the crack in the door. A strange triangular symbol was carved into the wood. She pulled the blinds down to get a better look.

Her mom's eyes shot up to the window. Penny gasped and ducked down. The motion tipped the already precarious ladder backward. She yelped and waved her arms uselessly as she fell into the neighbor's rose bushes.

The bushes tore at her arms and legs. She lay stunned for a moment before throwing the ladder off and rolling to her feet. Shouts drifted from the window. Pulling leaves from her hair, she dashed to the front of the house. Had they seen her? And what was up with that door? She looked down the street, just in time to see the school bus pull away from the curb. *Great, now I'm going to be late.* She grabbed her backpack from the porch and used the front step to climb onto her dad's bike. It was way too tall, but as long as she didn't need to stop, she should be okay.

She still felt a bit shaken as she rode toward school, but she couldn't afford to be late again. Her teacher, Ms. Puddlegum, already had it out for her.

Penny bent down over the handlebars and pretended she was being chased by a biker gang. She told herself if she could just make it to the train tracks, she'd be safe. They wouldn't dare follow her into rival gang territory. It would be suicide. Gunshots whizzed by her head as she revved the motor on her Harley. She was so close. She could see the tracks now. She leaned forward and pedaled with all her might. *I'm going to make it!*

"Hey, Penelope!" The familiar voice jolted her back to reality. She looked around in dismay wondering where the shout came from. It was the voice of Nancy Ferrill. Nancy was one of the prettiest girls in school, and unfortunately also one of the meanest. She and her gaggle of girls often made her life miserable. "Yeah that's right. I'm talking to you, Penny loafer!"

Her ears grew warm. She hated it when people called her that. Determined to get far away, she put her head down and pedaled faster, but it was no use. She didn't see Nancy 'til it was too late. Before Penny could react, Nancy stepped from behind a hedge and stuck a tree branch right through the spokes of her bike. With a yelp, she toppled off her bike into the neighbor's large duck pond.

"Well it looks like you're not a 'lucky Penny' today." Nancy laughed from the edge of the water. A couple of her impish friends stood next to her, giggling at their leader's wit. They all smacked large globs of pink bubble gum like cows chewing their cud. Nancy tossed her long, blond hair over her shoulder and sneered. "You do have some awesome bike skills though!" Her friends thought this was also a hilarious thing to say, because they flew into a new fit of laughter.

Penny clenched her fists. Why couldn't Nancy just leave her alone? "Thanks, maybe I'll teach them to you sometime."

"Fat chance of that, see you at school, hon...and don't worry, the wet look is in."

Penny got up and pulled the algae from her clothes and bicycle, as Nancy and her friends jogged toward school. At least her hair was probably lying flat now, she thought with a wry smile. Feeling a bit wobbly, she walked the bike the rest of the way.

Class had already started when she arrived. The teacher stopped speaking as Penny walked to her usual seat at the back of the room.

"Thank you for deciding to join us today, Miss Gilbert," said the deep, scratchy voice belonging to her algebra teacher, Ms. Puddlegum. Her teacher was likely born with a cigarette in her mouth. She would sometimes have bouts of coughing that forced her to go outside and, "get a drink of water," every hour or so during the day. When she would return, the odor of her cigarette left her smelling like a crowded bowling alley.

"Hey, did you wet your pants or something?" a freckled boy named Richard said, snickering.

Ms. Puddlegum glared back at them. "Is everything all right back there, Miss Gilbert, or do you need some time to chat?"

"I'm fine." Penny put her head down on her desk as class resumed, and wished she was transparent. The desk felt cool on her forehead and smelled like an eraser.

She liked sitting in the back. From this vantage point, she could see everything going on in the classroom. Better still, no one usually noticed her, including the teacher. She hated being called on. Not because she didn't know the answer. She hated it because she could never remember the answer on the spot. The solution would just jump out of her head, leaving her mind utterly and completely blank.

She also liked this spot because it was right next to the window. Her class was on the second floor, and she had a wonderful view of the whole schoolyard and the woods beyond. It was a perfect spot for daydreaming. She would always imagine herself out on the lawn doing all sorts of heroic things. She pictured herself fighting villains of all shapes and sizes, rescuing the hostages, and doing it all while looking completely cool and composed.

Today she was an undercover agent infiltrating an enemy warehouse. Right as she was about to detonate the explosives in the building, an enemy agent dressed in a black suit burst in and exclaimed in a raspy voice, "I'm not outside, I'm right here, Miss Gilbert. Miss Gilbert... Will you kindly join the class?" Penny was jerked back into reality by the words of Ms. Puddlegum and the laughter of the class.

"I'm sorry," she mumbled, feeling warm again. Her theory wasn't working well today. She was drawing more notice than ever. She wished she could just disappear until this awful day was over.

"Thank you. Now class, let's review yesterday's lesson, then I want to hear some presentations starting with the back row."

Penny's stomach dropped. *Presentations, oh no! How could I have forgotten? And of course they're starting with the back row today. Fire drill. Please let there be a fire drill.* She needed to get her mind on something else. What she needed was to somehow blend in like a chameleon so that she would be passed by. As the teacher's voice croaked on, Penny rested her chin on her desk, and tried to regulate her panicked breathing. She rather liked this view too. By resting her chin down low on her desk and squinting one eye, she could make it look as if the stapler on her desk was about to staple Ms. Puddlegum's fat head. She smiled, welcoming the distraction.

Her attention shifted to the stapler itself. She gazed intently at it, taking in every detail. It was a pleasant red and silver in color that looked cool to the touch. She thought about how it was made, how it worked, and how the metal felt in her hands. The bolt on the side was like a shiny metal eye staring back at her, calm and nonchalant. She almost envied the staplers of the world. *I'll bet you never have to worry about algebra,* she thought.

As she continued to study the object, the room seemed to spin. Her stomach felt funny. She tried to raise her hand to be excused, when she realized to her alarm that she couldn't move her arm. She tried to raise her head, but it felt as if it was stuck to the

desk. Had she spilled glue? Her heart raced as she realized she had absolutely no feeling in her arms or legs. What was going on? Was she paralyzed? She tried to call out to her teacher or her classmates, but her voice didn't work either. No one even glanced her way. Everyone's attention was focused on the student presentation at the front of the classroom. For some reason Penny was very aware of her mouth. Her jaw felt strong and powerful and she had the sudden desire to bite something.

"Where has Miss Gilbert gone?" Ms. Puddlegum asked. How could she not see her? She wasn't *that* short. The other children around her shrugged. Was she invisible? Nancy looked right at her. Could she see her? Why was she the only one who could? Nancy got up and strode over to Penny's desk, her fist raised. She realized to her horror that Nancy was going to hit the top of her head and knock her jaw into the desk.

She stood right over her now. Penny closed her eyes and braced herself for the blow. With a deft movement, Nancy shoved a piece of paper in Penny's mouth and slammed her fist down on her head.

Kachunk!

Startled, Penny opened her eyes. She was a bit dizzy, but other than that she felt unharmed. In fact, she felt great. She wanted to staple something else. Wait, staple? She wanted to do what?

A new wave of panic mixed with curiosity overcame her. Looking at the window, she could see the outline of her desk. She saw not one, but two staplers reflecting back at her. Swallowing, she now realized why she felt so odd.

She was the second stapler.

How could this have happened? She gave a start as the bell clanged.

"All right class, you can go. Don't forget to do problems one though twenty-five," Ms. Puddlegum said.

No wait... Don't leave me here! She tried again to call out to her fellow classmates. All the children pushed toward the door in a frenzy like a stampede, never even giving her a second glance. What if she remained a stapler forever?

This has to be a dream. Wake up! Please wake up!

With a sigh, Ms. Puddlegum waddled to her chair. "Ninnies, the whole lot of them," she said. "Why do I even bother teaching these nincompoops?" While looking through the papers on her desk, she absently thrust her finger deep into her left nostril.

Aw man, I did not need to see that. She wanted to look away from what Ms. Puddlegum was doing, but it was like a train wreck, and she couldn't take her eyes from it. Besides, she couldn't even turn her head if she wanted to, as staplers have no necks.

Just as she was imagining the rest of her life as a stapler, spending many a dull day stuck perpetually in math class, there was a knock at the door.

Looking up from her papers, Ms. Puddlegum croaked, "Yes, John, what is it?"

"Mr. Thompson would like to see us all in his office immediately. He says it's important."

"Yes, all right, all right. What is it this time? Did he lose his toupee again?" Ms. Puddlegum chuckled.

"Most likely," he replied with a snort.

Penny felt helpless. *Great, now I really am alone.* As she sat there on the desk that smelled of erasers in the room where she had spent many long, boring hours, she wondered if her parents would notice that she hadn't come home that night. *Will anyone notice?* That thought made her feel worse than remaining a stapler forever.

All of her life she wished that she were invisible. This wasn't what she had in mind. Glancing at the stapler next to her, she wondered if all the staplers in the world started out as children. Was this her last day of being Penelope Gilbert? Was she doomed to forever be a nameless stapler, spending her days biting paper? No, no it couldn't be. She could fight this. She knew she could.

Penny tried to recall if she had done anything to cause herself to turn into a stapler. *Let's see... I was leaning on my desk. I was looking at the stapler... Maybe if I imagine myself as me again, I can turn back.* Closing her eyes, she thought of the reflection she had seen that morning of the pale girl in the mirror. She envisioned herself sitting at her desk and concentrated on her limbs, her fingers, and her toes. Suddenly she felt lightheaded. Her whole body tingled, and she could feel her extremities stretching.

Just then, to her dismay, the familiar voice of Ms. Puddlegum drifted in from the hallway, breaking her concentration. "I forgot my cigarettes. I'll be right back."

Sudden unbidden memories of the algebra teacher with her finger in her nostril invaded Penny's mind. With a grimace, she opened her eyes to clear the image from her thoughts.

As the classroom came into view, she realized she could raise her head. She let out a cry of exclamation, or rather a croak. Wait, what was wrong with her voice? In just that moment, Ms. Puddlegum came through the door. Her teacher took one look at her, screamed, and fainted in the doorway.

Penny turned toward her reflection in the window, her chest tight with fear. To her utter dismay, Ms. Puddlegum's large frog-like face stared back at her from the glass.

Now that she had full use of her legs, she wasn't going to stick around that horrible classroom any longer. Jumping to her feet, she stepped over her fallen teacher and ran down the hallway. Bewildered students cleared out of her way as she dashed by the lockers, her dress billowing behind her like a giant cape.

Once outside, she paused a moment, wheezing. Years of smoking had sure taken their toll on her teacher's lungs. After regaining her breath, she waddled over to her bike and attempted to hoist herself onto the seat. "Maybe I was better off as a stapler," she muttered. With a loud grunt of determination, she managed to pull herself up and onto the bicycle.

She steadied herself for a moment, then turned her bike onto the road. As swift as her stocky legs would carry her, she headed home. Ignoring the curious looks of people nearby, Penny leaned forward and struggled to make her bulk move faster up the slope which now felt like a small mountain.

"Give her some air, Henderson."

"I know what I'm doing. I do teach biology after all."

"Maybe you should give her mouth to mouth."

"Er... I'm not qualified to do that! I'm only a biology teacher you know."

"But you said—"

"Quiet, she's coming to!" Ms. Puddlegum's eyes flickered open. Henderson and Vice Principal McConnell stood over her.

"Are you all right, Doris?" McConnell asked.

"Yes, yes, I'll be fine in a moment."

"I was just about to save your life by giving you mouth to mouth resuscitation," Henderson blurted.

McConnell rolled his eyes. "Come on, let's get her up onto her chair."

The two men huffed as they struggled to hoist her up.

Henderson took out his handkerchief and fanned Ms. Puddlegum. "What happened, Doris?"

She thought a moment before answering. "I...I saw myself."

"You what?"

"I saw myself just over there, sitting at that desk..." She pointed toward Penny's empty seat.

Henderson frowned. "Well you did hit your head pretty hard."

"No, I know I saw it!" she insisted.

McConnell's eyes grew wide. "I'll just get you a glass of water," he offered. McConnell shuffled down the hall as Henderson tried to calm Ms. Puddlegum.

"Maybe you should go home and lie down for a bit."

"I'm not crazy! I know what I saw. I need to get out of here before my evil twin comes back to finish me off!"

"Evil twin? Doris, can you hear yourself? Think logically. Why don't you go home, get some rest, and maybe even take a little vacation. Your work must be straining you more than you realize."

"But, but," she stuttered.

"Tomorrow, tell me all about it tomorrow," Henderson said in the most soothing tone he could manage.

"Oh, but I am interested in hearing all about it, Ms. Puddlegum," said the raspy voice belonging to Principal Thomson. He had been standing just outside the door. His eyes gleamed with excitement as he spoke. He stepped into the room with McConnell in tow. "I'm very interested indeed."

Chapter Two

Penny shut her bedroom door and heaved a sigh of relief. The relief was temporary however. One look into the small mirror on her dresser made her heart sink. The same gaze that she had spent every school day avoiding now stared back at her.

"Ms. Puddlegum," she moaned. Her chins jiggled with each syllable. It would have been fascinating if she wasn't so horrified. She had to fix this.

Maybe if I look at a picture of myself, it will help me focus. She looked around her room, searching for something suitable. Her parents didn't take photos. There were no pictures on the mantle, or family Christmas photos. Her gaze came to rest on a blue book on her shelf. *Ah, last year's yearbook. That should work.*

She took the book down from the shelf and settled down on her bed. The bedsprings creaked and complained under the pressure of her new posterior. Flipping through her yearbook reminded her of all her not-so-fond memories of that year.

She did have one real friend at her school however. His name was Connor Bryant. Connor and Penny had been friends since Kindergarten. He was tall, lanky, and a wee bit clumsy. Kids often called him Connor the Crane, or Crane for short, and the name stuck. If it wasn't for him, school would have been unbearable. She grinned as she ran her fingers over what he had written in her yearbook. "Keep this signature for when I'm famous. One day it will be worth its weight in ink!"

All right, no distractions now, she chided herself. Skimming through the pictures of her classmates, she found what she was looking for. Her pale, thin face stared up at her from the page. Why hadn't she combed her hair that day? She automatically reached up to smooth the hair that was no longer hers.

Looking close, she studied her features from her hazel eyes to the curve of her jaw. She started to feel lightheaded and sleepy. Her eyelids drooped. *No, I can't give up now,* she thought as she struggled against her grogginess. She sat back up and reached for the book again and stopped mid-reach. That was *not* Ms. Puddlegum's hand. Penny sprang from the bed and looked at her mirror. Could it be? She closed her eyes and tried again to be sure. Yes, yes it could. Her own face beamed back at her from the mirror. She never thought she would be so glad to be herself.

As she eased back onto her bed, she was pleased to hear the usual tiny squeaks that her mattress made. Now that she was herself, she wasn't quite sure what to do next. Her mind buzzed with all kinds of thoughts and questions. Should she try to get help? Who would she even go to? A doctor? A scientist? No, definitely not a scientist. Penny knew all too well from watching television that a scientist was the last person you wanted to go to. They would only do all kinds of experiments on you and give you shots. She shuddered at the thought. She had always been a little squeamish with needles…and blood…and doctors, not to mention clowns, pigeons, and turnips.

She should be able to trust her own parents. Then again, she didn't want to be their next experiment either. Maybe she was just going crazy. That alternative wasn't comforting.

Feeling drained, she soon drifted into a restless sleep. She dreamed that hundreds of stapler-wielding frogs, who all bore the face of Ms. Puddlegum, chased after her. She kept searching for a place to hide, but every time she thought she was safe, one of them would find her and croak, "Miss Gilbert, will you kindly join the class?"

She was so exhausted, she slept all afternoon and into the evening. She woke once during the night to find her heart racing and her body covered in a cold sweat, then drifted back to sleep, this time dreaming of scientists trying to make her eat turnips.

꙳

When Penny awoke the next morning, she felt as though yesterday had been a crazy dream. She almost had herself convinced.

Almost.

She checked her reflection in the mirror just in case and laughed at how silly she was being. Perhaps her imagination had gotten the best of her, or maybe she'd just been under too much stress. She decided to go to school that day as if nothing happened, and maybe it hadn't.

When Penny arrived at school, she noticed a man in a black suit standing just inside the door. The man stared at her for a long moment. His gaze made her chest feel tight. She couldn't seem to shake the ominous feeling that something dreadful was about to happen. She tried to ignore the knots forming in her stomach as she walked to class.

All thoughts of the mysterious man left her head as she went through the door. Jason was back from vacation. Penny had liked Jason Breedon since third grade. He wore a dark green shirt and his hair had the, I-just-got-out-of-bed-and-I'm-too-cool-for-a-comb kind of look. He gazed out the window with a bored expression on his chiseled features. She imagined what she might say to him, picturing how he might say hello, and maybe even say her name. Her thoughts of intellectual conversation and witty rapport came to a sudden halt as she tripped over the metal trashcan. She tried to catch herself, but her awkward flailing only made her feel more embarrassed. As she lay sprawled out on the floor, gazing at the room of laughing faces, she noticed Jason laughing along.

"A-ha-ha, what a klutz!" he exclaimed.

Penny put her head down and scrambled to take her usual seat. *Maybe Jason isn't so attractive after all. He does kind of look like a hyena when he laughs.* She comforted herself by imagining the whole class as a group of idiotic hyenas.

Class should have started by now. All of the students looked toward the doorway, waiting for Ms. Puddlegum to walk in. The class grew restless after several minutes ticked by. Ms. Puddlegum was never late. A woman finally entered the classroom. She was pale and thin. Probably in her late thirties. And she wore a starched, dark blue pantsuit and wore her auburn hair back in a tight bun. Another man like the one she had seen in the hallway followed close behind her.

"Good morning, class-s-s." The woman's voice came out in a sort of hiss. She bared her teeth in what she must have thought was a warm smile. It was more like a grimace of pain. "My name is Mrs. Snyder. Your teacher isn't feeling well. I will be teaching you in her absence. Perhaps you've noticed some extra security around here today." She nodded her head toward the man in the dark suit. "Don't be alarmed. We are just trying to keep you all safe."

"Safe from what?" a boy asked.

Mrs. Snyder ignored him. "Open your books to page ninety-seven." No one dared to tell her that they were actually on page one-twenty-four. The man in the black suit moved to the corner of the room where he stood with his gaze darting from student to student. What could he be looking for?

"Class, today you will all be taking a special test."

The class groaned in unison.

"What kind of test?" asked a girl.

"The test will not be like any that you've done in the past. It is...special. There is a prestigious school that only accepts a few students a year. It is a school for gifted children." Mrs. Snyder walked between the rows of students as she spoke. "Recently, a spot has become available, and we are looking for a suitable candidate to fill the position."

"But we haven't had any time to study," groaned a student in the front row.

"No study will be necessary. I will take you back, one at a time, starting with the first row. The rest of you, do the problems on pages ninety-seven through one hundred.

Penny's stomach felt queasy. Something wasn't right about this whole thing. She tapped her pencil as, one by one, she watched her classmates follow Mrs. Snyder down the hall. The minutes ticked by, matching the rhythm of Penny's pencil. The clock grew louder with each passing moment. She tried to focus on the math problems in her book, but the numbers all blurred together. Several hundred pencil taps later, she breathed a sigh of relief. Class was almost over. She wouldn't have to take the test until tomorrow.

Mrs. Snyder tapped on the desk. "Attention class. After lunch today, I want you all to come straight back so we may continue the testing. No one is to leave school today until they have taken this test."

"But I have a paper due in my biology class today," objected a short boy with glasses.

"No exceptions. This is a priority."

"But I—" he began. The bell rang, holding back any further objections the boy might have had.

"Remember," Mrs. Snyder called out, "straight back here after lunch." Penny's heart sank. She wouldn't be able to avoid the test after all. She got up from her desk and made her way to the front. She was anxious to escape the scrutinizing stare of Mrs. Snyder and her ominous-looking goon.

As she moved through the hallway, she realized that there was no escaping the men in dark suits. There were two standing on either side of the front doors, one standing by the water fountain, and she counted three more stationed throughout the hall. What was going on? No one else seemed to be the least bit bothered by the men, though one boy seemed a bit irritated that one of them was blocking his locker.

As she walked into the lunchroom, she tried to see if Crane was at their usual table. She spotted him lounging back in his chair, 'scoping out the place,' as he liked to say. His dark hair sometimes hung in his eyes, but it didn't seem to bother him. Not much ever did. He was laid back and never took things too seriously. He was the kind of boy who could be popular if he cared about that sort of thing. He didn't, and Penny was thankful for that.

"Hey, where were you yesterday?" he asked, as she joined him at the table.

"I had to go home and take care of something. It was nothing." She hadn't decided if she should tell him about yesterday. It seemed crazy, even to her. He studied her face for a moment.

"Are you feeling okay?" he asked. "You look like my neighbor's cat when it got cornered by a Doberman."

"Yeah, I guess I'm just nervous about the test today."

"What test?"

"I don't know. Some special test. Aren't you tak-ing it?"

"I haven't heard a thing about it."

"That's odd. I guess it's just our class. I wonder why."

"Beats me." Crane pulled out his usual peanut butter and pickle sandwich and began devouring it. Peanut butter was now smeared across his chin and some had mysteriously gotten in his eyebrow.

"You wanth thum?" he asked between mouthfuls.

Penny grimaced. "That's all right. I think I'll just go grab an apple at the counter."

"Your loth," he called after her.

She noticed two more men standing near the en-trance as she picked up a tray. For some reason their presence gave her goosebumps. She could feel their eyes watching her as she made her way back. Just as she was sitting down, she saw a large boy approach-ing their table. It was the self-proclaimed school bully and Crane's arch nemesis, Pete Sims. Crane liked to refer to him as, 'Potato Pete,' behind his back. He did indeed look like a giant potato. He was round and his face had scars from a bout of acne, leaving his face looking as if it were about to sprout.

He plopped himself at their table and began to eat Crane's chocolate pudding. "Hey there, Crane the Pain." He sprayed the table with pudding as he spoke.

"Whoa there, Petey. I don't think you need any more pudding there, pal. We wouldn't want you to outgrow your 'skinny jeans.' Oh wait..." He looked Pete up and down, pretending to examine his pant legs. "Those aren't supposed to be 'skinny jeans,' are they?" Pete scowled, but couldn't seem to think of anything to say in return. Instead he just sputtered and grabbed Crane by the collar of his shirt.

"Hey, let's all just calm down." Penny held up her hands, trying to pry them apart.

Pete pushed him back in his chair. "Lucky for you I don't have time to pound you right now. I have to prep for a test this afternoon. Oh, but here's your pudding back, pal." He dumped what was left of the pudding in Crane's lap.

"Yeah, thanks for that," he called as Pete stormed off. "Well, I'm glad I wasn't eating hot split pea soup like I was yesterday."

"Way to look at that silver lining." She handed him her napkin. "Hey, Connor, have you noticed those guys in black?"

He looked up. It wasn't often that she called him by his real name. "Yeah, I've noticed."

"They're kind of creepy aren't they? They just stand there staring. It looks like they're waiting for something to happen and are ready to pounce."

Shrugging, Crane went to work trying to get the large brown stain out of his jeans. "Naw, they aren't so bad. Maybe they just need a hug. You should try it," he said with a grin.

"But don't you think it's strange that they just appeared to 'protect' us from something?" she continued, ignoring Crane's attempt at humor.

"I'm sure it's just some crazy thing that the school board thinks is a big hazard." He kept wiping the stain on his jeans, but it only made the spot larger. He frowned and tossed the napkin on the table.

"You're probably right, but maybe we should do a little investigating. What do you think?"

"I say this sounds like a job for…" As he was speaking, he jumped onto the table. "…Super Crane! Oh, and I guess his little sidekick, Penny, too."

"Shh. Knock it off, you idiot. We don't want to draw attention to ourselves."

It was a little late for that. Curious students and faculty now were all looking toward their table.

Crane slid to the floor. "It's all right. Nothing to see here." Once everyone had lost interest, they lowered their voices to a whisper.

"Okay," she began, "we've got about twenty minutes left before class starts. We've got to hurry if we're going to find anything out."

"Right, but how are we going to sneak past those guys?" Crane nodded his head toward the men standing guard.

"I dunno. Maybe nobody is watching the hall. Let's check it out."

The hallway was empty except for one man. His body stood straight and rigid. A blank, unfeeling expression was on his pasty, white face.

"Well at least it's just one guy," she said.

"Yeah, but he is standing right in front of the office. He will see us, for sure."

Scanning the hallway, Penny's gaze paused on the girl's restroom. "Okay, so here's what we'll do."

Doreen Hadley liked her job, for the most part. She could file her nails between phone calls and even play a little solitaire. Being the receptionist for the principal gave her plenty of juicy gossip to talk about too. She heard everything that went on in Principal Thomson's office. Not lately though and that drove her crazy. The principal had been sending her away all day, just when something interesting was going to happen. Mrs. Snyder sat in the waiting room again. She'd been coming in a lot.

"Doreen?" Principal Thomson's voice came out over the intercom.

"Yes, sir?"

"Doreen, would you please send Mrs. Snyder in?"

"Right away, Mr. Thomson." Doreen sighed. She knew this was going to be another one of those conversations she was dying to listen in on but couldn't.

"You can go in now."

"Thank you, Mrs. Hadley," Mrs. Snyder replied in a soft, condescending tone. As Mrs. Snyder walked into the principal's office, Doreen felt a ray of hope. *Oh, he hasn't sent me away yet. Maybe I will get to have a little listen after all.*

"Oh, and Doreen," Principal Thomson's voice came over the intercom again, "would you please go pick up a turkey sandwich for me? You know the place I like."

Doreen crumpled a paper in her fist in frustration as she replied in a syrupy sweet voice, "Right away, sir." Her hand was on the door when she stopped. She just had to know what was going on with all the shady new personnel roaming the halls. Thomson could wait five more minutes for his silly sandwich. A person could learn a lot in five minutes if no one knew they were listening.

Penny was looking toward the principal's office with apprehension when they heard a shrill scream. The man in the black suit marched to the door and disappeared inside. She looked at Crane with raised eyebrows. He shrugged and shook his head. Moments later the man emerged and returned to his post as if nothing had happened.

Penny swallowed. "Okay, that was weird."

"You think? Are you sure you still want to do this?" Crane's eyes darted back to the safety of the cafeteria.

"Nope. Let's go." Penny made her way to the girl's restroom adjacent to the principal's office. Crane just needed to get the man to look away long enough for her to sneak across. He drew in a deep breath and approached the man in the suit.

"Hey, there is a girl stuck in a toilet in the girl's restroom upstairs!"

The man glared down his nose. Up close, Crane realized there was something odd about the man's eyes. They were...black.

"Go and get the janitor then."

"But, uh, it's an emergency! She's a piano player, and it's her most talented hand that's stuck. You wouldn't want to be responsible for ruining her career would you? Well would you?"

"Leave now, boy." The man spat out the words as if they were bitter in his mouth.

Crane racked his brain. They said they were there to protect them from something, but protect them from what? A threat to the school, perhaps?

"Well, sir. One more thing."

"Yes-s-s-s?" The man spoke without turning his head.

"She was acting...odd."

The man's head snapped toward him. "What do you mean?" he asked, his eyes now locked on Crane's.

"I mean like suspicious. She acted like she was up to something before she went in there. Everyone noticed. I mean, honestly, how does someone get their hand stuck in the toilet unless they are up to some sort of mischief, right?"

The man's eyes flashed. He turned and walked toward the staircase.

"Do you need me to show you the way?"

"Get back to your scheduled lunch break," the man barked as he hurried around the corner.

"Uh, yeah I'll get right on that, sure."

Penny peeked around the door. "Is the coast clear?"

"Yeah, it worked. I can't believe it!" Crane gave her a quick high five.

"All right, nice one! I guess we can both go in then. Come on."

They opened the door slowly and took in their surroundings. The waiting room was empty.

"Mrs. Hadley must be on her lunch break," Penny whispered.

Muffled voices were coming from inside the principal's office. She pointed toward the filing cabinet located next to the door. They both crept behind the cabinet and put their ears to the wall. Penny recognized Mrs. Snyder's voice on the other side of the door.

"Yes, we have found one," she said, "but the sensor detected two. I am confident that we will find the other child soon."

They heard some low mumbling that they couldn't decipher. It was the voice of Principal Thomson.

"Yes, I suppose they will," Snyder said. Principal Thomson must have been standing on the other side of the room. Penny motioned for Crane to follow her. The two crept closer and put their ears to the door as they listened.

"They can't exterminate them fast enough as far as I'm concerned," Thomson's voice boomed.

Penny's eyes widened. Were they talking about what she thought?

"They may be of some use first."

"Use or not, they are vermin, and they must be killed."

"Oh, they will be, but not until they have served their purpose. You didn't hear it from me, but Lord Esmond might use them in one of his special projects."

"Really?" Principal Thomson sounded surprised. "Well, after we finish the testing this afternoon, we'll hopefully have another one of them."

"Yes-s-s," Snyder hissed. "And it's about time. All this searching is growing wearisome. At least there are only a few left. The big extermination in Azure is next month. Will you be flying up for it?"

"I wouldn't miss it for anything," Principal Thomson replied with a chuckle.

"Speaking of the test, I should be getting back to it. I wouldn't want to keep my pupils waiting too long. They are so hungry for knowledge, you know." She let out a soft chuckle. "Ahsh Ahsh Ahshsh." It sounded like a snake with bronchitis.

Penny's heart pounded and her mind raced. Extermination? They must be killed? And where on earth was a place called 'Azure'?

"All right, keep me informed. The moment you find anything, send word to me at once."

"Oh, I will."

They saw the doorknob moving at the same moment, and both had the same idea to dive behind the secretary's desk to keep hidden. Unfortunately, they tried to dive to the same place at the same time. Penny gasped as they collided. They scrambled to the desk.

She made it first, looking back in the direction of the door. Crane froze mid-crawl, his jaw dropped. He pointed under the desk. Penny bumped into something warm and flowery scented. She turned to see the glazed, unseeing eyes of Doreen Hadley staring straight ahead.

Chapter Three

Doreen's mouth gaped open and her neck bent at an unnatural angle. Penny screamed and threw herself back, knocking her head into Crane's jaw just as Mrs. Snyder strode through the door. Her eyes bulged at the sight of them.

"Principal Thomson," she called out, "we've got a problem." The principal rushed to the door and gazed down at them as if they were two naughty children who had been caught with their hands in a cookie jar.

"It's a pity you two had to come in here."

"Yes a real pity," Mrs. Snyder agreed.

"Who us?" Crane managed to squeak. "We didn't hear or see anything. Me and my good buddy were just looking for my contact lens, and... Oh, there it is!" He pinched his fingers together as if holding a lens. "Well then, I guess we'll be getting out of your way now."

Principal Thomson moved quickly to the side of the desk, blocking off their escape.

"I'm afraid that we're going to have to keep you both after class today."

3

"Ahsh Ahsh Ahshsh." Mrs. Snyder chuckled. "What should we do with them, sir?"

Mr. Thomson ran his fingers through his hair. "Well, we can't take care of them here. There would be far too many complications. It's already going to be difficult enough getting one body out of here, let alone three. Let's just send them with the others. It's simpler that way."

Mrs. Snyder rubbed her chin before replying. "Yes, that would be the easiest, wouldn't it?"

Penny shook all over. They were both enjoying this moment far too much. Why couldn't she be brave like Crane who was staring defiantly ahead? He almost looked bored with the whole situation.

"Oh, wait a minute, sir. This girl was in Doris Puddlegum's class." Mrs. Snyder held out a boney finger.

"Well then, make sure that you get her tested before we load her with the rest."

Penny's eyes darted around the room, looking for an escape. Crane must have read her mind. As Principal Thomson stepped closer, he lunged forward, knocking Thomson back into Snyder. This left a small opening for a fraction of a second and they both took it. Penny slid across the desk and Crane slipped past while they struggled to get to their feet. They were all the way through the door when they realized what a hopeless escape it was. There were two men in black suits at the door and several more lined the hall. Aside from the men, the hallway was empty. Everyone had already returned to class.

"Stop them!" sputtered Principal Thomson from the doorway of his office. The men sprang into action. Penny decided to adopt a new method of escape. It was the new scream-your-head-off-and-hope-someone-comes-to-your-aid method. Meanwhile, her friend was living up to his nickname. He quite resembled a crane as he stood on one foot with his hands in the air. He was finally getting to put all of his knowledge of karate to good use. It was too bad that all of his knowledge came from late night movies, or it might have done some good.

The men rushed at them so fast that they didn't have much time to do anything. Crane's kick bounced harmlessly off the first man and made him cry out in pain as his foot struck the man's solid muscle. Penny swung her arms as she was lifted into the air. Her fist caught one of the men in the face, knocking off the man's sunglasses. He snarled and put them back into place, but not before she caught a glimpse of his left eye. It was...metal? The center bulged out slightly more than the rest, like a large, red cat's eye. She managed to get out a few good yells before something was shoved over her mouth and nose. She caught a glimpse of Crane falling to the ground just before everything went black.

Penny awoke to familiar surroundings. She was sitting in a chair in the nurse's office. She felt a glimmer of hope. Perhaps she had just been sick and brought in here to recover. Maybe this whole thing was just a hallucination. Her hopes sank when she realized that her arms and legs were tied to the chair. Her heart beat rapidly. She could feel her forehead breaking out in a sweat. If she were to make a list of all of the terrible scenarios that she would never, ever, want to find herself in—and she could imagine many—this would be at the top of that list. *Actually*, she thought, *being in a pit of flesh-eating zombies would be at the top, but this would be a close second.*

"Ah, you're awake." Snyder didn't bother trying to hide her devious smile. "We won't keep up any false pretenses with you, Penelope." Mrs. Snyder walked closer. "There will be no fake IQ tests or pretend medical examination for traveling overseas. No, none of that." Mrs. Snyder moved in so close, Penny could smell stale onions on her breath. "We just need your blood."

Chapter Four

"Hey kid, wake up," whispered a voice in Crane's ear.

"Wha...wha's a matter?" he mumbled, sitting up. His back was sore from lying in an awkward position, and his head pounded from whatever they had used to knock him out. He was in the back of some sort of vehicle. The air was thick with a stifling humidity that made it difficult to breathe. It reminded Crane of when he would play his handheld video games under the blankets in bed for too long. He filled his lungs with the stale air then regretted it. There was a sour, musty smell that made his stomach wretch and his hand fly to his nose. He blinked as his eyes adjusted to the darkness.

A boy about his own age was sitting next to him with a look of concern on his face. He could make out the shapes of several other people who appeared to be sleeping on the floor. A larger lump was whimpering in the corner. The voice that spoke to him belonged to a pale blond boy about Crane's own age. He looked like he hadn't eaten in a week. His clothes were tattered and worn, and he had a thin pair of spectacles perched on his nose.

"Where am I?" Crane asked the boy. "And who are you?"

"Haldor Lennox at your service," he replied with a tip of his imaginary hat, "and you, my friend, are in what we lovingly refer to as the death van."

"The what?" Crane asked, even more alarmed than before.

"Oh, they're taking us to be exterminated," Haldor replied in a matter-of-fact way. At this remark, the lump in the corner began whimpering even louder.

"What? Why?"

"Something about us makes us different. We can...do things."

Crane shifted. "What kind of things?"

"Well, that kid," he said, pointing to a mousy-looking boy sleeping in the corner. "Made his tuna sandwich levitate from his lunch bag to his mouth while he was listening to a history lecture, and I hear that the kid in the corner accidentally replicated into his teacher."

"I did not. Shut up!" said the lump. Crane sat up. He thought he recognized that voice.

"Pete, is that you?"

"Of course it is, dip wad," Potato Pete squeaked. His dark hair was disheveled and his broad face was streaked with tears.

"They told me that I did so well on the test, that I was going to get a scholarship, and then they shoved me into this stupid place. Someone is going to pay for this."

"That's what they do. They tell you that you're gifted and that they want to send you to some sort of special school. Then they clamp some weird collar on you, and toss you in the death van to send you off to be exterminated." Crane noticed the silver collars around all of the children's necks for the first time. "They keep us from using our abilities somehow," Haldor explained.

Crane cleared his throat before he spoke. "I'm sorry, but I'm having a hard time believing all of this. There must be another explanation. It sounds to me like you guys are all a bit crazy... No offense," he added.

"None taken, and I don't blame you. But you must have noticed that whatever you did to get yourself in this van didn't seem normal. What did you do anyway? And why aren't you wearing a collar?" Suspicion crept into his voice.

"Um, well, I don't have any so-called powers or whatever," Crane replied. "I just overheard some things that they didn't want me to hear."

Haldor let out a soft whistle. "Wow, I guess they must be getting careless. That's the first time I've heard of them taking a normal person. Usually they just—" His thoughts were interrupted by voices outside of the vehicle. "It's best to pretend you're asleep," he whispered. Crane nodded and assumed the position of what he hoped was a convincing slumber. The door slid open with a *thud*. Two men stood in the doorway. They were struggling under the load of a squirming Penelope Gilbert. One of the men had blood dripping from his bottom lip. He had a murderous look in his eyes.

❧

"Just toss her in already, you idiot!" the man with the bloody lip said with a snarl.

"You don't have to be cross with me just because the girl kicked your lip," the other man responded in a wounded tone. The two men heaved Penny into the van. She landed hard on her side. Her elbow landed on Crane's hand. He stifled a yelp and clenched his hand into a fist.

"Well, she wouldn't have kicked me if you'd been holding her properly."

"You said that you were going to grab her feet. How could it be my fault?" The bloody-lipped man slammed the door shut, and they could still be heard arguing as they climbed into the front of the van and started the engine. She sat up. Her head hurt and her thoughts were fuzzy. She swayed back as the van jolted forward.

Crane crawled over and helped her sit up. "Are you all right?"

"I think so..." She rubbed her eyes. "What's going on? Is that Pete? Why did they put us in here?"

"Well according to Haldor," Crane began, nodding in his direction, "they are rounding up mutants to take to a slaughter house or some such nonsense. Sounds crazy, right?"

Penny gazed down at her hands. This had to be related to the incident in class yesterday. The men, the test. They were after her. She looked up at the boy with glasses. "So why do they want to kill people like us?"

Crane shook his head. "Don't tell me you believe all this sci-fi stuff. There must be some other reason. There must be, right?"

"I have to believe it." She had made up her mind. Crane needed to know why they were in this situation. He had to know the truth. "I have to believe it because it's happened to me. I know it sounds silly, but I turned myself into a...staplagh," she said as she coughed.

Crane leaned forward and cupped his ear. "A what?"

"Staplagh," she said as she coughed again.

"What's a st-pla-gah?"

"A stapler."

"A-ha-ha, that's ridiculous! You actually had me going for a minute. I thought a 'sta pla gah' was some kind of mythical creature or something." Crane stopped laughing when he realized that he was the only one who thought this was funny. "You're serious then, aren't you?"

"I'm afraid so. That's not all either." She cleared her throat and went on. "After that, I accidentally turned myself into Ms. Puddlegum." Crane's mouth twitched as he tried to hold back a smile.

"All right, all right. If you say so, then of course I will believe you. But you have to admit, this all sounds quite unbelievable."

"Yes I know."

"All right, as long as you realize it."

The van turned onto a rough road. The children were being jostled around by the sudden turns and bumps.

"Hey," Haldor said, "you must be the student who turned into their teacher then. I thought it was that Pete fellow."

Pete let out a low growl. "I told you I didn't do it!"

"How did you hear about it?" Penny asked.

"We overhear all kinds of things from those guys." He nodded toward the front of the van. "I guess they don't feel the need to keep too many secrets from us seeing as we're headed for extermination and all." The van hit a bump that sent Haldor smack into Potato Pete. The larger boy growled and shoved him aside.

"Sorry," Haldor mumbled as he scrambled to locate his glasses.

Penny turned her attention to Pete. "So why are you here?" she asked. He gave her a withering look and then turned so that his back was to them all. The van came to a sudden halt, causing Haldor to fall once more into Pete, who again threw him off like it was nothing.

"Shh, listen," Haldor began as he struggled into a sitting position. "They are going to offer us food. Eat as little as you can get by with. There is something in it that causes you to sleep. All around them sleeping children were beginning to stir. They sat still as they waited for the doors to open.

Penny wondered if her parents had noticed that she hadn't come home that day. She doubted it. A tear ran down her face, and she wiped it away. She was on her own now, and she was fine with that. If her parents didn't need her, why should she need them? Pete's gaze met hers for a moment. She dropped her eyes and pretended to be absorbed in tying her shoe. A loud bang made her look up.

"Hey, that sounded like a gunshot!" Crane exclaimed. Another bang rang out, making Penny's ears ring. Several more shots went off, followed by angry shouts.

Chapter Five

The doors swung open, revealing the source of the noise. One of their captors was lying on the ground, and the other was struggling with a disheveled-looking man with a hooked nose. A woman, with turtles in top hats printed across her shirt, stood in the doorway of the van.

"Mom? Dad?" Penny was so stunned that those were the only words she managed to utter.

"Hurry, you have to hurry!" her mother cried. She ran to assist her father, who was now fighting both men.

Penny was brought to her senses by a sharp jab to her side.

Crane elbowed her again.

"You heard her, let's go!"

She looked from him to the others in the van. Some of them were still sound asleep. Haldor struggled to prod the still-groggy children.

"We can't leave without the others," she said. "Pete, you're the strongest. Help us carry them!" Without a word, Pete pushed past the others, clambered through the doors, and sprinted into the

woods. Penny called after him, but he was too preoccupied with putting as much distance between himself and the van as possible.

"Never mind him!" Crane shouted. "Help me out."
He grabbed the arms of a sleeping boy to his left
while Haldor and Penny hoisted up the boy's feet.
The children lifted with all of their might and managed to haul the boy out of the van and onto the
grass.

Zzaap!

Haldor went limp. One of the men stood over the
top of him with a triumphant look on his face. In his
hand he held a long rod with electricity pulsing between the menacing-looking prongs on the end. The
man slammed the van door, barring the other children's chance of freedom.

"No!" Penny cried as the man came for her. She
started to back away, but tripped over her own feet
and fell to the ground. The man sneered as he hovered over her.

"Time to teach you a lesson, dog!" he spat out.
Just as he was about to bring the electric prong
down on her neck, Crane threw the full force of his
body weight against him. The man stumbled and fell
back. They helped lift Haldor to his feet, then half-
drug him into the safety of the nearby woods. Penny
scrambled up onto a boulder to get a better view of
the van.

༄

"Garn, Garn, what are you doing?" Dirk turned
from the van to see Garn lying flat on his back. He

kicked him hard in the side. "Get up, you fool!" Garn sat up, rubbing the back of his head.

"Those stupid kids," he muttered. "I'll kill them! First your mouth, now my head."

"Forget it, we need to get going." The two men were already running behind schedule, and there was no way that Dirk was going to show up late again. Not after getting chewed out last time.

"They won't last long out there anyway. No one uses this logging road anymore." Garn nodded. He was still rubbing his head as he lifted the still-sleeping young boy back into the van.

"Get these two while you're at it." He nodded toward Penny's parents who were both lying on the ground.

"Boy, they are a lot tougher than they look. It's a good thing re-enforcements showed up when they did, eh, Dirk?" Two black cars were parked to the left of the van. They had been following them from a distance as a precaution since they left the school. Dirk shrugged his shoulders.

"Well it made things go smoother anyway, but I had them right where I wanted them." Garn started to laugh, but caught Dirk's eye and changed it to a cough.

"Are all the children accounted for?" A large gruff man by the name of Dane asked.

"Yes, sir," Dirk lied, "they're all still here."

"Good, I wouldn't want to be the one who has to answer to Lord Esmond for any missing prisoners. Now tie up the man and woman and bring them along. They may be of some use."

"Obviously, what kind of idiot does he take me for?" Dirk mumbled under his breath. To Dane, he said, "Right away, sir." Together, he and Garn bound Penny's parents and put them into the van.

"Hey," Garn whispered to Dirk, "we can't just leave their car here. The kids might use it." Dirk pointed toward the station wagon that they had been driving. He grunted in agreement, then took the keys from the ignition, and threw them far into the woods. Dirk then took out his knife and slashed through one of the tires.

"Hurry up, you two!" Dane shouted over to them. Garn cast one last look toward the woods where the children had gone before climbing into the front of the vehicle.

The children watched the entire scene from their hiding place. Haldor was back to his relatively normal state and was now nursing his leg where the electric rod had struck. Penny and Crane looked toward the van from the top of the boulder.

Penny's voice was shrill. "We can't let them take my parents. We need to help them!"

"It won't help them if we're captured as well," Haldor said. The van rumbled to a start and drove down the long dusty road.

With a sigh Penny climbed down from the boulder. "You're right of course," she said as she gazed after the van. She just couldn't believe that her parents had shown up. Had they come all this way just to rescue them? She had never considered her parents to be the heroic type. She never imagined that they would have been able to fight off those huge men for so long. Everything seemed upside down. She needed a moment to think. She scanned the area. They were in the middle of nowhere, all right. They were stranded on the side of a mountain. Woods loomed over them in every direction. An old logging road was the only sign of civilization that she could see. The road wound up the mountain like a giant snake and disappeared into the darkness. "I wonder where Pete disappeared to."

"Who cares? He made his choice," Crane scoffed. "We need to focus on our situation. For instance, what do we do now?"

"Yes what now?" Haldor echoed.

To Penny's surprise, they both were looking at her. She shook her head to clear her thoughts. "Well," she began, "does anyone know how to hot-wire a car?" Haldor raised his hand and rose to his feet.

The sun had long since sunk below the horizon and freezing rain fell around them. They all decided it would be best to get a good night's rest before attempting to start the station wagon. The giant rock provided some shelter from the rising wind, and Haldor was able to build them a small fire using the cigarette lighter from the car. The three of them sat huddled around the fire, in silence, for some time, each one lost in their own thoughts. The firelight danced off the children's faces and created deep shadows in the woods beyond.

Crane shivered and moved closer to the fire. He had just thought of a question that had been burning at the back of his mind. "Haldor?"

Haldor looked up. "Yes?"

"What happens to our families after they take us?"

"It depends on your parents," Haldor began. "If they buy the line about a special school for gifted students, then nothing happens. They just go on with their lives. If they get suspicious though, they..."

Crane leaned forward. "They what? They can't really kill them. Can they?"

"They killed my dad," Haldor spoke just above a whisper. "He didn't want me to go away to school. They didn't have time to convince him."

Penny's eyes grew wide. "What happened?"

Haldor cleared his throat before he began. "My dad owned a carnival. That is, my adoptive dad. He found me when I was young. Anyway, we traveled all around the United States. They never would have found me if I didn't enroll in public school this year. My father didn't want me to miss out on a normal life. I know now that I should have never let him convince me."

The fire was growing dim. Haldor stirred up the coals before continuing. "I discovered my talents early. Probably due to living the Carny life where you are always testing what you can do and trying to reach beyond your capabilities. One day, while performing a new escape artist trick that I had been practicing, I swallowed the key I was hiding in my mouth. I started panicking. The curtain was about to rise, and here

I was about to get my head sawed off. It was sort of a dangerous trick," he added as he saw Crane's mouth drop open.

"Anyway, I discovered that I could manipulate metal just by concentrating. I used my mind to bend the metal cuffs and chain off of my body. It was fantastic. An escape artist's dream! I was soon able to pull off more and more impressive stunts! I planned on telling my dad—I just never got around to it."

Haldor climbed to his feet and paced in front of the fire. "I never should have used my ability at school. I know that now. I'm pretty sure that's how they find us. They have detectors hidden in the classrooms or something. All I know is one day I am sitting in class bending staples into pretzels, and a week later these men in suits show up. They put me and my classmates through all these tests, and then they take some blood. They said it was to make sure we were healthy enough for overseas travel.

"That same evening, they showed up at the carnival and insisted I go with them to their special school. My father refused. I think he could sense something wasn't right. The next day our trailer blew up with my dad in it. The police said it was a gas leak. They said it was an accident, but I know better. Soon after that, a couple men showed up at the carnival and took me away while everyone was sleeping. I'll bet they all think I ran away..." Haldor trailed off as he sank onto a nearby log and stared into the flames.

"That's horrible." Penny put her hand on Haldor's shoulder in what she hoped was a comforting manner.

Crane's thoughts went to his grandmother.

"I'm sure she'll be fine," Penny said as if reading his mind. Crane had lived with his gran ever since his parents passed away in a car accident several years ago. He hoped that she wouldn't worry about him. She might even be excited, thinking he was attending a school for the gifted. She was always proud of him, even when he did nothing of significance.

Penny hurled a pinecone into the fire. "They can't just get away with kidnapping people."

Haldor frowned and polished his glasses on his shirt. "Apparently they can." With that grim statement hanging in the air, the children curled up around the fire and drifted into a restless sleep.

The next morning, they awoke to the sound of banging. Haldor was already hard at work under the dash of the station wagon. All they could see were his feet, which would occasionally kick in frustration.

Penny stretched her aching muscles and walked over to him. "How's it going?" she asked.

"Goongoomd," was Haldor's muffled reply.

Following right behind her, Crane walked a complete circle around the car. "Well, it looks like they only managed to slash one tire," he observed. "I hope there's a spare."

"If there is, it should be in the trunk." Penny walked to the back of the car and tried to pry open the lock with a stick.

Crane shook his head. "You'll never do it that way."

"Well are you going to help or just watch?"

"I am helping! I'm helping by telling you that won't work."

"You're going to have to get to it from behind the back seat," Haldor called in a muffled voice.

Penny tossed the useless stick into the woods and walked to the side of the vehicle. "How do you know so much about cars?" she asked him.

Haldor came out from under the dash to take a break. He wiped his brow with the back of his arm. "I read a book on auto maintenance."

"And it told you how to hot-wire a car?" Crane raised his eyebrows.

"Kind of. I also took the bearded lady's hot rod out for a spin once. I wanted to see if I could do it. Turns out I could!" he said with a crooked smile, then went back to work.

Crane rummaged around through the glove compartment, looking for anything that might be useful to them. He held up a long, metal object that had been wrapped in cloth.

"Can I take a look at that?" Penny asked as she reached for the brass contraption. She turned it over in her hands. It was about the size of her forearm, had a couple hooked pinchers on one end, and several gears along both sides.

"Looks wicked, doesn't it?" Crane said, looking over her shoulder.

She nodded in agreement. It was just like some sort of medieval torture device.

"What do you make of it, Haldor?" she asked as she handed it to him.

He studied it before responding. "I don't think it's a weapon, but I've never seen anything like it. There is no switch to turn it on, and it doesn't appear to take batteries or hook up to power."

"Well in any case," Penny said, "I guess we should keep it with us. I have a strange feeling that it's somehow connected to all of this."

They returned the object to the glove compartment, then got back to work. It took them just under an hour to get the car in working order, but try as they might, they couldn't seem to remove the metallic collars from their necks. Haldor tried to use his metal manipulation and was brought to his knees by a sharp pain in his head. Crane even tried using a hammer and screwdriver from the tool kit that they had found in the car. This accomplished nothing but to leave a large bruise on Penny's collarbone—Crane had apologized profusely for this. After that, they decided not to try anything else until they were able to

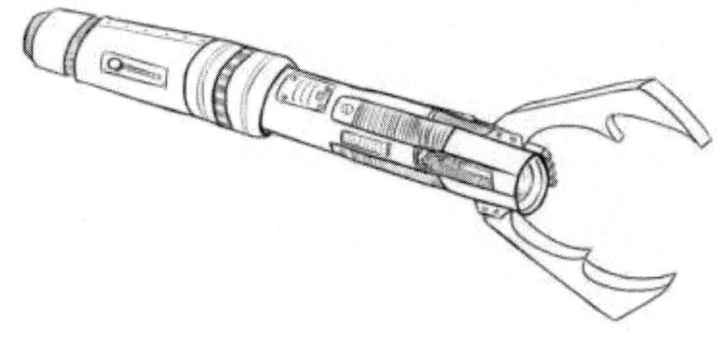

get ahold of some heavy-duty wire cutters.

"I guess they underestimated us," Crane said, looking at the car.

Penny rolled her eyes. "Right... They didn't know how well you could watch."

Crane feigned shock. "Well if I'm going to be driving you guys around, I need my rest!"

"Who said that you were going to drive? Haldor is the one who has experience with cars. It only makes sense that he should be the one to drive."

Haldor's eyebrows shot up. "I may have exaggerated my exploits before," he said as he slid his glasses back up his nose. "I sort of drove the car a few hundred feet and then crashed into a fast food establishment."

"You know, when they say drive-thru—" Crane began.

"I know how to drive," came a voice. Pete was standing at the edge of the woods. Penny and Haldor exchanged apprehensive glances as Pete strode over to the car and leaned against the hood. His hair was matted, and his clothes were spattered with mud.

"I said, I know how to drive," he repeated.

"No way!" Crane sputtered. "How can we even consider letting this creep drive after what he did? How can we even consider trusting him?"

Pete stepped closer. Crane flinched as if expecting a blow.

"I just did what I was supposed to do. That weirdo lady said run, so I ran. It's as simple as that."

Crane met his steady glare. "Don't you care about anyone but yourself? If you had helped, that weirdo lady might even be standing here with us now."

"That is highly improbable," Haldor cut in. "Several others arrived after we escaped."

"The point is that we needed you," Crane continued. "More of us may have been able to escape if you had thought of anyone but yourself."

Pete punched the hood of the car in anger.

Before he could respond, Penny stepped between them. "Everyone listen. First of all, that weirdo lady you're talking about is my mom. Secondly, we are all in this together. We need to learn to depend on one another. If we can't trust each other, then we will fail."

"Fail doing what?" Crane asked.

"Saving the others, of course. Who's with me?"

Chapter Six

"You're kidding right?" Crane ran his fingers through his hair.

She shook her head and tried to read the expressions on her companions' faces.

Haldor removed his glasses and polished them on his shirt. "This is going to be incredibly dangerous you know—"

"See, it's dangerous!" Crane cut in. "Dangerous means that we could all get killed!"

Penny cleared her throat. "I know, but I don't have a choice. They have my parents, Connor."

Pete, who had been listening this whole time, now spoke up. "There's no way I'm going to stick my neck out for total strangers. I'm getting in that car and driving straight home."

"Hey, potato head," Crane said, suddenly feeling loyal, "you can do what you want. We'll just leave you at the next town we come to. As for me, I'm with Penny!" With that, he walked over and put his hand on her shoulder. Pete glanced back toward the woods as if he was considering bolting once more.

"Listen, Pete," Penny began, "we can leave you at the next town if that's what you decide, but right now we need you. You are the only one who can drive, and those people are getting away."

Crane looked at her. "Hey! I said I would drive."

Pete's gaze softened, and he turned back toward the car. "Let's go," he grunted.

Penny raised her arm to slap him on the back, but changed it to a stretch when she saw the dangerous look on his face. "What about you, Haldor?"

"Oh, I'm in," he said, firmly placing his glasses back on his face.

With Crane still grumbling about the driving arrangements, they all piled into the station wagon. Haldor and Crane slid into the back, and, with a sigh, Penny climbed in the passenger seat next to Pete. The air was still, and the car was growing warmer by the minute as they pulled out onto the old logging road. The children scrambled to roll the windows down as the car began the long journey up the mountain.

"So what do we do if we catch up with these guys?" Crane asked from the back seat.

Penny hadn't thought that far ahead. She bit her bottom lip and ran her fingers through her tangled hair. "I'm not sure yet, but I'm sure we'll think of something." She hoped she sounded more confident than she felt. In truth, she was having some serious doubts.

Pete cocked an eyebrow. "The woman with the plan." He flinched as Crane's hand met the back of his head. "Hey! I'm driving here."

"Sorry, I was trying to give Haldor a high five. I guess I must have missed."

Haldor furrowed his brow. "I'll say you missed. I didn't even have my hand up."

Crane gave him a look of disbelief. "Shh, Haldor!"

"Ouch! Why did you kick me?"

Penny hardly heard the others as they drove. Her thoughts were elsewhere. As the station wagon wound up the large mountainside, she could feel her anger growing stronger with each curve. She still couldn't believe what was happening. Along with her anger came waves of nervousness that shook her body in spasms. She had no idea what to do next, and the others all seemed to be depending on her.

She had never been much of a leader. Penny recalled with embarrassment her younger days. She couldn't even lead well then. All of the kids in her class used to love to play follow the leader during recess. When it was her turn to be the leader, all the kids would get bored and give up. One day, after practicing her moves at home the night before, her turn came again. This time, she was ready. She hopped on one foot, summersaulted, walked like a crab, and did just about any other kind of acrobatics she could think of. The kids loved it! Penny was king of the leaders until they followed her through that poison ivy. She never got to be the leader again after that fiasco. Even their parents were furious at her.

"I'm hungry." Crane's voice drifted from the back seat.

"I'll be sure to pull off at the next drive-thru," Pete scoffed.

"Sounds good, but don't make your own drive-thru like Haldor did last time he drove a car," Crane said with a wide grin.

Penny had no idea how long they had been on the road. She dropped off to sleep to the sound of Crane and Haldor arguing about whether hamburgers or grilled cheese sandwiches were the most delectable type of food. She awoke several miles later when the car came to a halt.

Looking around, she expected to see a town or something, but trees still lined the road on both sides. "Why are we stopping?"

"Looks like this stupid car is out of gas," Pete mumbled. He leaned forward to tap the gas gauge as if hoping that would somehow change the situation. The car now sat alongside the desolate-looking street. They hadn't seen a single car the entire time they had been driving.

"Out of gas?" Crane sat up in alarm. "We're going to die of hunger out here!"

"We'll be fine. I just saw a sign that said there is a town just fifteen miles from here," Haldor said.

"Fifteen miles?" Crane's voice was shrill. "That will take forever!"

"Well I guess we better get walking then." Penny opened the door and swung her legs out of the car.

Rainey Carmichael sat slouched in the chair of the reception room in the principal's office. She sighed and pulled at a loose thread on the arm of her chair. This was the third time this week that she had been called in for fighting. Only this time was different. This time she had set fire to Gerald Butler's pants. She hadn't meant to do that part...Well, maybe she meant to a little. She had recently discovered that when she got angry or upset, things around her would sometimes combust.

At first, she thought it was just a coincidence, but now...Now she was sure she was the cause. It had only happened a couple of other times, and no one knew how the fires had started, but she had been labeled a pyromaniac problem child by the foster system. It had gotten her and her brother Derrick kicked out of their two previous homes, and now she feared it would get them rehoused again, sent to a facility, or worse yet, separated.

Derrick ran his fingers through his short, wavy hair, making it stand on end. Like his sister, Derrick had red hair, a pale complexion, and a dusting of freckles across his nose. Unlike his sister, he was quite tall. Rainey just came to his shoulders. Also, he was quiet and reserved. For the most part, because of his size, he was able to avoid conflict, but on days like today, he found himself unable to keep the peace. He sighed as he looked in Rainey's direction. It seemed like he was always trying to keep her out of trouble.

"What? It's not like I did it on purpose," she muttered as her gaze met his. "And you didn't have to get involved."

"Oh, like I'm just going to stand by and watch my sister get beat up by the biggest guy at school?"

"I was doing just fine."

"He was literally sitting on your back, and pushing your face in the mud."

"Well he won't be sitting on anything for a while now." She allowed herself to feel a small satisfaction in that at least.

"I thought we agreed you were going to keep your temper in check after that last fire."

"I know, I know. It's just...He was getting under my skin."

"What on earth could he have said that would be worth us possibly getting separated?"

Rainey hesitated "He...he told me to have a nice day."

"What?" Derrick gripped the arm of the chair 'til his knuckles turned white.

"Well you weren't there. You should have heard the way he said it! He was being a real jerk."

"How on earth..." His voice trailed off as the principal poked his head out of his office and called them in.

"Please sit down," he directed them as they walked in. Rainey was confused. He didn't seem upset in the slightest. In fact he was...smiling? Yes, he was trying to hide it, but he seemed happy, almost giddy. His bald head gleamed under the florescent lights and made Rainey's head ache.

"Peppermint?" he asked them, holding out a tin full of candy. Rainey shook her head. Derrick reached for the tin, but something made him stop.

"No thanks," he mumbled.

"Suit yourself." The principal sat down in his overstuffed, leather chair. It emitted a soft squeaking sound as he rolled forward. "I have made a few phone calls on your behalf today." He waited as if expecting a reply. When he received none, he went on. "You see, after the incident with the fire, we had the nurse draw some of your blood while you were in her office, and it turns out that it's special."

"Special how?" Derrick asked. "Like a rare blood type?"

"You could say that."

"So, why the phone calls?" Rainey wanted to know. This guy was acting weird.

"I told them to come get you, of course."

"To come get us? Wait, give us another chance," she pleaded. "We can't get kicked out of another home."

"Oh, not them. Your foster parents will be told you got rehoused."

"Then who is coming, and why?"

"They are, of course. Haven't you been listening? My people. They are coming to kill you. Isn't it grand?"

"Wha—" Derrick and Rainey looked at each other in disbelief. They knew they had to have misheard him.

"After many long years I can finally get out of here! I think I'll take a nice, long vacation."

Rainey let out a soft whistle and twirled her finger in a circle around her temple. "Cra-a-azy," she whispered.

Derrick nodded in agreement. They needed to get away from this lunatic, and fast. "We'll just wait for your people out in the hall. You seem quite busy," she said as they both stood to leave.

"Not so fast," the principal said. The door slammed behind them. They turned to look, and standing in front of their escape route was a big man in a dark suit.

In the back of the large, gray van, Penny's parents were still out cold thanks to a strong dose of tranquilizer. Dirk didn't want to take any more chances. It was early morning, and they had been on the road all night. In the front seat Garn was sleeping soundly. Dirk reached over and struck him with an old newspaper. Garn awoke with a start.

"Wake up! We have a couple more stops to go. There are a few more 'gifted' students that we need to take to the academy," he said with a wry smile. They arrived moments later at Garden Grove High School. Dirk drove the van to the back of the old, brick school building and turned off the engine. Dirk flipped through a large brown folder and furrowed his brow.

"There are two kids we need to pick up here," he said. "A Rainey and Derrick Carmichael. They're twins. Both with red hair. That should help make them easier to spot."

"Well at least we have plenty of room back there now," Garn said with a yawn.

"Don't remind me. If it wasn't for you, we wouldn't have lost them."

"Me? It wasn't my fault!"

"Just get out of the car. If you follow my lead, maybe you won't screw up this time." Garn frowned but said nothing as he opened his door and climbed down from the vehicle. The air was warm and the sun had begun to rise above the horizon as they walked up the cement steps toward the back entrance of the school. An eerie silence hung over the large, brick building. They walked up the steps and paused in front of the entrance, each one sensing that something didn't seem right. Dirk cleared his throat and knocked on the door. After waiting a few moments, he tried the doorknob. It turned easily.

"I guess they left the door open for us," Garn murmured. As they stepped into the empty hallway, a large explosion shook the building. They heard shouts coming from somewhere within. Dirk and Garn froze in the doorway. Another explosion rattled the building as a door near the end of the hall was blown outward. A small, red-haired girl emerged from the room, coughing. She glanced around, her eyes wild, then bolted toward the door where the men stood.

"Stop her," a voice called from the smoking room. A rather singed-looking, bald man hobbled into the hallway. "Stop her, I said!"

Dirk reached toward Rainey as she sped toward them. There was a strange glint in her eyes that Dirk didn't understand.

"Dirk, don't," Garn began. His warning came too late. As Dirk reached for her shoulder, his sleeve burst into flames. He let out a yelp and fell back into the lockers. Rainey's eyebrows shot up. She paused in indecision just long enough for Garn to step in front of the door, blocking her path. He'd come prepared. He thrust the electric prong he held toward her neck. She cried out in pain as it connected with her bare flesh, and crumpled to the floor like a rag doll.

Chapter Seven

Penny's throat ached from thirst. Beads of perspiration gathered on her forehead and threatened to roll down her face. They were still heading toward the town that Haldor had seen on the sign, but she didn't know if she could go on much longer without some water.

"How long have we been walking?" Pete croaked.

Haldor looked down at his watch and furrowed his brow. "Well, we've been walking for about two hours, and I would estimate that we are walking roughly two and a half miles per hour. We should be there by tomorrow at this rate... We did stop for a couple breaks though," he added, looking toward Crane with a raised eyebrow.

He pretended not to hear his remark and strained his eyes to see as far down the road as possible. "I think I see something!"

Sure enough, a small building was coming into sight. His weariness forgotten, Crane jogged toward the structure.

The roof was covered in moss, and the paint was peeling from the once-white walls. It reminded her of the summer she got a bad sunburn. The kids at school had called her 'Peely Penny' for weeks. The house gave the impression it was about to cave in on itself at any moment. The only thing that seemed to be holding it up was the chimney in the center of the structure, and even that seemed precarious. Several bricks had already fallen to the ground around the home.

Crane, who was the first to arrive, climbed up onto the woodpile near the house so that he could peer into the window. He cupped his hands to get a better look inside. "Looks deserted."

Penny guessed it had been deserted for a long time by the state of the house.

"Hey," Haldor called from behind the building. "I found some water, everyone! There is a river back here."

"Water? Outta my way!" bellowed Pete, needlessly pushing Penny aside in his hurry to get to the house. She stood up and brushed herself off, mumbling about Pete's manners, or rather the lack thereof.

Penny and Crane managed to find a few old canned goods in the cupboards of the rickety house which they brought outside to the others.

"Hey, we found this great bicycle in the toolshed!" Haldor said as they approached the outbuilding the two boys were sitting beside. The "great bicycle" as he had called it, was in about as rough shape as the house and toolshed. Haldor was definitely an optimist.

"Oh, I know it's not in the best shape now, but I'll bet I can get it working, and there is a trailer in there too. That means one of us can ride the bike, and three of us can be pulled. We can take turns!"

"*Puh,*" Pete scoffed, "it's a piece of junk."

"I'm sure it will be great. Good work." Penny smiled, though she was a bit doubtful he could pull it off. As Haldor worked on his new project, the others gathered wood for the fire. Without the cigarette lighter from the car, lighting the fire was proving to be difficult. Crane tried in vain to rub two sticks together to get the fire started, explaining all the while that he had watched a survival show and knew how to do this. Penny watched for several minutes but soon gave up on the idea of a fire.

"We may just have to eat these beans cold tonight. Hey, would you hand me that backpack with the tools from the car?" Penny asked. "I'm pretty sure there was a Swiss army knife in there that has a can opener on it."

"Can't now. I think it's getting warm!" Crane exclaimed, still rubbing the sticks together.

"Here," Pete said as he tossed her the bag. Penny turned the backpack upside down and began to dig through the contents. The mystery object from the glove compartment caught Crane's eye, and he abandoned the sticks with a comment about needing birch wood to do it properly. Lifting the object from among the pile of tools, he examined it again.

"Hmm, I wonder. Hold still a minute, Pete." He lunged toward him with the outstretched pinchers.

"Hey, hey, wha-a—?" was all that Pete managed to get out before toppling off the log he had been sitting on. He tried to rise to his feet, but Crane was upon him in an instant.

"Just...hold...still!" He clamped the pinchers around his metal collar. The object immediately started whirring as the gears began to spin faster and faster. With a loud click, Pete's collar fell to the ground.

"Well, who's next?" he asked with a triumphant grin.

Penny clapped her hands together. "Awesome job."

"Excellent indeed!" agreed Haldor. Pete was still sitting on the ground, looking shocked.

Crane gave a little bow. "Thanks, I'm glad it worked! I figured it would either unlock the collar, or kill him. I'm glad it was the first one."

Pete's eyes grew wide. "You're lucky it didn't kill me," he bellowed. "If it had, I would have killed you!"

Haldor pushed his glasses back up on his nose. "I would encourage you to examine that sentence for potentially flawed logic," he said.

"Yeah," agreed Crane with a chuckle. "You would have to catch me first and I'm kind of crazy fast."

Penny shook her head. "All right, let's get these collars off. You can take Haldor's off next. He's had his on the longest."

He was quick to oblige. With a whir and a click, the collars were both removed.

Haldor let out a sigh of relief and rubbed his neck where the collar had been. "Finally! It feels so good to get that thing off!"

"All right, Penny," Crane said, "now that you can use your powers, turn yourself into some chicken nuggets. I'm starving!"

She rolled her eyes. He did bring up a good point though. Now that they had their collars off, they could use their abilities!

Haldor rubbed his hands together with a smile. "Now this bicycle is going to be awesome!"

But something occurred to Penny that made her feel uneasy. "Wait, didn't they find us the first time because we used our abilities?"

"I don't think it should be a problem," Haldor said. "I am pretty sure that we would have to be in proximity to a sensor, and the sensors were only planted in the classrooms. Just to be safe though, maybe we should use our abilities sparingly."

Penny nodded in agreement. "I don't have much control anyway. I'm not even sure I could do it again."

"Sure you could," Haldor assured her. "It just takes practice." Without another word, he turned his attention to the bicycle. The metal shone with a luminous glow. The frame creaked and groaned in protest as the frame became straight and the spokes snapped back into place.

"Almost done," he said with a smile.

"That was fantastic!" Crane jumped up and down like a child. "Come on, do something else." As he continued to bring things for Haldor to bend—apparently both forgetting that they just agreed to be cautious—Penny looked at Pete.

"So, if you don't have any abilities, then why did they put that collar on you?" She prepared herself for an angry retort, but instead he shrugged.

He was quiet for a few moments, seeming undecided about something. Finally he spoke. "Well there was this fire, but I know I couldn't have been responsible for it. I never even moved."

"What happened?"

"I was in class, and Mr. Brady asked me to solve a problem on the blackboard. Well I hadn't done my homework. I made Johnny—I mean—" He cleared his throat. "Johnny agreed to do it for me."

"I bet he did," she mumbled.

"Hey, you wanna hear what happened or not?"

"Sorry. Go on."

"When I couldn't solve the problem, they all started laughing at me. It made me so mad! I was angry at their dumb laughing faces, angry at the teacher, and angry at the stupid math problem. I just wanted to destroy something. Then all of a sudden something just snapped inside of me. I felt lightheaded and warm, and the next thing I knew, the classroom was on fire!"

"Did that happen last Thursday?" Penny asked.

"Yeah, why?"

"I remember that day! We all had to evacuate. I thought it was a fire in the chem lab, but they were never clear on what happened."

"Yeah, I still don't know myself."

"Well if Haldor can control his ability," she reasoned, "then I don't see why we shouldn't be able to control ours."

"Maybe."

"Say, Pete, you think you could..." She gestured toward the firewood.

Pete's eyes grew wide in alarm. "I-I don't think that would be a good idea. I really have no control. Do you want to take the chance of bursting into flames?"

"I hadn't thought of that." She bit at her fingernail in thought. "What if the three of us go into the woods for a bit and let you have a go at it?"

"I guess I could try..."

"Only if you want to."

"Yeah, I'll do it."

Penny called out to Haldor and Crane, as he positioned himself on the ground in front of the firewood.

"What is it?" Crane asked. "Haldor was just showing me how he could turn a drainpipe into a ruler."

She motioned for them to follow her into the woods. "I'll explain in a minute."

❧

Pete waited until he couldn't hear them anymore, then turned all of his attention to the sticks in front of him. First, he tried squinting his eyes. Then he tried widening them. *Fire, fire, burn, spark, flame!* He yelled in his head, but nothing happened.

Maybe I have to be angry, he thought. He tried to imagine that the firewood was really annoying firewood, and that the bark was falling off in an extremely obnoxious way, but that just made him feel silly. How could burning firewood be annoying or obnoxious? Then he noticed a knot in the wood that looked like a face. He imagined the face was laughing at him. That thought brought back memories of that day at school. He remembered how upset he had been that day, and how embarrassed he had felt. He didn't have to pretend to be angry anymore; he was angry.

He could feel something now. His limbs tingled, and warmth rose from his feet. A feeling of exhilaration pulsed through his body. *Must...make...fire!*

Chapter Eight

Crane was the first to see the smoke from the forest. "Good old Pete, he did it!" he exclaimed.

Penny looked where he was pointing. She could see dark, billowy smoke starting to fill the sky. It seemed like a lot of smoke for a campfire. "I think we'd better get back," she said to the others. After retracing their steps and emerging from the woods, it didn't take them long to discover that Pete had overdone it. The small campfire had turned into an inferno in a matter of seconds, catching the rickety cabin on fire. Pete watched the scene. He stood motionless, his hands on his head. Penny was the first to come to her senses.

"Let's look for some buckets or something in the toolshed." She gasped. "Look for anything we can fill at the stream!" Haldor and Crane ran to the shed as Penny shook Pete, who had dropped to his knees.

"I told you I couldn't control it," he mumbled.

"Never mind that now. Help us put it out!" she shouted.

As if waking from a dream, Pete snapped out of his stupor. They ran to join the boys who were trying to get inside the small outbuilding to look for buckets, but the fire from the cabin was so hot they couldn't get close. Penny stepped forward. She could feel the intensity of the heat on her face. It made her skin feel tight as if she were wearing a mask. There was no way they were going to get in there. The flames were just too close.

Pete pushed her aside. "Move," he said with a grunt.

Penny reached out to stop him. "Pete, don't!"

He shook her hand off his arm then put his head down and barreled through the door of the shed. A gust of wind brought a shower of sparks down onto the roof of the building where Pete had disappeared. The dry wooden shingles glowed, threatening to catch fire any moment.

"Get out of there, Pete!" Crane yelled. Smoke engulfed the area around the cabin, making it difficult to breathe.

Penny covered her nose with the sleeve of her shirt and peered into the doorway, willing Pete to emerge. They were forced to take a step back as the flames spread across the brush and licked up the side of the shed. *Come on, Pete. Come on!* Through the smoke, she saw a flash of color as Pete stumbled out, coughing. In his hand he held a stack of clay flower pots. He teetered toward them and collapsed into another coughing fit.

Penny helped him to the edge of the forest while Crane and Haldor ran to fill the pots in the stream. Crane filled his bucket to the brim, then ran as close as he could to the cabin. He tossed what he hoped would be a gush of water, but it came out as a trickle.

He growled in frustration when he realized the pot had a circular hole in the bottom. He racked his brain to think of a solution. He looked around, then raised his finger. "I've got it. Haldor, we need to fill these holes. Let's gather some of the grass, then cake the bottom with mud. That should keep the water from—" He stopped short as Haldor dumped a full pot of water onto the fire.

"What did you say?"

"Doesn't your pot have a hole in it?"

"It does, but I just held my hand under it. Didn't you?"

"Yes-s-s...Of course. Just wanted to make sure you did, heh." His face felt hot from more than just the heat.

They all dumped pot after pot of water onto the flames. It felt like it would never end. Each pot caused the flames to sizzle, but it hardly made a dent. Sweat and dirt soon covered them all from head toe.

Feeling discouraged, Penny sank to the ground. "It's no use, guys. This isn't working." The others plopped down next to her. They were sooty and exhausted. Together they watched what was left of the cabin burn to the ground. They at least managed to keep the fire from enveloping the forest.

The next morning the gloom from last night seemed to be hanging over them. Crane and Pete were already squabbling over something and the sun had just risen. Penny walked around and surveyed the damage. The embers were still smoking on the now unrecognizable cabin, and the little shed was half gone. Pete's power was very volatile indeed. No wonder it scared him to use it. She stopped at the river to wash her face and arms. The cool water felt refreshing and invigorating. When she got back to the others, she was pleased to find that the arguing had subsided. All seemed to be forgotten as the boys devoured a can of peaches.

She sat down next to the others. "Hey, save some for me."

Pete handed her the can and she downed the last one. Eventually the topic of their next move came up. Penny realized that they were all looking to her. She cleared her throat and addressed the group as a whole.

"Um, well, we overheard Principal Thomson and Snyder talking about a place called Azure. They said that's where the extermination is going to take place. Haldor, have you heard of a town or city anywhere by that name?"

Haldor closed one eye and rubbed his chin. They could hear him muttering various names to himself. "No, geographically speaking, I've never heard of it."

Penny kicked a large rock into the woods, wincing at the impact. She hobbled back and forth, trying to shake off the throbbing in her big toe. "I've been thinking about it all night," she said, as she leaned against a tree and massaged her foot. "We may not know their final destination, but we at least have some idea where they might be next. It's a long shot, but since they seem to be taking kids from schools, I think we should visit all the local schools once we get to town."

Crane held up the empty can, catching the last drops of peach juice on his tongue, then wiped his mouth on his sleeve. "What should we do if we find them? Should we call the cops?"

"Do whatever you want," Pete cut in. "I'll be taking the first bus home!"

Penny replied as if Pete hadn't spoken. "Good question," she said. "There's no way they'll believe our story. What do you think, Haldor?"

"Well, I suppose that a van full of drugged kids is bound to look suspicious, no matter what. We could give an anonymous tip."

They all felt a little better now that they had some sort of plan.

"So," Haldor said with a smile after finishing his peaches. "Who wants to see the bike?"

The bicycle was completely different. For one thing, it was the first four-person bike Penny had ever seen. There were three seats in the back and one seat in the front, with a long steering column for the driver. There were four sets of pedals so that they could all pedal at the same time. The trailer had been fixed to the back. It would be perfect for hauling their food and supplies. The whole thing looked brand new. Not a ding or scratch on it.

"There were extra bicycle parts in the shed I managed to pull out before the fire," Haldor said.

"This is amazing!" Penny exclaimed as she hopped on.

"It's awesome! This time I'm driving," Crane announced.

Pete narrowed his eyes. "No way!"

After much arguing, they decided that the two of them would take turns driving. They loaded the supplies into the trailer and set off down the road with Crane taking the wheel first. As they pedaled down the winding road, Penny couldn't help remembering the follow the leader incident again. She couldn't seem to shake the feeling that she was leading them right smack dab into a big patch of poison ivy.

❧

"I'm going to throw up!" Rainey shouted from the back of the van. "Stop the car!"

Derrick tried to clap his hand over her mouth. "What are you doing?"

"I'm trying to get us out of here. Trust me," she whispered before shouting again. "Pull over!"

"Shut up back there!" shouted Garn.

"I can't hold it in any longer! I'm going to hurl!" She waited a few moments. After hearing nothing, she tried again even louder. "Pull over! I mean it you dumb, idiotic lackeys!"

That seemed to strike a chord. The children lurched forward as the vehicle came to a halt.

"Shh-h-h-h, are you trying to make them mad?" Derrick wanted to know.

"We can take them, don't worry."

The door slid open with a bang.

Dirk's face was distorted with rage. "What did you call me?"

Rainey didn't hesitate. She leapt at Dirk and swung wildly. "Run!" she shouted to the others.

Garn tried to slide the door closed, but Derrick jammed his body in the crack. He gasped for air as the door struck his chest. Several other children climbed over his frame. Garn dropped them like flies, zapping each one that emerged. Derrick managed to roll out onto the grass, knocking Garn down in the process. Derrick struggled to get to his feet. He could see Dirk with his hands around Rainey's neck.

"Let her go!" he shouted, preparing to punch Dirk square in the face. Before he could land the blow, he felt Garn tackle him from behind. Derrick toppled face-first onto the ground. He tried to twist away, but it was no use. Garn's large-framed body had him pinned.

"I am sick and tired of you kids trying to pull stuff," Dirk spat out. His eyes were wide with rage and his face was red as a turnip. "Let's teach this girl some manners so she'll never try anything again." He raised his fist to strike Rainey. She flinched and covered her face.

"No!" Derrick shouted. "Leave her alone! Hurting her won't accomplish anything."

Dirk paused. "You know, you're right—" He grinned. "—but hurting you might. Let the boy up." Garn stood up and Derrick leapt to his feet.

"Let this be a lesson to you, girl!" Dirk growled as he threw Rainey into Garn's arms.

"No, stop!" she screamed.

Derrick put his fists in the air, preparing for a fight. He didn't even see the first blow coming. Derrick gasped as the man's fist struck his stomach. He fell to the ground, gasping.

"Get up!" Dirk bellowed as his boot met Derrick's ribs.

Rainey struggled to free herself from Garn's grasp but it was no use. His hairy arms held her tight.

The next blow caught Derrick in the ear. Ringing filled his ears, and he could feel something warm trickling down the side of his face.

"That's enough, Dirk!" Garn shouted. "We've wasted enough time." Dirk stepped back. "Besides, they don't want damaged goods delivered."

"Fine, get them back inside. But if either of you try anything again, next time your brother will get more than a few bruises."

Once back in the van, Rainey moved to Derrick's side.

"I'm so sorry, Derrick." Rainey sobbed as she dabbed at his face with her shirt sleeve. The side of his face was beginning to swell, and it was taking on a purplish hue.

"You always jump into things before thinking. Why are you so impulsive?"

"I know. Everything is my fault! We wouldn't be here if I hadn't gotten into that fight. I...I'm sorry," she finished.

Derrick glanced at his sister's face. Her eyes were full of tears, and she gripped her knees against her chest. He sighed and tried to calm himself. Being angry with her would not solve anything. As her brother and only relative, Derrick felt it was his job to protect her. If anything, he should be the one apologizing. He had failed to do the one thing he was supposed to do. He had failed to keep her safe.

"It's okay. It's not your fault that we're in this mess. These people are crazy. Just please do me a favor. Next time you feel like doing something dumb, give me more of a heads up, all right?"

"Don't worry, I won't make the same mistake twice. Next time I'll have a plan."

Penny and the others made good time. They hadn't been traveling long before a sign that read, 'Welcome to Wilno' came into view.

"Finally, civilization!" Crane exclaimed.

Wilno turned out to be a small town. Everything seemed to be within walking distance. From the edge of town, they could see several rows of old, brick buildings with the town square in the center. They dismounted the bike and hid it behind a dumpster in the alley next to an old fish and chips restaurant and located the nearest telephone booth. Penny thumbed through the directory, then looked for the addresses on a half-torn map hanging from the phone.

"It looks like there is one school not too far from here. If we hurry, we can make it before it closes for the day." She jotted down the address and closed the book. As they began to head toward the bike, she stopped when she realized someone was missing.

"Hey, where's Pete?"

Crane shrugged. "He said he was going to take the first bus home. My guess would be the bus station."

"I guess so. I was hoping he'd change his mind."

"Good riddance, I say." Crane shook his head.

Penny took one last look around to make sure he was gone. "I suppose he did take off." She wasn't surprised, but she was disappointed.

"He had to make his own choice for what was best for him," Haldor said.

"I guess you're right."

Crane was already across the square. They had to run to catch up with him.

After retrieving the bike and pedaling furiously, they arrived at the school about an hour later. The schoolhouse was old and made of brick. The parking lot was quiet as they approached the building.

"I don't see the death van," Haldor said.

He was right. The van was nowhere in sight. "We should still check it out just in case."

"So we just stroll on in?" Crane asked.

She nodded. "That's the plan. If we act like we belong, then they'll assume we do."

They slipped in the front door. The hallway was empty and quiet.

"I guess everyone's in class," Penny said. "That's good, it will make it easier to—" Her words were cut short by a shrill bell signaling the end of class. Students poured into the hallway, in a rush to get to wherever they were going next. "Let's split up and see if we can get any information from the students," she said, trying to be heard over the noisy sea of kids in the hallway.

A skinny boy with blond, stringy hair was kneeling across from Penny. He was tying and re-tying his long shoelaces. "Hi," she said as she approached him.

"Do you think it looks better when I tie the laces in a quarter half-knot and then loop it under, or a three-quarter loop with a half twist over the top?" he asked.

"Um, the first one?"

"That's ridiculous! The half twist is obviously superior. Who are you anyway?" he said, looking up. "This is a small school, and I'm pretty sure I know every girl here. Not that you make much of an impression," he added as he looked her up and down.

"I'm new." She self-consciously tried to flatten out her wrinkled shirt.

"Hmmph," he grunted and went back to tying his shoe.

"My name is Pe...um, Pemmy." *Pemmy? Is that the best you can come up with?* she chided herself.

"Pemmy? Ha-ha, wow, and I thought Chester was a lame name. I'll never give my parents a hard time again."

This guy was starting to get on her nerves. "Yeah, well you laugh like a donkey choking on a cactus," she muttered under her breath.

"What did you say?" Chester asked, jumping to his feet.

"I said that... I like donkeys, and I saw a monkey on campus," she said with a tight smile.

"You are one weird girl, Pemmy," Chester said, shaking his head.

"Anyway," she began, "I just wanted to ask you—"

"Yes, yes, I suppose I could go with you to the dance," Chester cut in, "but you have to meet my mother first. Also, you would have to pay for yourself. I already spent my allowance on the newest Dragonlord booster pack. I already had the Yellow Knight Wizard set, which is the best by far. Now my deck is unstoppable!"

"That is *not* what I wanted to ask." She was starting to feel exasperated. Chester looked disappointed.

"Oh, well then, what do you want?" he asked.

"I was just wondering if you noticed any guys in suits hanging around the school lately."

"Oh, them. Yeah, it was kind of weird how they just showed up. Why do you ask?"

Her heart skipped a beat. "When did you see them? Are they here now?" she asked, looking around.

"Naw, they were here yesterday and earlier today. I think they were with the gifted program that was looking for students here. They didn't look hard. I am far more gifted than stupid Rainey and Derrick."

"Thanks," she said, and turned to look for the others. She saw Crane talking to a couple pretty girls standing near the water fountain.

"You're sure about the dance?"

"I'm sure. See you around, Chester."

"Your loss. See ya, Pemmy."

She made her way over to Crane who was just saying goodbye to two girls.

"I hope you had more luck than I did," he said. "I'm pretty sure those two were foreign exchange students. I could hardly understand them. I think they said that they liked the color of my elephant?"

"I did have some luck. Listen, we need to find Haldor and go someplace we can talk." All around them the kids were filtering outside. They spotted Haldor near the entrance. Penny directed them into an empty classroom.

"The only thing I found out was the special in the lunchroom," Haldor said once they closed the door.

"Well, the kid I was talking to told me they were here earlier today," Penny said. "He mentioned them taking some kids named Rainey and Derrick to a school for the gifted. I also kind of got asked to my first dance," she added with a wry smile. "Though I'll have to pay for myself since my date already spent his allowance on the newest Dragonlord cards."

"The new Dragonlord booster pack is out?" Crane asked, beaming.

"You play too?" Haldor's voice rose an octave. "I have the Purple Scales deck and the Green Elf set!"

"Nice! I have the Red Evil Gnome set."

"Ahem," Penny cut in, "can we get back on task and save the nerd speak for later? Besides," she added, rolling her eyes, "everyone knows that the Yellow Knight Wizard set is the best by far."

The boys exchanged surprised looks before following after her.

"Let's head to the principal's office and see if we can get any more information," Penny said as they walked down the empty hallway.

As they walked the sound of their footsteps echoed off the lockers. She felt a chill creep up her spine. Something seemed off. Crane spotted the principal's office first. They crept toward the door and listened. A man mumbled in a low tone. It sounded like he was on the phone. Penny put her ear against the door. The voice said something about progress reports and the school budget. Just normal principal stuff. She was about to suggest they leave, when they heard footsteps coming down the side hall.

"I hope your time here was enjoyable," said a man.

"Oh yes," replied a woman's voice that sounded quite familiar. "It's been very enjoyable indeed," the woman said with a hissing laugh. "Ahsh Ahsh Ahshsh."

Chapter Nine

They exchanged looks of horror as the footsteps grew closer.

Crane's eyes widened. "It's Mrs. Snyder!"

For a split second, they panicked. If Haldor hadn't had the sense to shove them both into a classroom, they would have been discovered. They hardly dared to breathe as they strained their ears to hear what was being said.

"I'm so glad that we are finishing ahead of s-s-s-schedule," Mrs. Snyder said.

"Yes, it will be great to leave this awful little town," they heard the man say.

Penny peered through the crack in the door to get a good look at the speaker. He was a balding man with a severe comb-over. He wore a loud checkered suit that looked two sizes too small, and when he smiled she could see his large buck teeth sticking out from under his mustache.

"Being assigned to this principal job for the past three years wasn't easy," the man went on. "I hate working with smelly children." They paused in front of the office. "Let me get rid of my assistant so that we can talk alone." He opened the door and leaned in. "George, what are you still doing here? Go home!"

"Yes, sir. I was just leaving." A small, mousy-looking man scurried out of the room as the other two entered. The door to the office swung shut behind them.

"How are we supposed to find out anything useful this way?" Crane asked. "We need to get closer!"

Penny paced back and forth. "I think I have an idea. I don't know if it will work, but it's worth a try." *All right, this is the moment of truth. I know you can do it.* Closing her eyes, she tried to picture one of the abductors in the van. She could see him now. He had been short and portly with a buzz cut. His name was Gary. No, Garn. If only she could recall the exact details of his suit.

"What are you doing?" Crane's voice broke her concentration.

"Shh, let her think," Haldor said.

Starting over again, she tried to recall how he talked, walked, and even smelled. She had gotten a whiff of him the day he had carried her to the van. He had smelled of B.O. and doughnuts. Now she wished she'd studied his face more because she couldn't recall if his eyes were brown or green. She was pretty sure they were brown. Then she tried to imagine her torso stretching, and her fingers lengthening.

She gasped as she felt the sensation of being lifted by her head up toward the clouds. Her limbs felt like they were all being pulled in different directions. A sharp pain assailed her stomach, but she gritted her teeth and kept envisioning herself as Garn. The pain grew into a dull ache. Her head was spinning. *Something must have gone wrong.* She decided she'd better open her eyes to clear her head before trying again.

Crane stared at her, his mouth hanging open.

"Sorry, it's taking me so long. I am still new at this," said a deep, foreign voice from her throat. *Did it work?* She was both excited, and terrified.

Crane took a step back. "P-P-Penny?"

Haldor's face broke out in a large smile. "Right on, you did it!"

With her heart racing, she turned to look at herself in the window. Garn's dopey-looking mug stared back at her in the reflection. "I really did it." Her rumbling voice took her by surprise again, making her jump.

Crane, who had been standing with his mouth open, found his voice. "Wow, you weren't kidding about this stapler stuff! This...is...*awesome!*"

Haldor cupped his hand over Crane's mouth. "Shh, keep your voice down."

"Right, sorry."

Penny straightened her coat, and opened the door. "Here goes nothing."

"Wait," Haldor called after her. "You forgot something," he said, pointing down. She looked at her feet. They were still their usual size, and she was still wearing her light blue sneakers.

"Oops," she said. "I guess that would look a bit suspicious." Penny shut the door and closed her eyes again. She tried to recall the man's shoes. She'd gotten a pretty good look at them when she was being hauled off. *Let's see, they were black leather shoes, about a size twelve,* she guessed. She opened her eyes and looked to see if it had worked. They were black, all right, and about a size twelve, but somehow she'd neglected laces. "That's going to have to be good enough. Wish me luck." She swung the door open and walked across the hall. Her hand shook as she knocked on the office door.

"The voices inside the room grew quiet." She panicked, realizing she had no real plan and chided herself for not thinking this through. Before she could change her mind, the door swung open, revealing Mrs. Snyder who was standing in the doorway with her hands on her bony hips.

"What on earth are you doing here?" she asked with a frown.

"I uh..."

"Well, don't just stand there, get in here." She frowned and tapped her foot.

Penny gulped and followed her inside. Once the door was closed, Mrs. Snyder rounded on her.

"Why aren't you in Porterfield at the drop zone with the other field agents?" she demanded. Her finger wagged inches from Penny's nose.

"We had some unexpected complications," she answered in what she hoped was a non-suspicious tone. "Darren lost the address."

"I thought your partner's name was Dirk," said the man in the plaid suit. Penny's face flushed.

"Right, it is Dirk," she said. "I call him Darren for short." To her surprise, this explanation seemed to satisfy them.

Mrs. Snyder shook her head in exasperation. "How could you lose an address twice in the same day?"

"I'm sorry, it's all Darren's... I mean Dirk's fault," she stammered. "He said that he didn't need to write it down. He thinks he has an amazing memory. Why, just last week he told me that he could recite this one book word for word. Of course I said it was impossible. Then he said—"

"Enough!" Snyder shouted, rubbing her temples. "If I write it down for you, will you shut up and get out of here?"

Penny nodded.

Mrs. Snyder snatched up a pad and paper from the desk and began scribbling down the address. "There," she said when she was finished. "If you lose it again, I'll write it on your forehead with a branding iron!"

"Oh I won't!" She assured her as she took the folded slip of paper. She was turning to leave when there was a sharp knock on the door.

"What now?" Snyder demanded. She pushed past her and flung open the door. Penny froze in horror. Standing in the doorway were two men dressed in black suits, and standing in front of them, with their arms held behind their backs, were Crane and Haldor.

"We found these two listening at the door," one of the men said.

"Is this chess club?" Crane asked.

Mrs. Snyder's eyes grew wide as she looked at him. "I know you!" she said in surprise. "Still listening to things that don't concern you, I see." She looked from one boy to the other. "Have you found a new partner in crime? What happened to your little girlfriend?"

"Oh I think she's in the restroom," Crane said with a cocky smile. "She said something about seeing your face and needing to throw up."

Snyder's eyes flashed for a moment before she regained her composure. "Ashs Ashs Ashsh," she hissed in her horrible laugh. "Well aren't you amusing?" She looked up at the men. "Tie these two up, then search the building for the girl. As for you," she said, looking at Penny, "how did you allow them to escape in the first place?"

Penny shook her head and tried to look annoyed. "Dirk must have not been watching them well. Don't worry though, I'll take these two straight back out to the van!" She reached for the boys, but Snyder put up a hand to stop her.

"Not this time. They are more trouble than they're worth." An evil grin spread across Snyder's face. She reached into the desk drawer and pulled out a lethal-looking object. "This time I'll take care of them myself!"

Rainey Carmichael and her brother Derrick were still bumping along in the back of the van. It felt like they had been driving for hours, but it was hard to tell just how long. From what Rainey could gather, they were all headed to some secret facility to be slaughtered. The two adults had finally woken up.

"Don't worry," the woman said, seeing the look of concern on her face. "We'll find a way out of here."

"Yes, indeed," chimed in the man. "Like we said, our daughter, Penny, and her friends are out there. They will find a way to help us. You'll see." As the van came to a stop, Derrick rubbed his eyes and sat up.

The van door slid open with a bang. Two men grabbed Penny's parents and led them away, while Dirk and Garn directed the children to get out of the van.

"Don't give up hope!" the woman called as they disappeared down the corridor.

Dirk held out the electric prong device. "Hurry up."

They all piled out of the van and were led down a long, dark, metal hallway. The stomping and shuffling from their shoes echoed off the walls as they were pushed along. After a few twists and turns, they arrived at an iron door. Garn removed a key from his pocket and inserted it in a hole to the left of the door. The door clanked and clicked as several internal locking mechanisms opened. The door swung inward, revealing a large, dome-shaped room full of children.

Rainey estimated that there were at least fifty kids, not counting the ones who had just arrived with her and Derrick. They all looked up at the newcomers as they entered. Several cots were against the far wall, along with blankets and straw on the floor. Most of the children looked skinny and malnourished. Without another word, Dirk and Garn turned and went back through the door they'd come in. The door closed with a loud *clang* that reverberated off the metal walls before going silent.

"Well at least we're out of the van," Derrick muttered.

"Yeah, out of one cage and into another." Rainey sighed.

"Hi there," said a boy with a long pointy nose. "I'm Reginald, but you can call me Reggie."

"I'm Rainey, and this is Derrick," she said with a nod in Derrick's direction. "Any idea where we are?" she asked.

"No, not really," Reggie replied. "Only that we seem to be waiting for something."

"Extermination day," Derrick said with a nod. "Yeah, we've heard about that."

Rainey looked around the room with a frown. "But why go through all this trouble just to kill us?"

"Beats me," Reggie replied. "They leave us alone in here for the most part. Once a day they give us some kind of gruel and water through those slats."

Rainey looked around at the many slats around the base of the walls. She knelt down to peer through one of the rectangular holes. She could see only darkness beyond.

"Any idea when extermination day is?" Derrick asked.

Reggie shook his head. "No, but I have a feeling that it's going to be soon."

Despite putting on a brave face, Rainey could tell that he was terrified. She looked around at all the others in the room. They all looked frightened. Most of them were either sleeping or talking in hushed tones. A small group was sitting in a circle playing cards, but even they kept looking around from time to time, a look of worry in their eyes. What they needed, Rainey decided, was some sort of hope. The words of Penny's parents came drifting back to her.

"Listen, Reggie," she said as loud as she dared, "there may be a chance we will get out of this yet."

"What do you mean?" Reggie asked in an excited whisper. "Do you have a plan?"

"No, not exactly," she said, "but Derrick and I heard about a possible rescue mission. A group managed to escape the van a couple days ago. As we speak, they are probably forming some brilliant escape plan! Maybe the police have already surrounded the building." She tried to sound more positive than she was, but in truth, she had her doubts. What were the chances that a few kids could even find them, let alone save them?

Reggie didn't take long to process this information. His demeanor changed almost immediately. "Well, it's a long shot," he said as he scratched his prominent nose, "but I suppose it is possible!"

"Tell the others," Rainey said. "If...I mean, when they come, we need to be ready to move." Reggie nodded. The word spread like wildfire, and, within just a few moments, the atmosphere was different. The room was abuzz with conversation, and a few people even smiled. She prayed with all her might that their hope wasn't in vain. They were relying on Penny and her friends now. They were their best and only hope of escape. "Please don't let us down," she murmured.

Chapter Ten

Penny's mind raced. Her friends were about to die, and she felt powerless to stop it. Snyder had lead them all outside to a secluded spot behind the school. She directed the men to tie the boys to a chain-link fence. As a precaution, she also put metal collars around both of their necks.

Snyder stood in front of them with a syrupy-sweet smile on her face. She seemed to be relishing this moment. "You naughty children must learn to stay out of the grown-ups' business. Didn't your parents teach you that it's rude to listen in on other people's conversations?"

"Didn't your parents teach you that it's rude to, oh, say...*Tie up children and kill them?*" shouted Crane.

"He's right," agreed Haldor, "it's quite rude."

Mrs. Snyder laughed in her horrible hissing fashion. Penny looked at the weapon Snyder was brandishing toward the boys. It looked like some sort of crazy camera/gun contraption. It was full of switches and dials with what looked like a giant lens for the barrel.

"Don't worry, it will all be over soon." Snyder raised the weapon to her eye and it began to make a high-pitched whirring sound. Crane and Haldor closed their eyes and braced themselves.

Penny's thoughts felt muddled and her head dizzy. She knew she needed to act now, so she did the only thing she could think of. Gritting her teeth, she prepared to run toward Snyder with Garn's six-foot, two-hundred-and-fifty-pound frame. Penny put her head down and ran with all her might, but something didn't feel right. Too late she realized that it was her own body hurtling toward Snyder now and not Garn's. To her dismay, the only part of Garn that remained, were his oversized, lace-less shoes. So instead of tackling Snyder like she had hoped, she stumbled over the large shoes and fell at the woman's feet. Snyder turned and gazed down at her. A look of recognition spread over her face.

"Well, well, isn't this interesting," she said with a grin. "Penelope, isn't it? Well Penelope, it looks like you volunteered to go first!" she said as she aimed her gun at her head. She struggled to get to her feet, but knew it was too late. Instinctively, she covered her face with her arms and waited for the end.

"Aa-a-ah-h-h!" Snyder screamed as her sleeve burst into flames. Penny opened her eyes to see the woman leaping around, waving her arm, which only caused the blaze to glow brighter. The man in the plaid suit chased her around, trying to help put out the flames. The two men in suits rushed toward Penny. One of them reached her first. She dodged to the side just as his coat burst into flames. The other man stopped dead in his tracks. His eyes grew wide with fear.

She glared at him and wiggled her fingers in her best impression of a magician. "Allacablooie!" she shouted.

The man stumbled backward, then got to his feet and ran as fast as he could toward the school parking lot. Penny rushed over to help her friends. She struggled to untie the knots, but they were stuck fast.

"Here, let me do it," said a voice nearby. As she turned, she saw Pete standing behind her.

Crane's jaw dropped. "What are you doing here?"

"No time to talk," Pete said as he cut the ropes, using the pocketknife from the backpack. The ropes slid from their wrists and the boys rubbed the spots where the ropes had cut in.

Their captors were still busy trying to extinguish the flames.

"Let's continue this reunion elsewhere, shall we?" Haldor said.

The others agreed, and they all ran toward the parking lot. From there, Pete led them to the spot across the street where he had hidden the bike. They climbed on and rode off as fast as they could. They turned left and right, ever watching for a vehicle on their trail. They only slowed down after they had put several miles between themselves and the school. They came to a stop at a quiet spot under a bridge where they could rest and stay hidden from the road.

Haldor perched on the edge of a rock and looked at Pete. "What happened to you anyway?"

Penny looked up at him as she removed the metal collars. "Yes what happened? We thought you must have taken the first bus home."

Pete scoffed as he covered the bike with leaves and branches to keep it hidden. "I just had to go to the bathroom! When I came back out of the super-market, you were gone. I looked all over town for you. When I couldn't find you guys, I looked up the ad-dress of the closest school myself. I hoped you'd still be there."

"A likely story," Crane interjected. "Why didn't you tell us where you were going?"

"I did!" Pete's eyes flashed and he balled up his fists. "I told you. Don't you remember?"

"You never told me anything."

Pete took a step forward. "Are you calling me a li-ar?"

Crane backed away, tripping over a fallen log. "Ow." He winced. "I guess it's possible you told me."

Penny shook her head. "Crane, how could you?"

"I'm sorry, but we were busy looking up schools and stuff. I can only think of a few things at once. Anyway, if I hadn't forgotten, Pete would have been captured too and we would all be dead."

"It did all work out rather well," Haldor said with a nod.

"Yes, it did. Good, bad work, I guess." She shook her head. "Oh, and great work, Pete!"

"You were spectacular!" Haldor agreed.

"That was pretty awesome," Crane chimed in, holding his hand out for a high five. Pete hesitated for a moment, then with a half-smile, slapped his hand with all his might.

"Ow!" Crane yelped, cradling his stinging hand.

Later that night, after eating a dinner of canned beef and cold beans—they didn't dare build a fire now for fear of being discovered—Penny and Pete sat alone near the stream.

"Hey, can I ask you something?" Penny began. "How did you know that you could set them on fire without hurting us?"

Pete watched a leaf float by. He spoke without looking up from the water. "I didn't."

Crane tossed and turned on the lumpy ground. All around him, he could hear the others dozing. Everyone else had something amazing to contribute to the group. They could all do such awesome things, and all he could do was bad karate.

As long as he could remember, he'd wished he had superpowers—even wearing a cape for his entire third grade career. He had called himself 'The Amazing Goat Boy.' His superpower was the ability to eat anything. It was an ability that got him into trouble after he gnawed off a large chunk of the cushion on his teacher's chair. Of course, he knew deep down that he could never really be a superhero. He'd given up the notion years ago that toxic waste was going to one day fall on top of him and bestow him with superhuman strength or a goat-like eating ability. Now however, he was faced with the fact that not only did powers exist, but his best friend and his archnemesis both had them, and he didn't. It wasn't fair.

Trying to push these thoughts out of his head, he closed his eyes tightly and tried to get comfortable.

The chilly night air made him shiver. Now he was too cold to sleep. Crane remembered he'd put his sweatshirt in the backpack earlier that day. He sat up and reached over Haldor who snorted when he bumped his head with the backpack.

"Sorry, buddy."

Haldor mumbled gibberish and rolled to his side. Crane pulled his sweatshirt from the pack. It was unusually heavy. In the rush to get away from Mrs. Snyder, he forgot he'd taken the weapon she dropped and wrapped it in his sweatshirt. He took it out and held it in front of him. In the light of the moon he could just make out some of the switches and dials. This could be his equalizer. If he could only figure out how it worked. Turning it over in his hands, he tried to discover where the firing mechanism was located. A snort from Haldor startled him. His hand slipped on the gun and he felt something give way with a click. He dropped it with a start as it let out a high-pitched whirring noise. A flash of light lit the sky as it struck the ground. Something resembling a lightning bolt snaked out of the end of the contraption and struck the boulder Pete was lying against.

Pete let out a yelp as his head fell to the ground. "What was that?" he bellowed as he bolted upright and looked around. The commotion also woke the others.

"Whatsamatter?" Haldor mumbled.

Crane looked from one face to the next. "Um, it was lightning. From the sky." He pointed upward. "Crazy weather, eh?"

Penny looked at him, turning her head to one side. She could tell when he was hiding something.

"Okay, okay," he admitted. "I accidentally dropped the gun and—"

"Gun? What gun?" Penny cut in.

"Oh, I took it from Snyder. Sorry, I meant to tell you, but I just remembered it myself. Anyway," he went on, "I dropped it and it went off. I guess it must have shot that rock Pete was against."

"You what?" Pete was aghast. He stood up and grabbed Crane by the shirt. "That could have killed me!"

"What rock?" Haldor examined the place where Pete had been sleeping. The boulder was completely gone. They all gathered around the charred ground in amazement.

Penny let out a low whistle. "Wow, that's some powerful gun."

"That was almost us today," Crane said with a shiver.

"It was almost me five seconds ago!" Pete scowled as he looked at Crane.

"Sorry, it was an accident," he said as he struggled to pull his shirt out of the larger boy's grasp.

Haldor bent down and picked up the weapon.

Pete gave a yelp and jumped behind them. "We should get rid of it!"

"No way," Crane objected. "It's awesome."

Penny shook her head. "I dunno, maybe he's right. What do you think, Haldor?"

"Well, I think I can figure out how it works, and it could come in handy." He looked closely at the machine. "I think this is the safety." He flipped a switch near the bottom of the gun. "There!"

"All right, I guess we can hang onto it for now," Penny said. "Sorry, Pete, you've been outvoted." With Pete still grumbling about his near-death experience, they returned the gun deep into the backpack for safe keeping. By this time, the sun was just starting to peek over the horizon.

"Well, we might as well stay up," she said with a yawn. She pulled out their last can of peaches and opened it with the pocketknife. They took turns eating from the container. The syrupy sweetness helped them wake up.

"So, where to next?" Crane asked between mouthfuls. "We heard something about an address yesterday." Nodding, Penny pulled the slip of paper from her jeans and handed it to him.

Haldor looked over his shoulder. "That's pretty far. I think it's just inside Clark County."

"Maybe we can take a bus," Pete suggested.

Penny kicked at the ground. "Not without any money. Let's just head in the general direction and see if we can figure it out along the way."

The others agreed and they soon had their things packed up and ready to go. It felt good to be riding through the sunny countryside. If it weren't for the fact that they were headed toward danger and possible death, it would have been quite enjoyable.

Chapter Eleven

It didn't take long 'til the countryside started to give way to a less rural area. They started seeing more and more houses along the road. The houses in this neighborhood were pretty nice, just like the ones that stood on either side of Penny's dilapidated home. It gave her a sudden pang of homesickness. She never thought she'd miss that tiny, brown shack. There were several people out in their yards today. Some kids were playing catch, an old man was mowing his lawn, and a young couple were bringing boxes from their home out to a large moving truck. That gave her an idea.

"Let's stop here for a bit," she said to the others.

Crane sighed with relief. "Good, because I think these other guys are getting tired."

Penny rolled her eyes and climbed off the bike. "Can you guys wait here a minute? I want to talk to that couple over there."

As she approached them, she tried to look like she was just out for a morning stroll. She could hear them arguing about something as she drew closer.

"The silverware needs to go in the box marked *p* for practical," the woman was saying. "And the coats go in the box marked *s* for items with sleeves! It isn't that hard, John," she finished in an exasperated tone. John looked like he was about to say something in return, but instead threw his hands up and strode back into the house.

Penny cleared her throat. "The neighborhood just won't be the same without you guys," she said in a tone that she hoped sounded sincere.

The woman looked at her in confusion for a moment and then smiled. "It's Sarah, right?"

"Good memory," she said with a smile.

"How is your sister doing?"

"Oh she's doing pretty good. She should be around here somewhere."

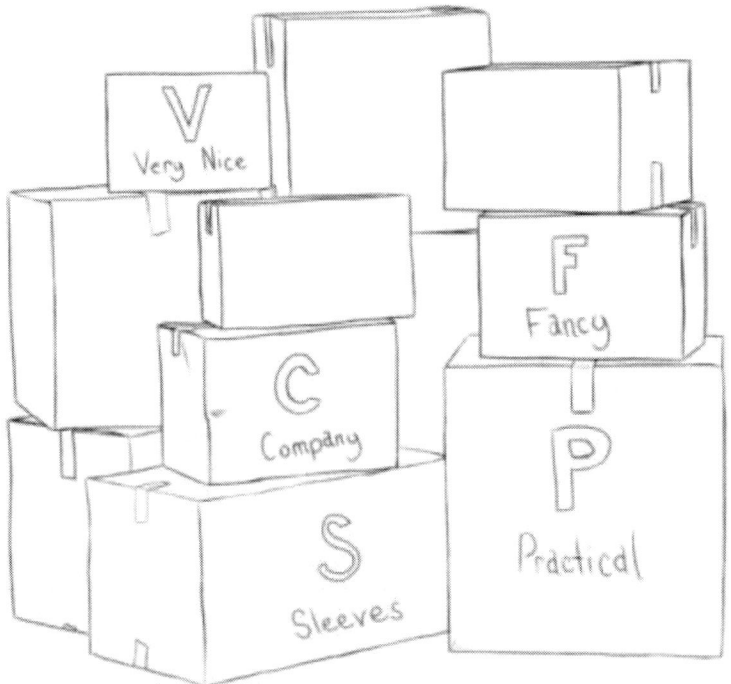

The woman looked confused. "I thought she was getting married in Hawaii today. In fact, I thought your whole family left for the airport yesterday."

"Oh, um, the wedding was called off."

"What? Why?"

"Oh you know, for the usual things, I suppose."

The woman leaned forward as she waited for further information.

"He, uh, had a gambling problem, an annoying laugh, and three other wives," she blurted.

"Oh my!" The woman exclaimed. She put her hand to her face and tried to look concerned, but her eyes danced with excitement over this new bit of juicy gossip. Penny couldn't help but feel a bit guilty about starting a nasty rumor. However, once she remembered the woman was packing and wouldn't be around to spread it, she felt a little better. The woman seemed to realize this as well, for her face fell as she looked down at the box in her arms. Penny took the opportunity of this momentary pause to steer the conversation elsewhere.

"Well enough about our drama," she said. "I hear you guys are moving to... Where was it again?"

"Oh we're moving to Carvel. It's in Clark County," she murmured absently. "It's a couple hours from here. John had a rather lucrative job offer!" she said, perking up. Penny was excited. She was pretty sure Haldor had said that address they were going to was in Clark County.

"Honey pot?" the woman's husband yelled from inside the house. "Does the fine china go into the box marked *f* for fancy, or *c* for company?"

"Excuse me, won't you?" said the woman as she walked back toward the house. "Neither!" she bellowed to her husband. "The china goes in the box marked *v* for very nice!"

Penny didn't wait to hear the rest of the conversation. She turned and went back to where the others were waiting. She could see that they had made themselves comfortable while she was gone. Haldor and Pete were both sitting cross-legged in the grass, while Crane was sprawled out on his back. He had taken the gun out of the pack and was examining it.

She plopped down next to him. "I think I found us a ride!"

He sat up. "You did?"

"I did. And you shouldn't be playing around with that."

"Don't worry, the safety is on...I think. Anyway, what about this ride?" he asked as he put the gun away.

"Those people over there," she said, indicating the couple, "are moving to Clark County."

Pete scratched his head as he looked across the street. "And they said we could ride with them? Just like that?" He sounded doubtful.

She shook her head. "Well, not exactly, but I'll bet that we could sneak inside that big moving truck."

"As always, I like your style, Gilbert," Crane said with a grin.

Penny passed an open can of mystery meat to Crane and they both chewed happily on it. They'd managed to sneak inside the moving truck and were now cruising along. It was so nice to be riding instead of walking or pedaling for a change. Pete and Haldor's soft snores drifted over from the other side of the truck.

"Hey, Penny?" Crane said.

She squinted toward him in the darkness. "Yes?"

"How are you doing with all this? I mean, we haven't talked about anything. It's all happened so fast. It's crazy, right?"

She thought about it. *How was she doing?* She hadn't taken the time to address this herself. "I'm scared," she said after a moment.

"Don't be. I won't let anything happen to you," he said as he gave her hand a squeeze. This gesture took her by surprise.

He cleared his throat and pulled his hand back. "After all," he said with a laugh, "I did complete the Ultra Flying Fist online karate school."

Penny grinned. "Indeed you did! I only made it to lesson three myself."

"Aw that's a shame. Lesson four is when you get your black belt." He laughed. "Seriously though, we'll get through this all right. You'll see."

Sighing, she let her muscles relax. The weight on her shoulders had lessened. It hadn't been lifted all the way, but it was more bearable. She realized for the first time that it didn't all depend on her. She had friends, and for that she was grateful. Penny closed her eyes and allowed herself to rest.

Penny jolted awake. She wasn't sure how long she had been asleep. She looked around the darkness in confusion.

Haldor fumbled to find his glasses. "I think we were hit by something."

They waited for several minutes. When nothing happened, Pete inched his way to the door and pulled it up a few inches. The light outside was blinding. She put her arm up to shield her eyes. They were on the side of a highway. She could see the woman and her husband standing just outside the truck arguing with another motorist. The man from the other vehicle looked like he was about to be sick. The front of his little red sports car looked completely smashed.

"Where did you learn to drive? Clown car academy?" the woman yelled to the nervous-looking man.

Pete slid the door shut. "Well it looks like we won't be going out that way."

Crane groaned. "We could be here forever waiting for the cops to show up."

"Not necessarily," Haldor said. He returned to the back of the truck and put his hand to his temple in concentration. The metal on the floor of the truck let out a creak and a groan as it curved upward, leaving a good-sized hole.

Crane blinked as he looked through the gaping hole. "Or we could just go out that way."

With Haldor leading the way, they dropped down through the hole, and crept to the side of the interstate. Haldor looked at the signs on the road and referenced his mental map. We managed to cover a pretty good distance before the accident. I think we're getting close to Clark County."

"That's good, because it looks like we're on foot from here on," Penny said.

Crane adjusted the pack on his back. "All right, let's get this over with.

After keeping a steady pace, the group managed to make it to the warehouse district in town by late evening. Graffiti competed with graffiti to get the last word on the old abandoned structures, and trash lined the quiet streets. A bold rat poked his head around a dumpster to get a peek at the travelers.

Crane swallowed. "This seems like a pretty shady part of town. Are you sure we're going the right way?"

Penny pulled the scrap of paper out of her pocket and examined the address. I think so. In fact, I think that's it..." Her voice trailed off as she pointed to a large, green structure that loomed in front of them. It seemed deserted and quiet with the exception of another rat scurrying by. The building was covered in rust and filth and looked like it hadn't seen use in years. They crept forward and crouched behind a low hill.

She looked from the address on the paper to the faded numbers on the building in front of them. "This has to be it. Are you guys sure you want to do this?"

They all nodded without hesitation. Even Pete agreed. Crane pulled the lightning gun from the pack, making Pete flinch.

He held the gun in both hands. "I'm ready. And don't worry," he added after seeing the look of alarm on Pete's face. "I'm pretty sure I know how to use it now." With those reassuring words hanging in the air, they made their way down to the warehouse.

They ducked behind some bushes just as a black luxury car approached. Penny tried to see who was inside, but the windows were too dark. The car stopped at the front of the building and a large door rolled up. It rolled inside and went down what looked like a giant hallway. She motioned for the others to follow her. They all ducked under the door as it was closing. Pete barely made it through before the door slammed behind them with a *thud.*

They stood in the entrance for a few moments, waiting for their eyes to adjust to the darkness. The inside of the building didn't look anything like she expected. Rounded walls made of dark metal lined the passage, and dim flickering lights with fixtures made of brass hung from either side. The air felt cold and dank, almost as if they were underground.

Crane put his hand against the metal wall. "Cozy." His voice echoed down the passageway. "*Cozy, cozy, cozy,* cozy," came the echo. Grimacing, he dropped his voice to a whisper. "Sorry."

Their footsteps echoed as they walked down the long corridor. A smaller passageway led down some steps on their left.

Penny looked from the large corridor and back to the steps. She bit her lip. "Maybe we should split up."

"No way." Crane shook his head. "That never turns out well in the movies."

"Well this isn't the movies. Besides, last time being split up saved our lives."

"I suppose, so," he admitted with a sigh.

"Well," Haldor chimed in, "Pete and I can keep heading straight if you two want to check out what's down the stairs. Is that okay with you, Pete?"

He nodded and so it was decided.

Crane led the way down the steps with Penny close behind. He had the lightning gun pointed in front of them in case any danger should appear.

Her heart raced as they went deeper into the passage. She was trying to be brave for the others, but inwardly she was terrified. This was just like the adventures she would daydream about at school, except in her daydreams, she was never afraid. She would swoop in, perform spectacular stunts, and save the day every time. Usually there were many Hollywood explosions involved, as well. Now that it was real, all she wanted to do was turn around and run. She couldn't believe when she was bored in class, she wanted to be somewhere like this. It seemed so long since then. Could it really just have been a few days ago?

She tried to push any negative thoughts from her mind as they pressed forward. Maybe if she told herself that this wasn't real it would give her courage. She tried hard to think of this as a big game. For a moment, she was bolstered by this thought. The illusion was broken however, as she stubbed her toe against the metal wall. This was no game and she knew it. There was no pain in daydreams, this was real, and she could get hurt.

Crane put his finger to his lips for silence and pointed around the corner. She peered around the edge. Two men were sitting at a table ripping off pieces of a loaf of bread and dipping it in some kind of grey gruel. Both of the men were dressed in mismatched leather armor and tattered clothes.

One of the men was bald and had some sort of mechanical eye patch over his left eye. The eyepiece looked retractable, like a telescope, perhaps. A black, leather strap held the eyepiece in place on the man's head. A metal ring hung from his nose. It made Penny think of a door knocker. The other man was huge and covered in tattoos. He also had a mechanical piece on his body. She watched as he ripped off a large chunk of bread with his metal arm. There were gears along the sides of the arm that must help move the fingers. A set of keys hung from the man's belt. The two men sat next to a large, iron door.

"Why do we always get the boring jobs?" the large one with the mechanical arm asked between bites.

She leaned in closer as they continued to talk.

"Well we aren't exactly suited for field work here," the bald man answered as he pointed to his eyepiece. "We wouldn't blend in, if you know what I mean."

"Still," the large man said, "I would kill to get some kind of action. All this waiting drives me crazy."

Penny had heard enough. They turned and walked back up the steps until they were out of earshot. "Those two might be guarding the prisoners," she whispered. "Do you have any ideas how to get by?"

He looked at his gun with a smile. "Indeed I do."

As it turned out, his plan was quite simple. She was to distract the guards while he got the jump on them with his gun.

"How do you think I should distract them?" she asked. "They are likely to just shoot at me and ask questions later."

"Who would they listen to? Mrs. Snyder maybe? You could turn into her."

"We don't know if they even know who she is. This seems like a pretty big operation. They might not have come in contact with her," she said, biting her thumbnail.

"I suppose you're right." Crane sighed. "Wait a minute, I've got it." He perked up as a thought came to him. "What if you were to try being an animal or something? You know, like a cat. Or how about an insect, like a spider? Can you even turn into animals, or just people and staplers?"

"I'm not sure, but I think so," she replied after a moment. "I think whatever I turn into, has to be something familiar. I have to have either just seen it, or felt it. It's like I need some kind of connection to it. It's not about looking like something or someone, it's about being them. I think that's the reason I had a hard time staying in the form of Dirk yesterday. It had been too long since I'd seen him. Our connection was severed." She shook her head. "I know it must sound weird."

"Well what is more familiar than a cat or a spider? Can you remember how they look well enough for it to work?"

"You don't understand. I don't think I can just become a cat or a spider. I have to be a particular cat or spider. Besides," she added, "being a spider sounds like a good way to get squashed, and I doubt a spider would be much of a distraction."

"Well a cat then! You should at least try it."

"All right, all right. I'll give it a shot," she said as she closed her eyes. In her mind, Penny tried to remember her neighbor's cat, Muffin. *I think he had brown and orange fur... No wait...he had white and orange fur.* She tried to think about how being a cat would feel, how her claws would retract, and how she would pounce on things and attack them with her sharp teeth. As she felt the familiar, dizzy sensation, she opened her eyes to see if it had worked. Crane stood against the other side of the wall as if he were trying to back away from her. Then the look of shock on his face turned into a huge grin.

"That is the best thing I have ever seen," he said in complete awe. Penny looked down at her hands. They were still her hands. She looked at her feet. Yep, those were still her feet as well.

"What are you talking about? It didn't work."

"You um, you totally have cat ears," he said.

Alarmed, she reached up to the top of her head. She could feel them all right. Furry cat ears were coming out of the sides of her head. Gasping, she dropped her hand.

"Also," he added as he looked behind her, "you seem to have a tail."

She reached behind her to see if it was true. Sure enough, a long, furry orange and white tail hung down from the top of her pants. Feeling self-conscious, she tried in vain to tuck the tail into her jeans.

He tried to hold back his laughter. "Don't worry about it. I've seen it all before. I have two cats."

Her face grew hot. "I told you it wouldn't work."

"It kind of worked," he said with a smile. "You would be a good distraction now."

"Or we could just do this," she said in exasperation. She reached into the backpack, pulled out a wrench, then strode down the steps.

"Wha...What are you doing?" Crane followed her down the steps.

"Be ready," she whispered. She stopped at the bottom step, then heaved the wrench with all her might toward the far side of the room. It hit the wall with a clang, and the two men jumped up and turned to investigate. This was just the opening that they had been waiting for. Penny gave Crane a little shove of encouragement, and he stepped around the corner.

"Freeze, dirt bags!" he shouted, pointing the gun at the men. "Keep your hands where I can see them and turn around slowly," he ordered. "I can't believe that worked..." he whispered under his breath. The men did as they were told and turned to face them.

"Why, you're nothing but kids," spat out the man with the metal arm. He took a step toward them. "At least, I think that's what you are," he added, looking at Penny's tail and ears.

"Stop right there!" Crane held out the lightning gun. The man's eyes grew wide as he saw what Crane was holding.

"You should know better than to play with guns," the other man with the eyepiece said in a mocking tone.

Crane ignored them. Who knew that watching all those cop shows on TV would ever come in handy? Next Crane directed them to sit back down in their chairs and put their hands behind their backs. "Um, do you happen to have some rope?" he asked.

Penny shook her head.

"Rats! I guess I'll have to shoot them after all."

"What?" both of the men yelped.

"You want to kill them?" No way was she comfortable with that. There had to be another way.

"Relax, I think most of these phaser-type guns have a stun setting somewhere," he said, fiddling with the nobs.

The man with the metal arm saw his chance. He grabbed Penny, spinning her around. "Don't even think about it. Now drop it, or the girl loses an eye." He held his strong metal fingers over her face to show he meant it.

"You heard him, Crane...Drop it," Penny said in a steady voice. She gave him a meaningful look and he seemed to understand.

"Okay, if you insist," Crane dropped the gun on the hard floor with a clack. It immediately started whirring. Penny drove her elbow as hard as she could into the man's stomach and whirled to the side just as bolts of energy shot from the gun, hitting the men. The electricity made their bodies spasm and dance. The men fell to the floor, still twitching. She checked to see if they were alive. Both of their chests rose and fell. Penny heaved a sigh of relief.

"Nice police work, Officer Bryant," she said, shaking her head. She leaned down and pulled a metal key ring from the man's belt.

"This must have the dungeon key on it." She rushed over to the door and put the largest key in a hole. It opened with a loud *click.*

"Are you coming?" she asked. Excitement was now radiating through them; they felt like they were actually going to do it. They were going to rescue everyone!

Chapter Twelve

Haldor and Pete had been walking down the corridor for several minutes when Haldor noticed a flicker of movement above them. A glint of light made the hair on his arms stand up.

"Pete, get down!" he cried.

Pete dove to the floor just as a beam of light shot over him. A wisp of smoke rose from Pete's hair where the ray had just missed his skull. "Stay down and crawl back this way," Haldor directed him. Pete made his way back to where he waited.

"What was that?"

Haldor pointed toward the ceiling. Several tentacle-like objects had emerged from panels in the wall. On the end of each one there was a firing mechanism.

"They are probably motion sensitive."

Pete wiped the sweat from his face with the back of his arm. "What now?"

Haldor removed his glasses and polished them on his shirt. "They look like metal. I might be able to bend them upward so they can't sense us. The only problem is that I need to get close to them to do it."

"That is a problem," Pete said. He looked around the corridor as if hoping a solution would present itself. Haldor sat down against the wall and closed his eyes to think. A loud creaking noise made him sit up and look around. Pete had torn off a loose panel from the wall and was now holding it with a smile.

"Why did you do that?" Haldor asked.

Pete held the panel out in front of him. It was almost as tall as he was and twice as wide. "I thought you could use a shield," he said.

Haldor stood up and slapped him on the back. "Great thinking!" he exclaimed. With Pete holding the shield out front, and Haldor ducking behind him, the two of them crept forward inch by inch.

"I think we are almost within range of the beams now," Haldor said. "I just need to get a few feet closer. I hope the beams don't penetrate metal."

"What?" Pete's eyebrows rose. "Maybe we should—" But his words were drowned out by the sound of the beams hitting the shield.

"It seems to be working," Haldor shouted over the racket. "We just need to get a little bit closer."

Pete closed his eyes as they continued forward. The shield was getting warm with the heat from the beams.

"I think we're close enough," Haldor yelled. He closed his eyes, and concentrated on lifting the sensors upward. It was working. The noise subsided as one by one each tentacle was pointed toward the ceiling.

When the last one had stopped firing, Pete let the shield fall with a *thud*. His legs shook with nerves, and he leaned against the wall for support. "Just in time," he said. "That metal was getting hot!"

Haldor looked down at the makeshift shield and was amazed to see that it was radiating heat. "There is no way you should have been able to hold onto that!" Haldor exclaimed. "Your abilities must have allowed you to hold something so hot. It sure is lucky, or we would have been fried! You know, I am beginning to think we didn't think that plan through very well," he added with a frown.

Pete was pale. "You think?" he said as his knees collapsed out from under him in a dead faint. Haldor leapt forward to catch him, but he was much heavier than he anticipated. Haldor only succeeded in getting trapped under him. He let out a muffled yell as he struggled to get free. He braced himself and gave a final shove with all his might. Pete rolled off and came to rest peacefully face down on the floor. Haldor stood up and straightened his glasses. He walked over to Pete and with a grunt, managed to roll him onto his back.

"Are you all right?" he asked as he shook him. Pete's eyelids flickered and he began to stir. Haldor helped him sit up.

"What happened? How many guys were there?" Pete looked around as if expecting to get jumped at any moment.

"I think you may have fainted."

"What? That's ridiculous," Pete sputtered. His eyes came to rest on the makeshift shield. "Oh yeah. Listen, brainy, if anyone asks, there were at least ten guys, got it?"

"Ten? I could have sworn I counted twelve," Haldor said with a smile as he helped him to his feet.

"You know, you're an all right guy." Pete slapped him on the back.

Haldor winced. "Thanks."

Both of the boys now watched for the motion sensors as they went along. They saw a few other passageways on their left and right, but they decided to keep to the main tunnel. They soon came to a huge doorway that stretched all the way from the top to the bottom of the corridor.

Pete gave the door a shake, but it didn't even rattle. He pounded his fist against it. "Looks like we'll have to turn back."

Haldor examined the lock. "I think I can open it."

"Do you have a magic key I don't know about?"

"Not quite." Haldor closed his eyes and tried to picture the locking mechanism in his mind. He concentrated on manipulating the metal pieces. The lock turned with a soft *click* and the door rumbled and shook. "Nothing to it."

But their triumph was short-lived. As the door rose, they could see a room filled with about twenty angry-looking men in uniform. Every eye was on them as they stood frozen in the doorway.

"Oh, hello!" exclaimed Haldor. "I do believe that we're a bit lost. Can anyone direct us to the highway?"

The men rushed straight at them. Pete fell backward but still managed to set one of the men coming at him on fire. The man screamed and batted at the flames on his pants. Before he could send another volley, two men grabbed Pete and held him down. Haldor tried to will the door to close again, but it was too late; they were overwhelmed in an instant.

"How did you manage to get out of your cell?" asked the man who held Haldor by his shirt. "And where are your collars?" The man's breath smelled like old gym socks, and Haldor couldn't help wrinkling his nose.

"Never mind, there is no time to worry about that now," said a large man with an orange beard. "We gotta get them back before the departure. Bring me two collars."

Pete gulped. He didn't like the sound of that. Where were they taking them now? He didn't want to be stuffed in another smelly van. They both jumped as a loud alarm bell echoed through the hall.

"An unauthorized lower prison breach!" the man holding Haldor exclaimed. "Jock and Flen, take these two back to the main holding cell. The rest of you, follow me!" Two blond, muscular men grabbed them and clamped the wretched metal collars around their necks. The men must have been twins because they looked almost identical.

"Move it!" the men said as they pushed them through the large doorway.

"I sure hope the others are having more luck than we are," Haldor whispered.

Penny covered her ears to dull the horrible ringing noise. They had been walking through the dark, dank dungeon for some time, looking for any sign of the missing kids, when the alarm sounded.

"The guards must have woke up and sounded an alarm!" she said.

Crane nodded. "Maybe I should have used a stronger setting. At least we thought to close the door behind us. Maybe they don't have another key."

The two of them picked up their pace, looking in one cell after another.

"Hey, over here!" Crane yelled.

She dashed over and peered into the cell. It was so dark that at first she could hardly see anything. "What is it?"

"There, in the corner." He pointed through the barred window.

Two lumps in the corner of the room stirred.

"Penny, is that you?" came a voice from one of the lumps.

"Mom? Is Dad with you?"

"I'm here," called out the other lump.

"What are you doing here?" her mother asked. "Did they capture you too? And why do you have cat ears?"

"I'll explain later," she replied as she began trying every key in the door. A loud *clang* echoed through the dungeon. Penny suspected it was the sound of the main door opening.

"Hurry," Crane urged. "I think they're coming."

"I'm trying." There were only three left. If it wasn't one of those, they were sunk. She inserted the next one. It fit in the lock but wouldn't turn. She tried to pull it back out, but it wouldn't budge. The key was jammed in the lock. "Oh no!" she cried in dismay.

"Let me give it a shot." Crane grabbed it and gave it a sharp tug. The key flew from the lock and landed at their feet, mixing it back in with all the others on the ring. They looked at each other in horror. They could hear footsteps coming toward them now.

Crane picked up the jumbled-up set of keys and said a silent prayer. Singling out what he hoped was the right one, he thrust it in the lock and gave it a twist. The door swung open, and he let out a cry of exultation. Her parents joined them in the hall, and the four of them ran deeper into the dungeon.

Penny glanced over at her dad. His clothes were wrinkled and his face was smudged with dirt. Likewise, her mom also looked like she'd been through a lot. Her hair was frizzier than usual, and one of the sleeves on her shirt had been shredded to the point that you couldn't make out the turtle print. They both looked exhausted, but still they pressed on.

"Is there another way out of here?" she asked as they ran along.

"There is at least one other," her father said with a huff. "We came in through a different door once after being questioned. It's like a maze in here. I don't know if I could find it again. I know it was farther left though." They took a passage to the left and continued moving forward. The group came to a T, took another left then took a right. Finally they came to a halt and paused to catch their breath.

Penny voice came in ragged gasps. "It looks like we've lost them for now, but how are we going to get out of here? Even if we do find another exit, they're bound to be guarding it."

"Maybe we'll have to make our own exit." Crane pointed toward the ceiling. There in the ceiling was a vent. A wonderful, beautiful vent. It looked just large enough for them to squeeze through.

"Stand on my hands. I'll give you a boost," Crane said.

He bent down with his hands entwined in front of him. Penny climbed on and he hoisted her up. She gave the vent a tug, and it popped open without too much effort. She let the vent swing out as she hopped down from his hands. The first person to be hoisted through the vent was Mrs. Gilbert. Crane and Penny winced as she tried to climb onto their out-stretched hands. Mr. Gilbert got behind her and pushed. Her mother's knee pressed sharply into her shoulder.

"Sorry, oops, sorry!" Mrs. Gilbert kept apologizing as she clambered up the human staircase. They helped her father up through the vent next. This was much easier.

"I hope we aren't all too heavy," Penny said. They could already hear a soft creaking noise above their heads.

"If we are, this could be a pretty short prison break," Crane said. He lifted Penny up next, then they pulled Crane through last. He made sure to pull the vent shut behind them.

The inside of the vent was quite dusty. Penny stifled a sneeze as they crawled along on all fours. She struggled to see in front of her in the darkness. She could hear her friend wheezing behind her. She had forgotten he was allergic to dust. A grate up ahead created dusty beams of light as they drew closer. She nearly ran into her father when he came to a sudden stop. Crane did collide with Penny, bumping into her backside with his head.

"Sorry," he mumbled. "Why did we stop?"

Mrs. Gilbert held up her hand for silence and moved to the other side of the grate so that the others could get closer. They all gazed down. A couple of guards walked below, holding two boys by the arms.

"Isn't that your friend, Peter?" Mrs. Gilbert asked in a whisper. Penny was shocked that her mom would recognize Pete, let alone remember his name. She didn't think her parents ever noticed anything about her life. Her shock gave way to alarm as the guards turned the corner. She could see that it was Pete, and Haldor was with him.

"We have to help them," she whispered. One of the guards paused just a few feet away from the vent to adjust the handcuffs on Haldor's hands.

"His wrists keep slipping out of these cuffs, Flen!" the man exclaimed in frustration. Penny studied the faces of the guards as close as she could from her hiding spot. The two men were identical in every way as far as she could tell. This gave her an idea.

"Never mind the cuffs, we're almost there," Flen said. After the guards had moved past them, Penny pushed open the vent and slid out, followed by the others. She closed her eyes and concentrated on the face of the man that she had just seen—from his blond hair to his Swedish-looking features. She had to get every last detail right this time if she wanted it to work. The dizzy, lightheaded sensation came over her, and she opened her eyes.

"Did it work?" she asked.

Crane nodded while her parents looked surprised.

"She is a Morphous!" Mrs. Gilbert said, as if to herself. Mr. Gilbert gave a nod of approval.

"So she is!" he said with a smile. Penny was about to ask what on earth they were talking about but stopped as she remembered the task at hand. Questions would have to wait a little longer.

"Everyone put your hands behind your back and follow my lead," she ordered. Her parents still looked a bit confused but obeyed without question.

"What are you going to do?" Crane asked.

"I'm going to take you to be exterminated, of course."

Chapter Thirteen

Haldor squirmed as the handcuffs dug into his wrists. He was pretty sure he could slip out of them again, but that wouldn't accomplish much aside from Jock making his cuffs even tighter. He glanced over at Pete. He had his head down as they walked along, looking utterly defeated.

Haldor racked his brain for an idea. There must be something he could do to get them out of this predicament. His thoughts were interrupted by a shout from behind. Their captors swung them around and held their spear-like weapons against the boys' heads. Haldor looked in dismay at the group behind them. A man who looked just like Jock and Flen held Crane and Penny's parents at gunpoint as he forced them to move ahead. Penny was nowhere to be seen. This gave Haldor a glimmer of hope.

"What's going on here?" the man with the gun demanded in a gruff voice. Flen and Jock both looked confused.

Jock scratched his head. "Who are you?"

"Who do you think I am?" the man bellowed.

"Jock?"

"Flen?" the brothers asked in unison.

"Yes, of course I am!" the newcomer exclaimed. "I was just bringing these prisoners to their cell when I heard the security breach. There is talk of a shapeshifter among us. One of you must be an imposter!"

Haldor smiled, realizing why Penny was nowhere to be seen. Flen and Jock both looked at her then back at each other with a scrutinizing gaze.

Flen took a step away from his brother. "I did think something seemed a bit off with you today. You didn't eat any pie this afternoon. The real Jock would never turn down pie."

"I-I had a stomach ache!" Jock stuttered. "Besides, I have nothing to prove to you, imposter." Jock grabbed Flen by the color of his shirt and slammed him against the wall.

"Get off me!" Flen batted his brother's hands away. Then rounded on Penny. "How do we know that guy isn't the imposter?"

She threw her large hands up in exasperation. "If I were the imposter, how would I know that my favorite number is...twenty-eight?"

Flen looked triumphant. "My favorite number is not twenty-eight, it's fifteen!" he shouted.

"Ah ha! Hear that, Jock?" Penny said. "He doesn't even know my favorite number. If you are going to impersonate someone, you should do your homework. Quick, Jock, grab him before he gets away!" Luckily her guess was right, and Jock was used to following orders first and thinking later. He seized his brother in his arms and wrestled him to the floor.

"Get off me, you idiot!" Flen sputtered. The two men rolled around on the floor, each one trying to pin the other. Haldor slipped out of his cuffs and handed them to Jock who clamped them around his brother's wrists.

"Great job, Jock," Penny said, then turned the gun on Jock. "Now if you wouldn't mind putting a pair of cuffs on yourself while you're at it. That would save some time." Jock looked up, furrowing his brow. He looked for his own weapon, but Haldor had already scooped it up.

"Next time when I say my favorite number is fifteen, maybe you'll believe me," Flen said from where he lay on the floor.

Haldor and Crane secured the brothers to a pipe on the wall while Penny removed Pete's handcuffs and the metal collars from the boys' necks.

Crane picked up the weapons that Jock and Flen had been using. They were thin and measured about five feet in length. They each bore a copper spearhead at both ends and a metal, lethal-looking, half-moon shape attached to the side. Jock had also been carrying an amber-colored knife with black leather on the grip. It was serrated on one side and razor sharp on the other.

Penny offered the weapons to her parents, but they both insisted the others have them. Haldor and Pete were only too happy to take the dangerous-looking spears. She handed the gun back to Crane then selected the amber-colored knife and strapped it to her waist. She didn't know if she would have the guts to use it when the time came, but it made her feel better to have it.

Penny was still in the likeness of Jock. She thought it would be best to stay that way in case they ran into any more guards. She looked around at their current surroundings. There were several corridors all leading in different directions.

"We must be getting close to where they are keeping the rest of them," she said with more confidence than she felt. She led them down the main corridor in the same direction the brothers were headed. She hoped it would lead them to the primary holding cell.

As they walked along, Penny's steps faltered. Every step felt like a tremendous effort.

Haldor was the first to notice her pale complexion. "Are you all right?" he asked.

Penny nodded before stumbling to the ground.

Crane rushed to her side, but didn't know how to help. "What's wrong with her?"

Mr. Gilbert knelt down next to her. "It's the form she has taken on. It is draining all her strength. It takes tremendous energy to maintain another person's form. It can kill you." Mr. Gilbert shook her shoulders. "Can you hear me?"

Penny's thoughts were foggy. She could hear voices, but it sounded like she was underwater. And she felt sleepy now. So sleepy. If she rested a moment, she knew she'd feel better.

"Penny, you need to wake up!" She looked around her. She was back in Ms. Puddlegum's class. Her classmates were laughing at her and pointing.

What was going on? Even her teacher joined the laughter. In her hands Ms. Puddlegum held out a full-length mirror.

She gasped as she gazed at her reflection. Her face was bloated and distorted. Her complexion had taken on a sickly green color, and her eyes were not her own. They looked like the eyes of a stranger, sunken and black. She raised her hands to shield herself from her hideous reflection and saw that her hands were covered in warts.

"No-o-o-o!" she screamed. *I must reverse this! I want to be me again!* In desperation she clawed at her distorted features. To her surprise, her skin fell away like scales. She could see her own pink skin appearing under the hideous face. She tore at her hands, her arms, her neck. Each tear burned and stung like being bitten by a thousand fire ants, but she continued. She peeled off the last bit of green-tinted skin from her hand and looked at the mirror with grim satisfaction. She was herself again. She sighed and let the darkness wash over her.

She opened her eyes. She could see the faces of her friends and family hovering over her in concern. She raised her hand to her face, then breathed a sigh of relief. She was back to normal.

Crane embraced Penny. His arms were wrapped around her so tight she found it hard to breath. "We thought you were a goner."

"I'm okay now." She squeaked and gently pried him off.

"You stopped breathing for a moment there."

"I did? I had such a strange dream. It felt so re-al..." Her parents helped her to her feet. She was a little shaky, but stable.

Pete's chest rose and fell as he tried to slow his breathing to normal. "Don't do that again, Gilbert!" He looked angry, but she knew better.

"Well I will try my best." Penny leaned against the wall.

Her father was still holding her arm as if he expected her to collapse any moment. "You need to learn how to gauge your energy levels. Everyone has a limit. You need to figure out where that limit is and not cross it or you could go into a coma or worse. Do you have any food with you? Food can help."

She frowned. "We're all out. We've barely eaten in days."

"That explains the sudden drop you experienced." Mrs. Gilbert patted her hand. It was the most mom-like gesture Penny could ever recall her doing. It felt foreign, yet somehow familiar. "You should at least rest for a few moments," her mother urged.

The wall behind her shook. "There isn't time," she said. "Something big is happening." The floor rumbled as she stood. "We need to keep going."

Mrs. Gilbert steadied her by putting her hand on her daughter's shoulder. "If you're sure you can."

Penny nodded and they half-ran down the corridor, with her dad still holding her arm. They came to another large door. Haldor concentrated on the lock. It was the same as the last one, so it didn't take him long to open it.

"Amazing!" Mr. Gilbert exclaimed. Haldor slid the door up, taking care to peek underneath before opening it all the way. The room on the other side was huge, and it was full of large, strange ships. Many of them already had their propellers spinning. The room was shaking with the vibrations. A few people ran around, adjusting ropes and pulleys. In the noise and confusion, no one seemed to notice the newcomers. Haldor nearly hyperventilated as he looked around the room in amazement at the monstrous ships. Even Penny forgot her fears as she gazed at them in awe. The one that caught her attention was the ship directly ahead of them. The front was constructed of pieces of glass held together by metal strips and heavy-duty bolts.

Four massive wings were along both sides and a row of portholes ran just above them. The front two wings each had a large propeller at the end. The back of the ship looked a bit like the tail of a lobster. The fin was made up of several metal joints to allow it to bend. There were several identical ships standing nearby. Another ship had a large, cloth balloon overhead and a strip of small propellers lining the hull. Yet another ship had three balloons attached to the top of a large, oblong cabin.

This ship looked a bit rougher than the others. It was dented in here and there, and the metal was corroding around the bolts. A canvas rudder hung from the back of the large metal monstrosity. There were no portholes or windows on the ship except for a small square window at the front for the pilot. There were several rectangular grates spaced at about five foot increments along the bottom of the ship. The grates looked like they had bars on them. *Bars?* Penny was brought back to the present as she realized what she was looking at.

"I think that's a prison ship!" she yelled to the others over the noise.

"They did say something about a departure," Haldor yelled back.

Pete nodded, remembering the words clearly. So this was what they meant.

The ship was already rising above the ground.

Penny looked up and saw that the ceiling of the room had opened outward, revealing the night sky. "Hurry!"

She raced toward the ship, her weariness forgotten. She could just see into one of the floor grates as the cabin rose higher. It was full of people. She saw many new faces along with a few she recognized. "Hey!" she called out to a redheaded girl. The girl looked around in confusion for a moment, searching for the source of the voice.

"Down here!"

The girl stooped down. A look of understanding and excitement appeared on her face.

"Hi, I'm Rainey. You must be Penny! Do you have a key? You have to hurry. I'm not sure what's going on, but we seem to be getting higher."

"You're on an airship of some kind," Penny said between breaths. "Don't worry though," she said, seeing Rainey's eyebrows rise, "we have something better than a key. Haldor, can you open up this big tin can?" But Haldor was already concentrating on the door. After a moment he opened his eyes.

"I can't seem to unlock it!" he cried in frustration. "The whole thing must be made of something besides metal..."

"It must be tathium," Mr. Gilbert said. He gave the side a sharp rap with his knuckles. "It's a rare type of metal that can't be manipulated."

"How do you know these things?" Crane asked.

"No time to explain now." He was right. As they were speaking, the transport had risen almost above their heads.

"Don't worry," Penny called after the ship as it lifted out of reach. "We will find a way to rescue you!" Many of the other ships were also lifting up off the ground, causing gusts of wind to swirl around the small group. She brushed her hair out of her eyes and looked around. The ship to their left was just starting to rise. Ducking under the ship, she scanned the bottom of the transport for a way in. A hatch under the wing was just out of her grasp.

"Allow me to try," Haldor said. He put his hand to his temple and the hatch swung open. Pete leapt up through the opening. He reached down, grabbed Haldor by the hands, and swung him up. He hauled Crane up next, then leaned down for Penny and her parents. Penny barely grabbed his fingertips when the ship gave a sudden lurch upward. She lost her grip and fell to the floor.

"Penny!" Crane shouted from above as the ship rose higher. He looked around for a rope or anything that he could throw down to them. Seeing nothing, he made a split decision to use himself as a human rope. "Grab my ankles," he ordered. Pete and Haldor both obeyed. He scooted himself farther through the hatch, but even reaching as far as he could, there was still a good-sized gap between his hands and the three below.

"We'll never make it," she cried in dismay as the ship continued to rise. Her parents nodded to one another as if coming to an understanding.

"We won't, but you will," her mother shouted over the noise of the propellers.

"How?"

"Do you remember when we took you to that circus years ago?"

"Yes, but what does that—"

"Remember the acrobats you tried to imitate for weeks afterward?"

Penny had forgotten all about that. It now came back to her in a flash. She had nearly broken her neck trying to imitate the flying Visooli brothers with Crane in their backyard when they were kids. She nodded to her mother in understanding though she didn't feel too confident in her acrobatics at the moment. Especially since the last time ended in a trip to the emergency room. She had to have five stitches in her chin from where she'd hit the driveway.

"What about you? I won't leave you behind."

"We'll be okay," her father assured her. "We will find another way out of here. But right now you have to go. Nothing is more important right now than saving those prisoners. We believe in you!" She looked from her parents to the others drifting higher above.

"Climb on our hands before it's too late."

Penny climbed onto their hands and steadied herself by holding their shoulders.

"On three!" she could hear her mom shouting. "One, two..."

No, she changed her mind. The ship was too far away now. She just knew that she was going to die.

"Three!" her Mom finished. Penny held her breath and jumped.

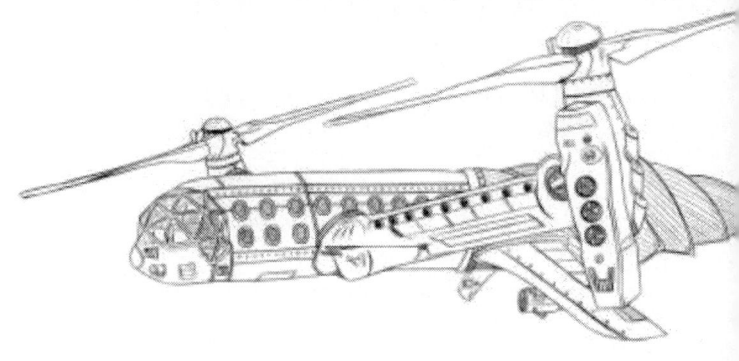

She sprang forward with all her might as her parents flung her upward. Her stomach dropped as she flew toward the ship. Crane's eyes grew wide as Penny shot up. He was so surprised that he almost forgot to grab her. Luckily he came to his senses in time to clasp her outstretched hands. They swung back and forth as the ship continued to rise. "Pull me up!" he cried. Pete and Haldor heaved with all their might. Soon all four of them lay in a heap on the floor of the vessel.

"That was so cool...We're so cool." Crane gasped between breaths.

Penny watched as her parents shrank in the distance. She hoped they knew what they were doing.

"How do your parents know so much about everything?" Crane asked. They were all sitting around the open hatch, watching the buildings grow smaller and smaller.

She'd been wondering that same thing herself. "I don't know. Everything about this day makes zero sense."

Penny thought that she had her parents figured out, but now their lives seemed like a puzzling mystery. They'd never been close. Up until a few days ago, she wasn't sure they remembered her at all. Now not only were they risking their lives for her, but they seemed to have a keen understanding of things the rest of them knew nothing about.

"We should close the hatch," Haldor said, interrupting her thoughts. "We don't want any of the other ships to notice us."

Nodding, Penny slid away from the hole as they latched the door back into place. "We need to get moving anyway. This doesn't seem like a safe place to hide."

They were under a walkway in a long hall. The walkway offered no cover. It was made of crisscrossing bars that you could see straight through. If anyone were to walk by and look down, they would be spotted. There was a single doorway at each end of the hall. Crane volunteered to scout ahead and see what lay beyond the door to their right.

"Be careful," Penny said as he pulled himself up onto the walkway.

"Always am, aren't I?"

She didn't answer. Crane was seldom careful. He would rope her into helping him with elaborate pranks that he never quite thought all the way through. As a result, they would almost always get caught.

"All clear," he whispered from above. The three of them joined him at the door with their weapons ready, just in case. The next room appeared to be the dining quarters. The tables were scratched and dented, and the floor looked like it could use a good mopping.

They salivated when they became aware of a wonderful smell wafting through the air.

"I smell food," Pete said, searching the room with his eyes. It smelled kind of like garlic and fried chicken. It was heavenly. They were feeling so ravenous that almost anything would have smelled heavenly at that moment. Pete ventured through a door near the back.

"It's the kitchen," he exclaimed. "And there is food cooking in here."

"I don't know, you guys," Penny began, "we don't want to get trapped in there when the cook comes back." She was eyeing another door nearby that led farther toward the back of the ship.

"Oh don't worry, we'll be fast," Crane said.

Haldor's stomach let out a loud growl. "I could use some nourishment myself."

She hesitated. It did smell pretty great, and she was so hungry. "Okay...But let's just grab something and go." Pete was already chowing down on some bread and cheese. Penny grabbed an apple from a bowl on the counter and then opened the door a crack to keep watch. "We should fill up the backpack with lots of little items that won't be missed," she said between bites.

"Already on top of it!" Crane stuffed his mouth with a roll as he tossed several apples into the bag. They didn't realize how hungry they were until they started eating. The boys were devouring everything in sight. There was no way the cook wasn't going to notice.

Penny sighed. "Let's get going," she urged them. "I have a bad feeling about this."

She turned to look through the crack again and froze. Someone was entering the dining quarters. A broad-shouldered man with a grease-stained apron muttered to himself as he made his way to the kitchen.

"Uh guys," she whispered, "I think we're trapped." The boys stopped mid-chew.

Bits of chicken flew from Pete's mouth as he spoke. "What do you mean trapped?"

"I mean that there is someone out there, and he's coming this way!" She scanned the room, looking for a place to hide and spied a small door in the corner.

"There!" she cried. They all just managed to get inside and close the door behind them before the man entered the kitchen. The little room that they had found was a large pantry. Bags of potatoes, barrels, and sacks of flour lay all around them.

"Oh man. I left the gun in the kitchen." Crane put his head in his hands.

Penny groaned. "Never mind that. We're really stuck now."

"Who has been in *my* kitchen?" They heard the man growl from the other room. "Stupid, greedy pigs! Can't they wait till supper? Now I'm gonna have to start from scratch."

Haldor risked a peek through the pantry door. "Better get comfy," he said. "It looks like he's about to cook a turkey. I'll keep watch for a while," he offered. "You guys can relax."

"What if he needs to come into the pantry to get more supplies?" Penny asked.

"I'll keep a lookout and tell you if you need to hide."

She sighed and sat down on the floor. Crane settled down on a lumpy sack of potatoes next to her, and Pete sat down on a bag of flour near some crates.

"Hey, Pete. I'm sitting on your relatives," Crane said with a grin.

Pete narrowed his eyes. "Shut your face, or I'll sit on you."

Suppressing a smile, Penny leaned back on her elbows and tried to get comfortable. "Well, I guess this spot is as good as any to hide and wait to get to our destination. Wherever that is."

Crane rested his chin on his knees. "I wonder if we'll ever see home again."

Penny had been wondering the same thing ever since they boarded this ship. "I don't know," she said. "I miss it. Mostly I miss not worrying about being killed every second. But you know, I kind of miss going to school. I even miss that awful Nancy."

"Who is Nancy?" Haldor asked from across the room.

"Nancy Ferrill. She's the prettiest and most popular girl in our school. Anyway, she lived to make my life miserable, but at least she wasn't trying to kill me."

Crane grimaced. "I for one do not miss Nancy," he said.

Haldor sat up straight. "Everyone hide."

They all jumped to their feet. Penny ducked behind some crates while Crane and Pete hid behind some large barrels. Haldor tried to hide behind a sack of flour, but realized only half of his body was hidden. He saw a good spot behind a shelf, but before he could reach it, the door to the pantry opened with a bang.

He froze mid-step not even daring to move his eyes. Maybe if he stayed still the man wouldn't see him. The burly chef stormed into the room, still muttering about his fellow shipmates. He walked straight toward where Haldor stood with his arm raised. Haldor's breath caught in his throat. *It's no use, he's spotted me!* The man reached past him and selected a can from a shelf before turning back toward the kitchen. He slammed the pantry door with a *thud.* Haldor let out a nervous giggle and relaxed against the shelving. The others all saw the shelf wobble at the same time. Each of them sprang from their hiding places to steady it, but it was too late. Haldor thrashed his arms as he and the shelf crashed to the ground.

"Dem stupid vermin!" the chef exclaimed, bursting through the door a second time. This time with a cleaver in his huge fist. I'll chop 'em to bits, then serve it to the crew..."

His voice trailed off as his eyes went from Haldor who was lying sprawled out on top of the canned food, to the three standing in the middle of the room. Penny's mind went blank. She could think of nothing to say. She just stood there with a strained smile on her face, then let out a nervous laugh. The others joined her in her impromptu giggling. The man's eyes gleamed. He leaned back and let out a loud belly laugh. She shot Crane a confused look. He shrugged and kept laughing.

"A-ha-ha, stowaways!" the man boomed. "Ha-ha, I *kill* stowaways!" He continued to laugh as he raised his cleaver high above his head. Penny ducked to the side as Pete blocked the blow with the spear, knocking the cleaver from his hand. The man seized Pete and the two began to grapple over the spear. Crane rushed over and helped Haldor to his feet. The two then turned a barrel onto its side and rolled it at their attacker. The man yelped as his feet were swept out from under him. Seizing the opportunity, they leapt over the fallen man and raced into the kitchen.

"The gun is gone!" Crane cried. "I know I left it right here."

"We'll have to get along without it," Penny said. She pulled him toward the door and glanced behind them. The chef was already back on his feet, his mouth twisted in rage. She swallowed and quickened her step. They all burst into the dining room. Two crewmen were sitting at a table playing cards. The men looked up as the group entered. They were seated right next to the door leading back to the hatch.

I guess we'll take our chances with door number two, she thought and veered to the left.

"Stop them!" the cook yelled. Pete slammed the door behind them and wedged his body against it. Penny turned around and froze. They stood in some sort of war room. Maps and charts hung from the walls and various sharp-looking weapons were spread out over the tables. No less than six crewmen looked toward them.

She let out her breath through pursed lips. Why did people keep following her? It was the poison ivy incident all over again.

A man with an eye patch lunged for Haldor who thrust his spear in front of him. The half-moon shape cut into the man's shoulder, making him recoil. Penny drew her knife and managed to fend off a blow from another crewman, but they were not deterred. Two men rushed Crane at once. He sidestepped a blow, tripping in the process. The other man raised his large axe. Just as he was about to bring down a blow to his neck, the man's shirt burst into flames.

"Thanks, Pete. That was close."

Pete nodded from the doorway. Haldor swung his spear around with his eyes closed. It was surprisingly effective. None of the men could even get close to him. A portly man with a beard had Penny cornered. He took a step forward and readied his blade. Crane, seeing her from the other side of the room, rolled under a table, and grabbed a sword from the assortment of weapons. He swung it at the portly man who dodged to the side, but not in time to evade injury. The sword cut the end of the man's foot clean off. He screamed and hopped up and down, spreading blood around the cabin. Crane felt nauseated. He held his stomach and leaned against the wall to steady himself.

"Look out!" Penny cried. But the warning came too late. Crane looked down to see a spear poking through his side. A man had thrown it at his back from across the room.

His eyes glazed over. "Ow," he said, sliding down the wall. Wincing, he pulled the spear from his body. Penny dashed forward to help him. Haldor glowered at the man who had thrown the spear and ran at him, flailing his weapon wildly. Startled, the man fell backward, striking his head against a metal table. Haldor stopped short and glared at the last man standing. The man turned and ran down the hall and out of the room.

Pete grabbed a weapon that had fallen at his feet and wedged it into the door handle to prevent it from opening. "That won't keep them for long," he said as he walked over to help support Crane who looked pale and solemn. With Haldor leading the way, they continued to head toward the back of the ship. They finally arrived at a cargo hold at the very end of the vessel and helped Crane sit down against some bags on the floor.

"I'm fine," he said, but his voice was weak.

Penny wasn't convinced. Her heartbeat drummed in her ears as she looked at the growing red stain on his shirt.

"What should we do?" Pete asked. "Should we keep his feet elevated, or put ice on it?

Haldor gathered some cloth that he'd found in a box.

"Here," he said, "hold this against him to slow the bleeding.

Penny pressed the cloth against his side, making him wince. "Sorry," she apologized. She turned toward Haldor. "They aren't going to stop looking for us now. We need to get off this ship."

"Well I think this opens the cargo doors," Haldor said, indicating a red button. Penny stood up for a moment to look out the porthole. They were flying over the top of a forest, still way too high to abandon ship. Pete joined her at the window.

"How are we going to get down?" he asked.

She thought for a moment. "Maybe we could construct a glider? Haldor, what do you think?"

"Well there are some pipes I could shape. And there's plenty of canvas." Haldor picked up the folded fabric. "I'm not familiar with glider design though. It would take quite a bit of time."

"Guys," Crane interrupted.

Penny put her hand on his shoulder. "Shh, you should rest."

Pete lifted the boxes off the metal pipes and laid them out on the floor.

"This isn't enough." Haldor scrunched up his face. "Maybe I could use part of the ship."

"Guys," Crane cut in again.

"What's wrong?" Penny leapt back to his side, expecting the worst. "Are you all right?"

"I'm fine. I was just thinking that maybe we could use the parachutes I'm lying on."

"Or that," Haldor said, dropping his eyes to the floor. "That could work."

There were only two parachutes behind him and they both looked quite old. Hopefully they still worked. It was decided that Crane and Pete would both wear one, and she and Haldor would each cling to one of them.

Haldor stood by the control panel on the wall. "Ready?"

"Ready," they answered.

He pressed the large red button, and the floor began to open downward. Several crates slid down the ramp and disappeared into the sky. The wind *wooshed* around them. They were higher up than Penny realized. Looking down was making her dizzy.

"On three?" she asked. The others nodded.

"One, two—"

"Not so fast!" boomed a voice from behind them. They turned to see several guards standing near the doorway. One of them held the lightning gun out in front of him.

Crane frowned. "Hey, that's mine."

"Slowly step away from the opening and place your weapons on the floor," the man with the gun commanded as the crew began to advance on them.

"I won't ask you again!" The man shouted over the noise of the wind. Penny couldn't believe their rotten luck. They were so close to escaping, yet so far away. It looked like surrender was now their best option for survival. She began to step toward them when something odd happened. Before her eyes, the gun in the man's hand began to change. The metal groaned as the barrel of the gun bent backward until it was aiming back at the man.

Haldor smiled.

The other crewmen dashed forward, but they were too late.

"Three!" Penny yelled.

Chapter Fifteen

Penny gasped as they flew through the air. It was both exhilarating and terrifying. She could see that Pete and Haldor had already opened their chute and were now drifting to the ground.

"I think you should pull the cord!" she shouted.

Crane swallowed. "I did."

She looked down in horror. The ground was swiftly rising up to meet them. She reached up and tried to pull the cord herself. "I think it's just stuck. Help me!"

Together they pulled the rip cord as hard as they could. She felt something give way and, to her immense relief, the parachute ballooned up above them. They were still falling too fast. Opening the parachute late meant that there wasn't much time for it to slow their landing. She flinched as the branches of a large tree whipped at her arm and legs as they fell.

The parachute got tangled around the tree limbs, causing them to come to a sudden stop. The inertia was too much for Penny and she couldn't hang on. She screamed as she fell, breaking branches the whole way down. She hit the ground with enough force to knock the wind out of her. She gasped for breath. A dark circle clouded the edges of her vision, growing larger.

"Are you all right?"

She sat up with a start to see Haldor and Pete standing above her.

"Are you all right?" Haldor asked again.

"I think so," she said as she got to her feet. She was sore all over and her head was throbbing, but at least nothing seemed to be broken. "Where is Crane?"

"Here I am," came a weak voice from overhead. They looked up and saw him softly swinging back and forth above. Penny scaled the tree and cut him loose, while the two boys attempted to catch him. He cried out in pain as he landed with a *thud* on top of them.

"If it wasn't for that tree, you guys would probably be dead!" Haldor said with a whistle.

Crane grimaced. "Who says we're not?"

Penny bit her lip as she glanced at him. He wasn't looking good. He was still pale and his wound had started bleeding again after the fall.

They decided to set up camp right where they were so that they wouldn't have to move him any farther that day. Haldor and Pete went to gather some firewood while Penny helped Crane sit against the tree. She gathered some water in an empty can from a stream nearby then gave it to him. After he had drunk his fill, she turned her attention to his wound. She braced herself for the worst as she pulled the rag away from Crane's side.

The sight of the painful-looking hole made her cringe. "At least it looks like it's far enough to the side, that it didn't pierce any major organs."

"Except my poor epidermis!" He flinched as she poured water over the puncture. She then tore some fabric from the parachute and wrapped the wound up nice and tight. He looked faint, but he didn't complain once. She hoped that she had done a good enough job. Her medical knowledge was quite limited. She wasn't sure if for a wound this size, she should have used some sort of antibiotics.

She looked up at the sound of something coming their way, but relaxed as soon as she saw it was just her friends. They'd returned with plenty of firewood, and thanks to Pete, they soon had a nice warm fire. That night they ate better than they had in a long time. The food from the ship provided a wonderful meal of bread, cheese, chicken, and apples. Penny knew they should conserve their food, but at the moment, she didn't care. It had been a rough day, and they deserved some comfort food. The food made them feel content, despite their still dire circumstances.

"Well, it seems that we are right back where we started." Penny sighed. "Except now Crane is injured."

"Not quite," Haldor said as he pushed up his glasses. "Have you noticed the plant life here?"

She looked around. Come to think of it, the trees did look odd. The leaves looked strange, and the bushes around them also looked foreign to her.

"Botany was a hobby of mine for a few years," he went on, "and I don't recognize any of these."

"What does that mean?" she asked. "Could we have traveled to another country? I didn't think we were on the ship that long."

"You misunderstand. I am familiar with plants from all over the world, and I've never seen any of these before."

"What are you saying?"

He pushed up his glasses. "I'm not sure. Maybe these are some sort of new species that haven't been discovered. All I know is they are new to me."

They were all silent as they mulled over this new bit of information.

"Guys, we can figure stuff out in the morning," Pete said with a yawn. "Right now, I'm tired."

He had a good point. They were all pretty exhausted and it was getting dark. They all huddled next to the fire under the parachutes to keep warm.

"I think I'll stay up and keep watch for a while," Penny said. She selected the most comfortable-looking log and tried to settle in. "I'm not tired anyway."

Haldor stretched and lay down. "If that's what you want."

She could soon hear the boy's rhythmic breathing from across the fire. It was as though they were synchronizing their snores. Crane, on the other hand, couldn't seem to get comfortable. He just kept tossing from one side to the other. She wondered if it was because of the spear wound.

Tilting her head back, she gazed up at the sky. The stars were bright tonight, and the moon almost seemed close enough to touch. This day had been a crazy one. She still half-expected to wake up from this dream at any moment. It all seemed so unbelievable. Crane let out a moan of discomfort.

"Are you all right?" she asked.

"I'll be all right. This ground is just lumpy." He groaned again as he rolled to his back.

"How is your side feeling though?"

"Oh that. Well not great, but I'm sure it will be better by morning."

"Yeah, I'm sure it will be." Her words didn't hold the conviction she hoped. She hated to even think of the prospect of losing her best friend. When she saw him get stabbed by that spear, she'd been so scared. At first, she was sad that he had gotten mixed up in this whole thing, but she was grateful he was here now. This whole experience would be much worse without him.

"Hey, Penny?" he asked after a few minutes of silence. "You know how you were talking about Nancy Ferrill earlier today?"

"Did you change your mind?" she joked. "Are you missing her now?"

"No it's not that." He cleared his throat. "It's just I thought you should know."

"Know what?"

"That Nancy isn't the prettiest girl in our school." An awkward silence followed. She waited for him to say more. But he was quiet after that. She wondered if he was waiting for her response, but she didn't know what to say. After a few moments she could hear him breathing softly in his sleep. She felt confused. Had he just complimented her?

Penny didn't remember falling asleep, but she must have at some point. She woke up the next morning with a crick in her neck from sleeping while sitting up.

"Morning," Crane said from his spot by the tree where he carved a stick that he had found nearby with the pocketknife from the backpack. It was as if the awkward moment last night hadn't happened at all. Haldor was already cooking something over the fire for breakfast. Pete was just starting to stir.

She stood up and stretched her back. "That smells great! What is it?"

"Just some leftover chicken from last night, along with a couple potatoes."

"Well it looks delicious." She closed her eyes and inhaled the buttery aroma.

Crane stood up, forgetting to be careful of his side.

"What is it?" she asked.

"I thought I saw something gleaming up in the trees." He bent down and picked up a rock.

"So you're going to throw a rock at it?"

"Well it could be a weapon. It was a sinister gleam," he added. Taking careful aim, he drew back his arm and threw the stone toward the object with all his might.

Clang!

"I hit it!"

The object clanged a few more times as it bounced off the branches on its way down. It hit the ground with a *thud*. Penny couldn't believe her eyes. It was a small, mechanical owl. The little bird kicked his feet furiously as it tried to right itself. Bending down, she picked up the squirming owl, being sure not to grip it too hard.

Haldor stopped cooking the food and came to stand next to her. "Amazing..." He breathed. "I've never seen such a complex little machine."

The bird was a tarnished brass color, and it looked like he'd seen better days. He was a bit dented, but still impressive. When he lifted one of his wings, Penny caught a glimpse of several gears underneath controlling the movement. One of his metal eyelids drooped down a bit giving him an almost sleepy look.

The owl began to shake as he looked from one person to the other.

"I think he's frightened." Haldor pushed up his glasses and leaned in closer. "A frightened machine? Is that possible?"

"Well you would be scared too if someone just knocked you out of a tree with a rock." Penny shot a look at Crane.

He shrugged. "For all I knew, it was something that was going to try to kill us. I'm sorry, little guy," he said and walked over for a closer look.

"Poor thing." Penny stroked the bird behind his ears. She remembered that a parakeet her parents used to own loved to be scratched there. The owl squinted his eyes and began to hoot contentedly.

As she pet him, she noticed that the bird had a fresh chip broken out of his left ear. "Aw, he must have gotten this when he fell."

"At least now we know what to call him." Crane said.

"What's that?

"Chip, of course!"

She looked into the owl's eyes. "He does look a bit like a chip, doesn't he? Well I guess we should let you be on your way, Chip," she said as she placed him on a branch. The little bird turned his head and blinked several times at them before hopping to the edge of the branch and fluttering back to her arm.

"Hey, it looks like you have a new friend," Haldor said with a smile. "Have you seen this amazing little guy?" he called to Pete who was already stuffing his face with the breakfast Haldor had made.

"Can I eat it?" he asked between bites.

The little owl let out an alarmed hoot and buried his face into Penny's arm.

"Well no," Haldor said. "At least, I wouldn't recommend it. The metal would get stuck in your throat."

"Then I don't care," he said, and went back to eating.

Penny coaxed Chip out of hiding, and he hopped up her arm and settled on her shoulder. She offered some breakfast to the owl, but he wasn't interested.

"You probably only drink oil, eh?" she asked. The owl hooted and bobbed his head up and down. "I think he said yes. Well, we'll just have to get you some."

"Don't be stupid. He's just a machine." Pete grunted.

"And you're just a blockhead, yet you manage to talk," Crane mumbled. Pete stood up and marched toward him.

Penny held out a hand between them. "Guys, relax," she said. "Boy, it seems like you both get along better when we're in imminent danger."

"Speaking of imminent danger," Haldor chimed in, "I suppose it's time we went looking for more."

"I guess you're right." She looked around their comfy little campsite and sighed, not quite ready to leave their safe haven. It was obvious the rest of the group felt the same way, as they slowly packed up their supplies. Chip flew to a tree branch and watched, tilting his head to the side before settling once again on Penny's shoulder. Once everything was ready, they gave their safe little camp a parting glance and set off into the unknown.

Chapter Sixteen

"Whoa..." Crane whistled as he arrived at the top of the large hill. They had been walking through the dense terrain for hours without a sign of life, and now this.

Penny came to a stop next to him. "Whoa is right."

The others soon joined them, and together they all gazed down at the most magnificent city any of them had ever seen. The place was made almost entirely out of clocks and bridges. She had never seen so many clock towers in her life. An intricate system of bridges crisscrossed throughout the town, leading to various shops. Even most of the shops had clocks above them.

"You would never have to ask for the time if you lived there," Crane said. "You would be all, 'I don't have time to do that.' Then they would be all, 'Yeah actually you do!' Be...because of the, um clocks," he finished.

"Uh, yeah." Penny nodded with a laugh. "Anyway, should we get a closer look?"

"Absolutely." Haldor rubbed his hands together.

Pete hesitated. He didn't like the looks of this place at all. It reminded him of something out of a crazy dream, or worse yet, a nightmare. He shifted uncomfortably at the thought. "I dunno. It seems weird. I think I'll wait out here."

"It will be fine," Penny said. "Besides, we may need you if things get tricky in there."

Pete nodded. He supposed he could go in after all. *These weaklings needed someone to protect them,* he thought to himself. The entrance to the town was over a large bridge that was in the shape of an arch. They stayed alert as they walked up the cobblestone path. For all they knew, this town could be full of those horrible guards or men in dark suits. The front gate was closed and locked from the inside.

"Well, we tried," Pete said and turned to go back.

Haldor strode forward and put his hand to the gate. "I'll take care of it."

Penny put out her hand to stop him. "I think we should be cautious about using our abilities in public. Besides, there is some sort of booth over here. Maybe there's someone in it." She walked over to the booth and peered inside. To her surprise, there appeared to be a man made out of iron sitting on a bench.

"Um, hello?" The man didn't move.

"Maybe it's just a statue," Crane suggested.

"It's odd to go through the work of crafting a statue only to hide him in a building," Haldor thought aloud. He examined the booth. On the outside of the structure, there were several buttons and switches that he hadn't noticed at first, along with what looked like a windup key. He clicked several of the buttons. They kept returning to their original position every time he had moved about seven or eight of them.

"Hey guys, check this out," he said. "I think it's some sort of combination lock." The others gathered around him.

"How will we figure out the code?" Pete asked. Haldor brushed his fingertips along the switches and furrowed his brow.

"Well right away, we can eliminate these eight buttons," he said, "because they aren't worn like the others. That just leaves these four buttons, and these five switches. I think it's just a matter of flipping them in the right order, and then turning the crank."

"That will take forever to figure out," Crane moaned.

"No it won't," Penny said with a smile. She was holding up a small piece of paper in her hand. "I found this next to the booth. Looks like someone was using a cheat sheet and got careless with it." She handed the paper to Haldor. On it were nine numbers printed in scrawled handwriting. He held them up to the lock and activated the buttons and switches in the order indicated. When he was done, they all stood back and waited for something to happen.

When nothing changed, Haldor smacked his forehead. "Of course, the crank! I forgot to turn the crank." He bent down and gave the crank several turns clockwise.

They were all startled when the man in the booth stood up.

"He's moving." Pete gasped as the man turned toward them. With his hands at his sides, he began to march. He raised his left arm as he approached. In his hand he held a rusty metal blade. "I knew this was a bad idea," Pete said, stumbling backward.

Haldor helped him to his feet. "Just wait."

They watched as the figure marched mechanically toward the bridge. Another metal man met him coming from the other direction. In unison, they turned and marched to the gate. Once at the door, the two machines turned around to face the group. They both gave a sharp salute as the doors creaked open. Pete was still looking warily at the metal men as they entered the town. The doors closed behind them with a slam, making him jump.

Penny took a good look around them. Some of the towers and buildings were so close that they were touching. There were several different levels of cobblestone bridges that ran throughout the city, intersecting here and there. A large fountain stood in the center. It was constructed of various intertwining pipes.

Because of the many clocks, a soft ticking could be heard all around them. As they walked farther down the path, they soon became aware of one strange fact. The city was completely empty.

Penny chewed on her thumbnail. "Where is everyone?"

Aside from the ticking and sound of the fountain, it was silent. It gave Penny the creeps. A crow swooped down from the sky and came to rest on a lamppost. It let out a single rasping caw that was magnified by the silence around them. Chip, who had been dozing on Penny's shoulder was brought to attention by the sound. The little owl hopped down Penny's arm and buried his face in her shirt.

Crane peered up at the bird. "Hey, he's made of metal just like Chip."

Only this bird didn't look nearly as friendly as the owl. There was something about his red eyes that didn't sit right with her. The bird tilted his head toward them as he studied the small group. His razor-sharp talons seemed to be cutting into the lamppost. It was soon joined by another bird, and another, until they were surrounded by the ominous-looking crows.

Penny licked her dry lips. "Let's um...let's go this way."

The little mechanical owl shook with fear. She tucked him away inside of her jacket and led the way down a narrow alley, hoping the buildings would provide some cover from those searching eyes. They could hear the crows cawing behind them as they picked up their pace. They were soon sprinting down the alleyway. They turned left, then right.

"I think we lost them," Crane said as they slowed to a jog. They stopped and listened. All was silent.

Haldor took off his glasses and cleaned them on his shirt. "That was odd. At least they seem to have lost interest in us."

But their moment of peace was broken by a shrill caw. They saw the bird too late. It swooped down out of nowhere and clipped Penny with its sharp claws. She swung at the bird and put her hand to her forehead. She could feel the warmth of the blood as it dripped down into her eyes. The horrible racket resumed just as quickly as it had stopped. It seemed to be coming from everywhere. Crane pulled off his sweatshirt and gave it to Penny to hold against her head as they began to run again.

"Hey, you there, stop!" yelled a man from a bridge in the distance. He and several other men dressed in the same guard uniforms as the men from the ship were now running toward them. The friends ducked down another alley.

"A dead end!" Pete slammed his fist against the wall. They could hear the shouts of the guards as they drew closer.

Penny gritted her teeth. "Looks like we may have to fight."

They turned and readied themselves for battle.

"Psst, down here," came a voice near their feet. They looked down to see a man with a pointy nose and a grey top hat looking up at them from a manhole.

"Hurry," he whispered, "follow me." They didn't wait for a second invitation and followed him without question down the ladder that led beneath the street.

"Thank you," she said once they had all reached the bottom of the ladder. "That was a close one."

"You're lucky I happened to be nearby. The penalty for being out during curfew is death. Why are you out this time of day?" The man spoke in an accent that Penny couldn't quite place. Hungarian perhaps?

"Curfew? But it's still light out."

"During Freedom Week, we're only allowed to be outside from nine in the morning 'til one in the afternoon. You should know better."

"Freedom Week? That seems ironic."

"Well it's not celebrating our freedom. It's celebrating Lord Esmond's freedom from the Pythians. He wants us to remember his victory in silence."

"The Pythians?" she questioned.

"Yes, the magic users. But you know that," he said, removing his hat and scratching his head.

"Well we aren't exactly from around here," Penny said.

The man looked them up and down. "Well that's apparent from your clothes. Are you from another city or province, or did you come all the way from another island?"

She shrugged. "We're a bit lost."

"Well, where are you staying? You can't be out wandering the streets. Especially during Freedom Week."

"We just arrived in town. We aren't staying anywhere." The man looked at them for a moment and then grunted as if he had made up his mind.

"Well we can't have you running about getting killed. Follow me." They went through a series of catacombs and then up through a small tunnel with homemade footholds made of pipes bolted to the sides. The tunnel opened right up into a cozy living room. They stepped out onto green, well-worn carpet.

Penny unzipped her jacket, allowing Chip to return to her arm. The walls of the room were covered with white and yellow wallpaper that was peeling here and there. A torn velvet duvet sat in one corner next to a shiny brass phonograph. A fire was crackling in the fireplace. The man clicked an armchair into place over the tunnel, disguising it completely.

"Mother Potts, I'm home!" the man said as he hung up his hat and coat. "And I've brought visitors!"

A woman in a flowered apron burst into the room and put her arms around him. "Welcome home, Father Potts!" she gushed. She spoke in the same unusual accent as her husband. "Who are your friends?"

"Well I seem to have forgotten to make proper introductions. I am Phineas Potts, and this is my wife, Clara."

"Glad to meet you. I'm Penny, and this is Haldor, Crane, and Pete," she said as she indicated each of them.

"They're new in town," Phineas told his wife.

"Do you have a place to stay?" she asked. "If not, you must stay with us."

"I was hoping you would say that." Phineas nodded with approval.

"Oh my!" Clara exclaimed as she noticed the gash on Penny's forehead. Come into the kitchen, dear, and I'll fix you right up. The rest of you can make yourselves comfortable."

As Penny followed Clara, Haldor noticed for the first time a strange contraption on the window sill.

"What is this?" he asked. He walked over to the window for a closer look.

"Oh that is one of my projects," Phineas said as he picked it up. "I'm a bit of a tinkerer." The object looked like a large spider with a compass in the center. He flipped it over and turned it on with a small key that he had taken from his pocket. Once he set it on the floor, the spider became animated and skittered across the carpet.

Haldor practically squealed with delight. "That's remarkable!"

"If you like that, you should see my workshop."

"Workshop?"

"Follow me," he said. "I think I have a few things that you would be interested in." With Haldor trotting behind him, Phineas walked down the spiral staircase leading to his workshop.

"I'm going to check on Penny," Crane said.

"Fine with me." Pete stretched out and made himself comfortable on the duvet.

In the kitchen, Clara was just finishing up.

"Oh Crane, I was just going to come get you," Penny said as he walked in. "Clara used to be a nurse. I think she should take a look at your side."

"I'm fine," he insisted, but he allowed Clara to unwrap the bandage anyway. He flinched as she pulled away the last bit of cloth. The skin underneath was puffy and an angry shade of red.

"It's not too bad yet," she said, "but another couple days untreated, and this could have been serious. How did this happen?"

Crane began to tell her about the incident, but changed his mind when Penny shook her head. "Just got careless," he replied.

"And landed on one of the bishop's spears? It leaves a distinctive cut you know," she added when she saw their surprise. "I have treated far too many of them in the past." Her eyes became fierce. "Don't worry though, any enemy of Lord Esmond is a friend of ours."

They both breathed a sigh of relief.

"We kind of hitched a ride on one of their ships, and had to abandon it after we were discovered," Crane explained.

"The guards on the ship are called bishops?" Penny asked.

"Yes, they are named after Lord Esmond Bishop. He rules all of Azure. Those men you met are his loyal guards."

"Excuse me, but where is Azure?" Crane asked. "Are we somewhere in South America?"

"South America?" she said, pronouncing each syllable slowly. She stood without warning and rushed to the living room. When she came back she was holding a dusty leather book. She opened it on the table and flipped to a page with a map on it.

"Is your South America somewhere on this?" she asked as she pointed to the map. The map was old, and the only writing on it was in Latin.

"This map is different than I am used to, but yes, that is South America." Penny nodded as she pointed to a spot on the map. She was so glad to see something familiar. "Where are we on the map right now?" she asked. "Can you point to where we are?"

Clara's face was pale. She collapsed onto a kitchen chair. In response to her question, she raised her finger. But rather than pointing to a spot on the map, she raised it toward the ceiling. "Up."

Chapter Seventeen

The others had joined them soon after Clara's strange declaration. She and Phineas had gone into the other room to talk for some time. They were all sitting around the kitchen table now eating hot soup. Phineas had produced a small bowl of oil for Chip, who drank it up, hooting with contentment. Clara still seemed a bit shaken even now.

Penny was afraid to upset Clara again, but she had to know what was going on. "What did you mean earlier about us being up?" she asked.

Clara and Phineas each exchanged a meaningful look before she answered.

"There have long since been rumors of a land called Terra. The legends say that Azure was once a part of Terra, and that Terra now lies beneath us."

"Beneath us?" Haldor asked. "As in underground?"

"No, not underground," she answered. "You see, Azure is a floating colony made up of several different islands. They say Terra is beneath us, but using ancient technology, the builders created an aura of storm clouds that prohibits us from being seen by the inhabitants of Terra. Consequently, we can't see them either, and the harsh winds they created make it impossible for anyone to get in or out. Most people now consider Terra to be a myth."

"But we got here somehow," Penny said.

"Yes and that is puzzling."

"But how did Azure come to be located here?" Haldor asked. "You said it was once a part of Earth? I mean Terra," he corrected himself. "And what's a builder?"

"I think my husband can explain that better than I can," she said. "Do you mind, dear?"

"Not at all." Phineas cleared his throat. "It's a bit of a long story, but according to the legend, our islands were once one giant island that was located in Terra's ocean. Our great city was built primarily by a mysterious race that we call the builders. We were a peace-loving people. Our city was a great and wonderful place. We were ahead of the world in innovation and our economy was thriving. However, other nations, seeking to steal our resources and kidnap our builders, forced us to close our borders to outsiders. An all-out assault on our land forced us to take drastic action.

"The builders worked night and day and created a machine powerful enough to lift our island into the air. One night, after forcing our enemies to retreat back to their borders, we lifted off into the night sky. So that our enemies wouldn't come looking for us, we left evidence behind to suggest that we had sunk into the depths of the sea. It is said that the separate islands came into being when the island broke apart as it was lifted from the sea."

"Well, your island didn't happen to be called Atlantis at some point, did it?" Crane asked with a laugh.

"We have been known by many names in the past," Phineas said in all seriousness. "It is possible that could have been one of them. It is said that our name became Azure the day we left for the sky. Up until today, the story was just a story in my mind. I mean, I hoped that it was true, but to actually meet people from Terra is something else altogether!"

"Fascinating," Haldor said as he cleaned his glasses on his shirt. "The idea that a whole island could rise into the sky is...well it's—"

"Amazing," Penny finished his sentence.

"Yes, quite," he agreed.

Pete scoffed. "More like crazy."

"I admit, it does sound a bit crazy," Phineas said. "But as crazy as it seems, here you all are. The builders are capable of amazing things. Like that remarkable bird you have with you, young lady," he said looking toward Penny. Chip had finished the oil and was making a soft cooing sound as he looked around the room. "Where did you get such a creature?"

"My friend sort of hit him with a rock while we were in the forest." Penny answered.

Crane shrugged. "I thought it had an evil gleam."

Phineas leaned in closer to get a better look at the little owl. "He is quite intricate. He must have been the work of a builder."

"Really?" Penny pet Chip behind the ears.

"Yes, without a doubt. Builders put a life into their machines that I can never manage."

Crane rubbed his face with his hands. "So why does this guy Esmond want to be free of Pythons, or whatever they're called? You said that was what Freedom Week was about, right?"

"Pythians," he corrected. "In order to answer your question, I must first tell you a little more about the builders and how they came to live with us here. The builders are a special race. They are full of magic and wonderful abilities. I have read some literature from Terra, and I believe that on Terra, they are called gnomes, or leprechauns in some cultures. Usually they remain in hiding, but for some unknown reason, many of them came out of hiding to work with humans and build our great city. Some people say that we caught them and blackmailed them, or threatened their families, but I like to think they just decided to give the human race a chance. It's said that most of them chose to leave Terra with the island, though a few remained behind."

"So we have gnomes living among us on Earth?" Pete guffawed. "Give me a break."

"Shh, Pete!" Penny gave Pete a scathing look. "Sorry, go on," she urged. Pete frowned but said no more.

"Anyway," he continued, "regardless of their origins, humans and builders have lived alongside one another for many years here on Azure. Once upon a time, the builders even wed and had families with humans. A half-builder, half-human is known as a Pythian, or a magic user.

"A child who is a Pythian possesses certain magical abilities. If a person who has magic in their blood has a child with a human, that child may or may not possess special abilities. Sometimes in the same family, one child is born with abilities while their sibling is not.

"For a long while, we all lived in peace, both the magic and non-magic people. Lord Esmond changed that however. Esmond was born into the noble family that governed Azure at that time. His father was a human, and his mother was a Pythian.

"Esmond was born with no magical abilities and it enraged him. At the young age of thirteen, he left home in search of power. He soon formed an anti-magic movement. I guess he thought if he couldn't have special abilities, no one should. His parents thought it was nothing more than a rebellious phase that would pass, but in just a matter of three years, he had gathered such a large following that his parents could ignore it no longer.

"They sent out a group of soldiers to stop the rebellion and bring their son home, but they were too late. Esmond's followers not only killed the soldiers, but next they came after the noble family. A bloody and long battle ensued for many days. When Lord Esmond finally seized the empire, his first act in power was to eliminate all of the Pythians."

"That's awful," Penny said. "Did the builders help them?"

"Well, yes and no. You see, many of the builders, not wanting to get involved in human politics, decided to instead hide in the mountains and forests. A handful, however, chose to stay and help the

Pythians take a final stand against Esmond. Fearing they would lose their lives, some of the magic users pleaded with the builders to help their children escape if the battle was lost. The builders were their only hope, for it was rumored their elders knew of a way to navigate through the intense winds around the borders of Azure. They agreed to send the children down to Terra where they would be safe while the Pythians held off Lord Esmond's forces. The magic users made a valiant stand and wiped out half of Lord Esmond's army, but in the end, they were overpowered. Their final stand began at nine in the morning and ended around one in the afternoon."

"The same time that you are allowed outside on Freedom Week," Haldor said.

"Exactly." Phineas nodded. "Those that escaped with their lives sought to blend in with the non-magic humans. There are many who still live in hiding to this day."

"What happened to the builders who didn't go into hiding? The ones that tried to help. Did they all die?" Crane asked.

"Once Esmond learned of the builder's involvement in helping the children, he hunted down, and killed the remaining elders," he replied with a frown. "The other builders were forced to become slaves for Lord Esmond. They are like his personal pets. The only ones that remain free are said to be hidden in a place called 'Sanctuary.' For all we know, they might all be dead by now too."

Penny rubbed a knothole on the table with her finger. "Did the children ever get to Terra?"

"No one knows for sure. Without the help of the elders, no one can leave Azure to find out. The winds prevent anyone from coming or going. Like I said, before today, I was unsure that such a place even existed."

"Oh it exists all right," Haldor said solemnly. "And I am convinced that the children made it there."

"How can you be sure?" asked Clara.

"This is how," he said as he held up his spoon. Haldor closed his eyes and concentrated on the metal. The spoon twisted and turned until it resembled a corkscrew. Clara and Phineas both gasped. He returned the spoon back to normal and set it on the table.

Clara's eyes filled with tears.

"Oh, Phineas, could it be that our Tom is alive?"

"Yes, Clara, yes I believe that he could be!" he cried as he embraced his wife.

Penny and the others soon related to them the events prior to that day.

Phineas tipped back in his chair and whistled. "Esmond must have found a way past the winds. But how?"

"There is another thing that I don't understand though," Penny began. "Pete and I both have parents, so how could we be part of this?"

"I don't have parents," Pete corrected, "just a lousy foster family."

"But I thought I met your dad when we were like eight. Didn't he come to career day?"

"That was my foster brother. He owed me a favor."

Penny closed her eyes and rubbed her forehead. Could she have been adopted? The thought that her parents might not be her real parents made her feel betrayed. She didn't like being lied to.

"So they have brought the children here?" Clara asked.

Penny's thoughts snapped back into the present. "Yes, and we're not sure why they bothered to bring them all the way here just to kill them. We heard Snyder mention that this Lord Esmond guy might be planning to use them in one of his special projects. Any idea what that means?"

Phineas set his jaw with determination. "I have no idea, but I think I know how we can find out."

Clara raised her eyebrows. "Do you mean the underground?"

Phineas nodded. "If anyone knows what Esmond is up to, they will."

"What's the underground?" Haldor asked.

"The underground resistance. It is made up of magic users and non-magic users alike who hope to someday overthrow Lord Esmond and his bishops. They have spies in Esmond's fortress that they use to gather information."

"Then let's go see them right now." Penny jumped up from her chair, nearly knocking it down.

"Well I wouldn't act too rashly," Phineas said. "I think it would be best to wait until tomorrow. You see, this is the last day of Freedom Week. By tomorrow, curfew will be back to ten p.m. and getting around will be much easier."

"Besides," Clara added, "Crane needs to rest."

"I'm fine." He rose to his feet, winced, and sat back down. "Well, maybe a little rest couldn't hurt."

"All right. I suppose we can wait till morning," Penny said with only slight reluctance. She was rather worn out after their day of walking through the countryside after all.

"Come with me and I'll show you to your rooms," Clara said after they were finished clearing the table. They followed her up a set of narrow stairs and down a hallway with various paintings covering the walls.

"A hobby of mine," she said as they passed. "I am still an amateur."

Penny gazed at the pictures in awe. "They are wonderful," she murmured.

She was no expert on art, but the paintings looked beautiful. They were extremely intricate. One was of the front gate of the city. It was complete with the mechanical men saluting by the double doors. Another one was of the fountain in the town square. A few of the sinister-looking crows were perched atop the fountain. Their eyes seemed to be following her as she walked down the hall. She gave an involuntary shudder at the sight of them.

"Why did those birds attack us like that?" she asked.

"They are spies for the bishops," Clara explained. "They were made by the builders that Lord Esmond enslaved. He says he had them made to 'keep us safe.'" They came to a stop in front of an old oak door. "Here we are!" she said as she turned the knob.

The little room was furnished simply with a double bed taking up most of the room. An old stuffed bunny sat in the window seat near the foot of the bed. There was a small dresser and what appeared to be a bassinet crammed into the corner of the room with a sheet laying partway across the items. Clara walked over and pulled the sheet the rest of the way over the furniture.

"You boys can stay here in the nursery, and Penny, you can follow me to the guest room down the hall."

"Nursery?" Haldor asked.

"Yes, this was Tom's room once." Clara stroked the stuffed bunny's ears and looked around the little room. She shook her head as if remembering that she was not alone. "I'm sorry, Penny, dear. I'll bet you're tired. I'll show you your room now," she said with a smile. "I can bring up a couple cots for you boys a little later."

"I get the bed," Pete announced as Penny followed Clara out the door. The guest room was just down the hall from the nursery. It contained an old four-post bed with a fluffy comforter covered in flowers. A carved wooden chest stood at the foot of the bed.

"I hope you will be comfortable here."

"Oh yes, I'm sure I will be. Thank you so much for letting us stay with you."

"Of course. Feel free to come down for some tea and cookies when you get settled."

She could hear Clara's footsteps on the wooden floorboards as she walked back down the hall. Penny walked over to the window and sat on the seat. Chip fluttered down to the window sill and together they sat gazing at the streets below.

The view from here was amazing. She could see nearly the whole city. The sun was starting to set, and the orange light was gleaming off the faces of hundreds of clocks. Her eyelids were beginning to feel heavy. Maybe she would lie down for just a few minutes, she thought as she moved to the bed. It was so comfortable. She breathed in the sweet smell of the comforter as she stretched out on the bed. It smelled of lilacs and lavender.

She knew that tomorrow would be filled with more danger and trouble, but for now all she wanted to think about was sleep. She tried to clear her head, but her mind went automatically to the resistance. Could they help them? Would they know Lord Esmond's plan? And what was going on with her parents? Were they even her parents? Did they manage to escape from the warehouse? Her thoughts soon turned into garbled-up nonsense as she drifted to sleep. Her last sleepy notion was that they might be able to beat Lord Esmond if they could only find a dance teacher and a pumpkin willing to travel abroad.

Chapter Eighteen

"Good morning," Crane chirped as Penny entered the kitchen the next day. "Or should I say afternoon?" The boys all sat around the table gulping down breakfast while Clara was busy at the stove.

Penny rubbed her eyes. She was still tired, but felt much better after having freshened up and washed her hair. "Is it that late? What time is it?"

"Really, you have to ask? Really?" Crane joked as he pointed out the kitchen window at the sea of clocks.

"*Pshh,* it's only eleven-thirty," she said after a glance outside. "Afternoon isn't until, you know, *after*-noon."

"Technically, she's right," Haldor chimed in.

"And technically these flour cakes taste exactly like pancakes, but they don't call them that here. So...yeah," Crane said, as if that somehow settled it.

Penny sat down in one of the empty chairs. "Flour cakes?"

"Yeth, they are delithious," Crane said after taking another bite. They were indeed delicious. She savored the honey flavor that flooded her taste buds as she took a bite.

"Where is Phineas?" she asked before reaching for seconds. Clara turned and set a new hot batch of flour cakes on the table. The boys immediately pounced on them.

"He's been up since the crack of dawn, out looking for information about the resistance," Clara replied. "We used to be more involved in the underground, but in recent years, I'm ashamed to say that we had rather given up hope. I'm sure he'll be able to find them though. We still have many of our old connections." Just as Clara finished speaking, they heard a door close in the other room.

"I'm back!" Phineas said.

Everyone filed into the living room after him. Phineas had plopped down into the easy chair and was fanning himself with a newspaper.

"Did you find them?" Penny asked.

"Yes, I spoke to my friend Derbisher McHenry. He lives across town and is still very much involved in the resistance movement." Phineas paused to light his pipe. "Apparently there is a meeting tonight, but because it's on the other side of town, we might have a difficult time making it back before curfew. I know of ways to travel unseen through the city at night, but I have never taken such a large group. I'm afraid it will be dangerous if we choose to go."

"I don't mind staying here," Pete spoke up. "You know, if it will help," he added.

Clara looked at Crane. "You should stay behind too. The more you can rest, the better."

"No way am I missing out on the action!"

Penny put her hand on his arm. "Please stay. You need to be ready for the real action when the time comes."

He sighed and banged his hand against the wall. It took a bit of persuasion, but finally, a sulky Crane along with Pete and Clara were bidding them farewell.

Clara gave her husband a quick kiss. "Be careful."

"Don't worry, dear," Phineas said as he put his hat on. "No one will even notice us."

Penny shifted uncomfortably in her outfit. She wasn't used to wearing a skirt. Mr. and Mrs. Potts had lent them a few articles of clothing to help them blend into their surroundings. Penny felt rather like a lady pirate. She wore a dark blue skirt with shiny brass buttons along the top, and a cream blouse under a leather laced bodice. It accentuated her chest in a way she wasn't quite comfortable with. Chip turned his head upside down, taking in her new look. She pulled the neck of her shirt up, feeling self-conscious.

"I know I look silly. You don't have to look at me like that." She had also traded in her sneakers for some sturdy boots. At least those were comfortable. Haldor was wearing simple grey breeches with a white shirt with black suspenders. Phineas had also lent him one of his old bowler hats which was a little too large for his head.

"Ready?" Phineas asked.

Penny gave a shrill whistle and Chip flew to her shoulder. They waved goodbye and walked down the steps to the street. The city was far from empty now.

The streets were bustling with people hurrying from here to there.

"Right after Freedom Week, everything is busy," Phineas explained. He led them over bridges and down alleyways and streets. It was easy for Penny to forget the terror she felt yesterday with the bright sun shining and the people all going about their business. She looked up to see a metal crow staring down at them from a lamppost. Shivering despite the warmth of the day, she picked up her pace.

They were passing through an outdoor market-place now. The venders were mostly selling fruits and vegetables. Some of the produce looked familiar, while others, like the bright blue, spikey ovals a man was selling in a cart, looked foreign. A woman, who was hurrying by, bumped into Penny who was thrown off balance. She stumbled to the side and bumped into a table holding something akin to pota-toes. Several of them fell to the ground.

"I'm sorry," she mumbled to the scowling vendor. Haldor and Phineas were getting farther and farther ahead as she scrambled to pick up the potato-like objects. They were just starting to disappear around the corner as she picked up the last one.

"Sorry," she said again and raced to catch up. Pen-ny scanned the busy streets. She couldn't see them an-ywhere. A feeling of panic was beginning to make her throat feel tight as she walked to the top of a bridge in order to get a better view. Chip flew from her shoulder.

"Oh, you're not leaving me too are you?" Chip fluttered to the top of a lamppost and began turning his head in all directions. He let out a loud hoot and flapped his wing toward the street below. She looked in the direction he was pointing and spotted what looked like Phineas's top hat disappearing into the crowd.

"What a smart little guy."

Chip flew back to her shoulder, and they made their way toward where she saw the hat disappear. She was so fixated on keeping her eyes glued to the spot, that she didn't notice the group of bishops until she ran headlong into them.

"Hey, watch it you!" One of the men snarled. The man had a mouth full of metal teeth which he clanked together. It reminded her of a mutant shark.

"I think you need to be taught a lesson in manners," a tall bishop with a surly face barked.

"Hey wait," the man with metal teeth said, "don't she look familiar?" His face became thoughtful. "Where were you last night?" The man was so close to Penny that she could feel his hot breath on her face. Chip didn't like this man one bit. And he certainly didn't like the way he looked at his friend. He leaned forward and gave the man a sharp peck on his porous nose. "Ahhhg!" the man cried, jumping back. "Why, I ought to—"

"I'll tell you where she was," came an unfamiliar voice. "She was lounging about the house avoiding work as usual!" Penny turned toward the voice. A boy a few years older than her lounged against the railing. He had jet-black hair and a tan complexion. His eyes were what caught her attention the most. They were a light, penetrating sky blue. "Mum sent me to find you. You are supposed to be helping her bake bread for market!" he scolded. "Was she bothering you gents?" he asked, shaking his head.

"I was just—" Penny began.

"Quiet, you!" the boy snapped with a glare.

"No, no," the toothy bishop said. "We just thought she looked familiar, but come to think of it, the other girl was much taller."

"Yes, taller," the other guards agreed.

"Come on then, mum is waiting," the boy said. He took her by the hand and pulled her away.

"Thank you," she whispered once they were out of earshot.

"No problem," the boy said with a smile that made her stomach flutter. "You should watch yourself around the bishops. It doesn't take much to anger those tiny brains. By the way, my name is Griffin."

"My pain is Nenny, I pean, Menny," she fumbled. "I mean, Penny is me," she finished. Her face flushed red.

"Well, Nenny, Menny, Penny," he said with a laugh. "It was great to meet you, but I need to get going. Hopefully I'll see you around."

"Yes, thanks be to you again." She shook her head. "I mean, thanks again."

"I'll be needing all of me though," he said.

Penny looked down and realized that she was still holding his hand. "Sorry," she mumbled as her cheeks flushed a deeper red. Without another word, the boy disappeared back into the throng of people, leaving her standing alone.

"There you are!" Haldor exclaimed as he clapped his hand on her shoulder. She jumped, thinking for a moment that the guards had come after her. "We've been looking all over for you."

"Glad to see you're okay. We were afraid something happened," Phineas said. He sounded relieved.

"Something almost did." She related to them the incident with the guards and the boy who had helped her as they walked. Phineas gave a start.

"Sounds like that guard recognized you. At least they weren't able to get close enough to you yesterday to be sure."

Penny took another calming breath. "Yes, but if that boy hadn't shown up, things may have gone much differently."

"This should be the place," Phineas announced. They had arrived at a dingy-looking, little shop. A bell jingled on the door as they stepped inside. The store was dimly lit. From floor to ceiling it was jam-packed with various knickknacks and oddities. The three wound through the aisles like a maze 'til they reached the front counter. A balding, white-haired man was slumped forward on the counter making a dreadful racket with his snores. Phineas gave him a gentle shake.

"Excuse me..." he began. The man sat up with a snort and looked around in bewilderment. He was wearing an eye patch that appeared to be made out of an old metal spoon with the handle cut off.

"We're closed," he mumbled after looking them up and down.

"Actually we're here for the meeting," Phineas ventured. The man gave them a searching look as he scratched his prominent nose.

"Don't know what you're referring to."

"Ah, well you need the code right?" The man folded his arms and didn't answer. "I think McHenry said something about clouds." Phineas closed his eyes in concentration. "That's it," he said, snapping his fingers. "A head in the clouds is better than a cloud overhead!"

"Why didn't you say that in the first place?" The man jumped down from his stool. He was much shorter than he had first appeared. The top of his head only came to Penny's elbow. "Better hurry then, the meeting is about to start," he said, gesturing for them to follow. They entered a door near the back of the shop and went down a set of stairs into a storeroom.

Haldor glanced around. "This is quite a small room for a meeting."

"It would be, if it were going to be here." The man shook his head. "You're a silly lad." Standing on a stool, the man reached up, opened an old grandfather clock, and twisted the minute hand two turns to the left, and the hour hand one turn to the right. They watched in amazement as the stairs that they had come down lifted upward, revealing a hidden passage. "Go on in," he said. "I've got to get back to watching the front desk in case we have any other late folks." With Phineas leading the way, they entered the passageway.

Penny strained her eyes to see where she was going. The candles flickering on the walls were the only light in the cramped walkway. Chip hooted nervously on her shoulder.

"What's wrong?" she whispered. "I thought owls liked the dark." Chip nuzzled her hair and leaned in closer as they continued to walk. They soon reached a tall wooden doorway. Phineas swung the door open to reveal a room filled with a dozen or so people. A man with spectacles stood at the head of the table. Penny thought that he must be in charge. No one even noticed their entrance. They appeared to be in the middle of a rigorous discussion.

"That is out of the question!" exclaimed a tubby man with a large mustache that looked like it was trying to take over his face.

"But if we are to succeed, we must refine our methods!" a woman wearing a bright red shawl argued.

"Now, now," the spectacled man said. "There is no need to raise our voices. Let's discuss this calmly. A training academy would be a dangerous proposition," he said. The tubby man nodded in agreement. "But if the alternative is never mastering our abilities," he went on, "we may have to take that risk." A murmur of assent could be heard from several people. Haldor, who was listening intently to the conversation, was bumped from behind by the door. He stepped to the side as two others entered the room. One of them was the man from the front desk. Penny looked at the other newcomer in surprise. She recognized him. It was the boy she had met earlier.

"Griffin, what news do you bring?" asked the man with the glasses. Griffin walked over to the table and addressed them all as a whole.

"Well according to our lookouts, a whole fleet of ships were seen late last night flying toward the north. One carrier was identified as a prison ship."

"A prison ship?" said a large-nosed man. "What can this mean? Could they have found the builders?"

"It is doubtful that the builders would let themselves be found," said the man with glasses. Phineas cleared his throat. Everyone looked toward them as if noticing they were there for the first time. Griffin spotted Penny and a look of confusion appeared on his face. It was soon replaced by a wide grin.

"Phineas, my dear fellow!" the man with glasses said. "It's good to see you. What brings you here tonight?"

"It's good to see you too, Horace," he said with a smile. "It's good to see all of you. What brings me here tonight, is some news that I've recently heard. It is good news and bad news. I suppose it depends on how you look at it."

"Well, out with it," said the tubby mustached man.

Phineas fidgeted. "The good news," he said, "is that our children survived the war, and there is a good chance that they are still alive as we speak." Murmurs of excited amazement rippled through the group. Phineas held his hand up for silence.

"Unfortunately," he went on before they could interrupt, "our children are the ones being held in the prison ship."

Chapter Nineteen

The room was noisy with chatter as everyone tried to register what Phineas was telling them.

"That is preposterous," the tubby man said as he stood up from the table, his mustache bristling out in indignation like a porcupine. "Where did you get this information?"

"Sit down, Barton," Horace said in a tired voice as he removed his glasses and leaned back in his chair. "Phineas, I don't doubt that you believe what you are telling us, but I don't see how this could be possible. In a moment of desperation, we sent our children to a place that doesn't exist with a group of individuals that we never saw again."

"But it's true," Phineas exclaimed. "And these two are proof," he said, waving his hands in a grand gesture. Penny gave a start as all eyes looked toward them. "Show them," Phineas urged.

They stood in silence for a moment. Finally, Haldor walked over to a map on the wall and removed a pin. He took a deep breath and closed his eyes. They all watched, but nothing seemed to happen. He opened his eyes and gave a nod of satisfaction. He set the pin on the table and returned to his spot by the door. Barton bristled and swiped it from the table. His look of ill humor gave way to surprise as he examined it.

"Why, it's bent in the shape of a word," he said, squinting his eyes. "Howler?"

"It's supposed to say Haldor," he corrected him. Barton passed the pin around the table so the others could see.

"A young Pythian? What can it mean?" murmured several voices.

"It is a sign!" croaked a wrinkled old woman. She drew back her black hood revealing a mop of tangled, white hair. Her eyes gleamed wildly. As she spoke, she looked at Penny. Her gaze was piercing and made her feel uneasy, but she couldn't look away. "The prophecies tell of the children's return to Azure. It is a sign of our liberation," the woman went on, spitting bits of froth as she spoke. "It is a sign of the coming of the chosen one."

"The chosen one," scoffed Barton.

"When that which was lost is returned," she went on as if he had not spoken, "the chosen one will lib-

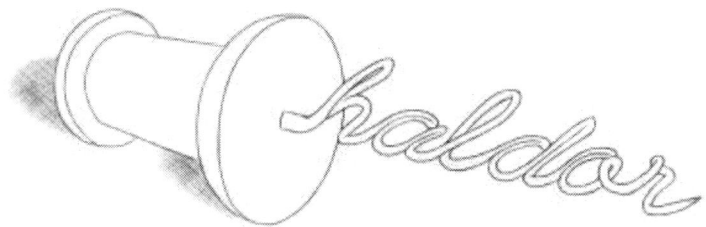

erate us with great power. That's what the prophecy says. I can feel it. The chosen one has come to Azure at last."

"The prophecy is an old wives' tale. Just like Terra," Barton interrupted again. "It means nothing. It's some kind of trick." The old woman sat down, but she kept her gaze locked on Penny. She shifted uncomfortably, wishing the woman would look away. "They could be spies from Lord Esmond!" Barton continued. "Besides, even if they do have abilities, not all of the Pythian children were sent to Terra. Griffin here is proof of that."

"Yes," Horace began, "but Griffin is one of very few exceptions. His abilities were not known until later," he said, stroking his chin. "But I suppose it is possible that he also was not sent to Terra."

He looked at Penny now. "Is she one as well?"

She swallowed. *All right, that's your cue,* she said to herself. She lifted Chip from her shoulder and set him on the table, then closed her eyes and tried to concentrate on turning into the man with the mustache, but all she could think about was the fact that everyone's attention, including Griffin's, was on her. She opened her eyes. Everyone still looked at her expectantly.

"Did it work?" she whispered to Haldor.

"Did what work?"

Penny took that to mean no. She let out a nervous laugh. "Must be an off day," she apologized. She felt so stupid. Shrinking back, she leaned against the wall, wishing that she was nothing more than a piece of furniture like the battered wooden chairs in the room. Anything to get people to stop looking at her. Penny's body became rigid with embarrassment. She wondered why they kept looking at her. The woman with the red shawl gasped and pointed.

"Where did she go?"

"I believe she is the chair," a man sputtered.

Penny thought she felt stiff. *So this is what a chair feels like.* At first she was intrigued, but then she panicked when she realized that she could no longer move. It was such a claustrophobic feeling. She was trapped! It felt like the stapler incident all over again. She wanted to turn back into herself right away. She tried to focus and visualize her body once more. She tried to remember the feeling of her limbs, the texture of her hair, even her goofy crooked smile. She sighed with relief as she felt the familiar dizzy feeling come over her. She opened her eyes and smiled as she gazed at her own wonderful fingers. Her relief gave way to complete mortification however as she became aware of a peculiar draft. Looking down, she gasped in horror. Apparently she had neglected to remember clothing. She let out a yelp and toppled behind Phineas and Haldor.

Phineas offered her his cloak, which she threw around her shoulders. She pulled it down over her head in embarrassment, then closed her eyes and concentrated as hard as she could on regaining her clothing. Penny could feel her clothes materializing over her body. She racked her brain to think of some offhand comment that she could say when she emerged to hide her utter mortification. *Who nude that would happen? No, no... Too corny,* she thought. *Don't worry, the buck stops here! Yeah, like that is any better.* In the end, she thought it best to just be silent. She gave herself a quick once over before she ventured a peek out of the cloak. Everyone seemed to be preoccupied by something the woman in red was saying. A few people looked toward her as she drew the hood back all the way.

"Who nude that would happen!?"she blurted, then slapped her hand over her mouth. Her comment was met with silence and some confused looks. Penny pulled the hood back over her face and slipped into the hallway, closing the door behind her. Once in the hall she slid down the wall onto the floor. She would wait for Haldor and Phineas out here. The stone wall felt cold against her back. She pressed her warm face against it to cool her blushing cheeks. The door opened again and Griffin stepped into the hall.

"You forgot this little guy," he said, holding Chip out to her.

"Thanks," she mumbled, taking the owl without looking up.

"That was quite a performance," he said. Penny didn't dare look him in the face. He closed the door and sat down next to her. "Don't worry," he said, "I'm sure everyone *bare-ly* even noticed."

She smiled in spite of herself.

"Shut up," she muttered.

"You're lucky though," he added.

"And why is that?" Penny asked, rolling her eyes.

"Turning into an object is dangerous. You are lucky you were able to turn back at all."

She looked up at him, her embarrassment forgotten. "Really?"

"Of course!" he said, suddenly fierce. "That is one of the first things you should have been taught."

She held out her hands. "Well nobody taught me anything. I just kind of taught myself."

"I'm sorry," he said in a softer tone. "I don't mean to sound harsh. You just scared me back there. I think you scared everybody."

"But why is it dangerous?"

"No one knows for certain. There are theories though. Some people say that it's because objects are non-organic and your body can go into some kind of shock when you make the change. I think of it a little differently though. I think that shape-shifting is ninety percent mental and only ten percent physical. You have to be able to feel and understand what you change into. It's pretty hard to understand the motivation of something that has no motivation. And on top of that, if you don't hold onto the feeling of your humanity, you can easily forget and become lost in the object forever. I know it sounds silly, but it can happen. I've seen it myself."

"What about clothing? Isn't that considered an object?"

"Yes and no. Clothing can be a bit tricky as you discovered tonight."

Penny dropped her gaze and pretended to be interested in a hang nail on her finger.

"However," he went on, seemingly oblivious to her discomfort, "clothing seems to be more of an extension of the person than an object. I don't pretend to understand it all though," he added. "I'm still learning things myself."

"How do you know so much about it?" she asked, looking up from her imaginary ailment.

"Well, I, like yourself, am a Morphous. It is a type of Pythian. I've been practicing my abilities in secret for several years now."

"Isn't that dangerous though?" she asked. "Aren't those crows everywhere?"

"I just have to be careful. Even so, some members of the resistance don't think I should risk it. It's causing quite an issue right now," he finished and stood up.

"But if you don't all practice, how can you hope to overthrow Esmond?" she asked as Griffin helped her to her feet.

"Exactly!" He nodded. "We need more people like you in our meetings. Sometimes it seems like we aren't making any progress at all. It's the reason Phineas and Clara left. They got tired of things growing stale because people were afraid to take any kind of action."

"I wondered what happened. Hey, what's up with the wild-looking woman in there? Is she crazy?"

"Oh you mean Widow Johnson? She's a little eccentric, but she's all right."

"What did she mean about the chosen one and the prophecy?"

"Well we have a few ancient documents that we managed to save during the war. Esmond burned or stole everything else. Widow Johnson has devoted her life to studying and trying to interpret the meaning of these documents. She sees herself as some kind of a medium. Growing up, she used to tell me all sorts of stories and prophecies of things to come. Most people write her off as crazy, but I, for one, think she may know more than any of us."

"We need you both back in here," said Phineas as he opened the door.

"After you," Griffin said, waving her in front of him. She took a deep breath and walked back inside. It seemed like everyone in the room was talking at once.

"What's going on?" she asked Haldor who was still standing near the door.

"It seems that a few people believe us, but many do not. They are about to take a vote on whether or not they should help us," he yelled over the noise. The room was split. Heated arguments were erupting all around them. Horace stood up, banging his cane on the table for silence. The room grew quiet as everyone returned to their seats.

"Now, I believe you all know the motion on the floor. Let's get on with the vote," he said. "All in favor of putting our trust in Penny and Haldor, and helping them on their way, raise your hand." Several hands went up around the room, including Griffin's, Horace's, and Widow Johnson's. "All opposed?" Several other hands shot up. The tubby man named Barton was among the opposed. "That's odd, it seems we have an equal number of votes for and against," Horace mused. "Ah, I see. Someone wake Fitz," he said, pointing toward the short man from the front desk.

"I'm awake," Fitz muttered as he was shaken from his slumber.

"You missed the vote," Horace chided.

"Oh, I know, I know. I was just resting my weary eyes. I was tired of all this arguing nonsense. I say, of course we should help the children. What have we to lose?"

"That settles it then," Horace said. "Now, who will volunteer to accompany them?" This question was met with vacant stares.

"I will donate funds for their travels," offered a woman. Several others chimed in with similar sentiments.

"I'll go," Griffin said, stepping forward.

"But we need him here!" Barton objected. "He's our primary look out."

"It will be fine," Horace said. "Those who are staying behind can fill in. There are certainly plenty of you," he said, looking around the room. "Anyone else?"

His question was met with silence.

"Well, okay then." After Horace was done speaking, they took up a collection of money and various items to ease their journey. "I'm sorry we can't do more, old friend," Horace said, handing Phineas a large knapsack.

"This will help a lot. And come to think of it, our smaller numbers might work to our advantage. Our best strategy will be to sneak in and out again before they even know what's going on."

"Yes, I hope you're right. Good journey then," Horace said with a wave. As they made their way to the exit, Phineas stopped to talk to Griffin about the details of the journey. A rough hand grabbed Penny's arm and pulled her aside. She turned to see the old woman from before. The woman grabbed her shoulder and pulled her down to her level. Their noses were almost touching as she spoke.

"Beware of your friends as well as your enemies. The prophecy speaks of malice from within. When the chosen one returns, a malice from within will threaten to bring about death."

"Okay... I will," she murmured, trying to move toward the door. Widow Johnson had a surprisingly strong grip.

"Remember!" she urged, releasing Penny, who stumbled backward into Haldor.

"Sorry," she said. When she turned to look back, the old woman had melted back into the group. Penny shivered. She could still feel those eyes on her. *What a strange character,* she thought as she wiped the spittle from her face.

After talking with Griffin, it was decided that they would all meet early tomorrow morning at Phineas's house. Next, they began the arduous task of returning home without being seen by bishops or crows, for the meeting had gone way past curfew. It was no easy feat. Many times they had to slip under the street and into the sewers, or wait for a crow to move to another spot. When the three returned to the Potts's home, they were exhausted. As they sat around the table, they explained to the others what had happened and their plans for the morning.

"Tomorrow morning seems so sudden!" Clara said with surprise.

Phineas nodded. "I know it does," he said, "but we don't know how long the prisoners have. Time is of the essence."

"Well then what time do we leave?" she asked.

"Well we leave at eight o'clock, but, Clara, I need you to stay here," he said. Clara's face fell.

"But I couldn't bear staying here, not knowing if something terrible has happened to you!"

"But you know the laws that prohibit unauthorized travel. If no one is here when they come to take the census next week, they'll come looking for us. One of us needs to be present. You can lead them to believe that I am at home, taken ill." Seeing the sad look on Clara's face, he added, "If you want to come though, my dear, we can certainly take that chance."

"No, no. It will be much easier for you to travel if you aren't a wanted man. But please be careful."

"Of course," he assured her, giving her arm a squeeze.

"Can Locksley still obtain travel documents?"

"Yes, Griffin said he would bring them over tomorrow," he said with a yawn. He stood up and stretched his back. "We have a big day tomorrow. We had better get some rest." They all agreed and went up the stairs to their respective rooms.

"So what is this guy like?" Crane asked once they were in their room. "Do you think he will be helpful?

Haldor turned from where he was setting up his bedroll on the floor. "His name is Griffin, and I think he will be quite helpful. He knows a lot about air travel and getting from place to place. He thinks that we should be able to charter a ship with the money that the resistance gave us."

"Does he have any idea what Esmond's plans are?" Crane asked as he plopped down on the end of the bed.

"My bed!" Pete pushed Crane to the floor.

Ignoring the sharp pain shooting through his elbow from hitting the wooden floor, he brushed himself off and sat on his makeshift bed on the window seat.

"No, he hasn't heard any recent news, but he has strong ties to the resistance and says they have connections on the inside."

"I just hope all these old geezers we're picking up don't slow us down," Pete muttered.

"Oh, actually Griffin is just a little older than we are," Haldor said. "Penny and he seemed to hit it off quite well."

Crane sat up. "What do you mean? Does she like him? Is he good looking?"

"Oh I don't know, I suppose she does. He is a likeable fellow." Haldor yawned and stretched out on the floor.

"But I mean like, like. Does she like, like him?" He sat on the edge of the window seat, waiting. His question was met with a soft snore.

"Would you shut up so that I can sleep?" Pete said.

"Yeah, yeah." Crane slipped down under the blankets. He didn't know much about this Griffin guy, but he already didn't like him. What a stupid name. What did he think he was, a flying lion? Actually now that he thought about it, it was a pretty cool name. *Aargh!* Why did he have to have such a cool name?

Chapter Twenty

The next morning came early. Especially for Crane who had tossed and turned most of the night. Penny, on the other hand, had slept well. She felt extra chipper that morning. Crane looked alarmed, watching her whistle a catchy little tune as she buttered her toast. Chip sipped his morning bowl of oil beside her.

"Why are you in such a good mood this morning?" he asked.

"Oh, I don't know. I just am. Probably because I got to take a nice hot bath this morning."

Crane wondered if he ought to do the same. It had been over a week now since he'd had a proper shower. He supposed that Griffin probably smelled super manly, like a hardware store, or leather, or perhaps bagels. They seemed a manly sort of food. Crane lifted his arm and pretended to stretch so he could sneak a whiff under his arm without anyone noticing.

"Blech!"

"Is something wrong with the eggs?" Clara asked.

"Oh no, everything is great! I just, uh, remembered something," he said and slipped off to the bathroom. Phineas, who had gotten up an hour earlier than everyone else to buy supplies at the market place, arrived back just in time for the end of breakfast.

"Any left for me?" he asked as he walked into the kitchen.

"Yes, I saved some for you," Clara said, reaching for a plate on the counter. "I hope you got plenty of food rations, these boys can eat!"

"It's hard not to indulge with food as delicious as yours," Haldor said between bites. Pete grunted in agreement. Just then, a knock sounded at the door.

"That will be him," Phineas said as he went to open the door. Penny smoothed her hair, and brushed a few crumbs from her shirt.

"Come in. We're just finishing breakfast," Phineas shouted. Griffin strode through the doorway. He was carrying a well-used metal crossbow with leather wrapped around the grips and a rather deadly-looking spiked mallet around his waist. "Are you hungry?" Phineas asked. "We have plenty of..." He paused as he looked at what food remained on the table. "Butter," he finished with a shrug.

"That's all right," Griffin said with a laugh as he sat down at the table. "I stopped for a bite at the market this morning. Hello again," he said as he smiled in Penny's direction.

She drew a blank on the proper response to hello. She instead found herself waving like an idiot.

"And it's good to see you, Mrs. Potts," he went on.

"It's wonderful to see you again," Clara said. "And my, you've grown tall!"

"I think the only people you two haven't met yet are Pete and Crane," Phineas cut in. "This is Pete."

Pete gave them a nod. "And where is Crane?" Phineas asked, looking around.

"He said he forgot something and took off," Penny said.

"Well it's good to meet you anyway," Griffin said, extending his hand. Pete seemed not to notice the gesture. Griffin cleared his throat and sat in the vacant chair next to him. He pulled some papers from the bag hanging over his shoulder. "Here are our travel documents. Locksley was able to whip them up last night after the meeting," he said, spreading the papers across the table for them to examine.

"These are great!" Phineas said. "I see old Locksley hasn't lost his touch." He thumbed through the documents and started to hand them out to their corresponding people. "In case we get separated."

"This says Mildred Grousebottom," Penny said as she studied her papers.

"Yeah, sorry about that," Griffin apologized. "It was a rush job after all. From now on, where the law is concerned, you are Mildred Grousebottom."

She grimaced but said no more.

"Who wants to be, Franklin Findley?" Phineas asked.

"I could see myself as a Franklin," Haldor said and took his documents.

Phineas sifted through the remaining papers. "That leaves, Gordy Thomas, Seth Barnes, and... Poppy McField. Is this last one serious?"

"It was a rush job," Griffin said with a shrug.

"I'll take, Gordy." Pete decided.

"Well, I guess I get to choose next then. Just call me Seth," Phineas said and tucked the papers into his jacket.

"There is something wrong with that bath," Crane said as he entered the room with sopping wet hair. "I couldn't get any hot water from the pump and..." He stopped short as he noticed the unfamiliar faces in the room.

"This is Crane, the last member of our party," Phineas explained.

"Welcome aboard," Crane said as he walked forward and shook his hand. Griffin unfortunately was about how he imagined. Stupid perfect hair, stupid perfect face. It made him feel sick.

"Something wrong?" Griffin asked.

Crane realized that he was glaring at him. "Oh, no," he said and relaxed his face. "Just trying to warm up after that ice bath."

"Sorry about the water," Clara said. "You have to open the pipe that allows the water to flow over the furnace."

"That's okay, it was quite, um, refreshing."

"Hey there, Poppy," Pete jeered.

"Um, hey. I didn't realize we were giving each other new endearing nicknames. I think I'll call you, Sparkles Diamonds!"

Pete frowned. Why was he always ruining his fun?

"Poppy is your new alias," Penny explained as she handed him his traveling documents. "Poppy McField, to be precise."

"Wow, that's kind of great. I sound like a large man who sells baked goods."

Griffin unrolled a large map onto the table.

"Now that the documents are figured out," he said, "let's take a look at the map and decide where we're going." He pointed to a spot on the map. "Here's where we are now. If we want to take the quickest way to the docks where we can charter a ship, we need to head north over Hangman Hills, and then take the eastern road to the town of Pankor.

"But Hangman Hills is dangerous," Phineas said. "Can't we take the northeast path?"

"We've had reports that the bridge is down on the northeast path. There are treacherous cliffs and nearly impassable forests if we try to go round any other way. It would add at least three more days to our journey."

"All right then, I suppose we'll just have to chance it," Phineas said.

Griffin had brought a few extra weapons and bits of armor which he offered to the others. Penny donned some leather wrist guards and selected a slender rapier with an ornate carving of a little bird on the handle, mostly because it reminded her of the small dagger she already possessed.

Pete chose a large sword with jagged sides and a blunt tip. He also put on some shoulder armor that came partway up his neck. Crane selected two large daggers. He liked the idea of dual wielding. After careful thought, he decided to wear a shield on his back, as well. He did not want to be stabbed from behind again. Haldor was content with the spear scythe that he had gotten earlier from the guards on the ship. It had served him well before, after all.

Once they double-checked their supplies, they all said a final goodbye to Clara—who for the fifth time that morning, begged them to be careful—and exited down the hatch in the living room. Once beneath the streets, Phineas led them to a manhole near the far side of the city.

"We'll be less likely to be noticed if we don't go through the main gate," he explained. After climbing the ladder, he lifted the manhole then motioned for them all to follow. Penny climbed the ladder last. The light was intense compared to the darkness below. She squinted her eyes against the blinding sun and looked around. They were partially hidden from view by a large cart. A young boy sat by the cart, staring toward them, eyes unblinking.

"Hurry," Crane whispered. Most of the others had already disappeared through the side gate. They closed the manhole and turned to follow, but a bishop appeared around the corner, blocking their way.

"Well, well, fancy seeing you again!" the man said with a toothy smile. She realized to her dismay, that it was the man from yesterday with the metal shark-like teeth. "You weren't going to run off without a proper goodbye, were you?"

"We are traveling to see our mother," Crane stated. "She's gravely ill."

"Yes," Penny nodded. "Gravely."

The man leaned in and looked at Crane, as he clicked his teeth. "You're not the boy from yesterday. He was older."

"Well I have more than one brother," Penny said.

"I am the younger, better-looking one." Crane flashed a smile.

"And I thought your mother worked at a baker's shop in town," the man went on.

"She, uh, she did. I mean does," Penny fumbled. "It is our grandmother who is ill. Did he say mother? Sorry, it's our grandmother." The man circled them, once again reminding her of a hungry shark. Chip flapped his wings and let out a warning hoot. The man drew back, covering his still tender nose.

"Well then I suppose you have papers?" he challenged. *"Humph."* The man sniffed, but seemed appeased after seeing their documents. "Wait," he said after a moment, "why do you have different last names?"

"We have different fathers," Penny said. "You see my father met an untimely demise when he was trying to clean the outside windows. At least that's what Mom told us. I have my theories though. You see, I think that a band of mercenaries was sent to hunt him down for his famous pie recipe. He made the best triple cherry, whipped, double dip pie à la mode that you ever tasted! At least that's what I was told. Anyway, on that fateful day—"

"All right! Enough, you can go," the guard said, turning and walking back toward the square, muttering some unpleasant remarks under his breath as he went.

Pete crossed his arms as they joined the others. "What took you guys so long?"

"We got a bit held up, but everything is fine now," Penny replied.

Before they could get into any more detail, Phineas had taken the lead, and the little group was on the move. They all trudged along in silence for a while, wanting to make as much progress as possible before sunset. The countryside was rocky and barren here. Every so often, they would come across a lonely tree. When they did, Penny would slow her steps to enjoy the momentary shade on her back. Of course that put her behind the others, and she would have to run to catch up, making her even warmer than before. They came to a stop at the foot of a large cliff reaching to the clouds. There were broken steps zigzagging against the wall, all the way to the top. Many of the steps were rusted and bent at awkward angles making their use all but impossible. Griffin walked over and stood next to Penny.

"This was once a great stairway," he commented, "with a waterfall on both sides and water wheels churning the water to all corners of this valley."

She could see the remnants of the wheels at the base of the cliff. There were also a few metal ramps resembling waterslides snaking here and there up the sides. "What happened?"

"Esmond re-directed the flow as a war tactic, so that the people would need to come to him if they needed water."

"How awful," she murmured as she gazed up toward the top of the cliff. "So what now?"

"We climb."

Crane's hands shook. He'd never told anyone, but he had a bit of a fear of heights. Once when they were younger, he and Penny had climbed to the top of a huge tree because Penny wanted to pretend they were giants. He lost his footing while pretending to stomp on his uncle's car and fell straight down, breaking several branches on the way. The branches had left him battered and bruised, but had probably saved his life. Ever since that incident, heights made him a wee bit uncomfortable. He had surprised himself and jumped out of the ship the other day without hesitation, but only because the alternative was to be shot. And with the parachute malfunctioning and all, it hadn't boosted his confidence. He took a deep breath and tried to steady his nerves. It didn't look like a safe climb.

Pete, who wasn't crazy about heights either, also had his doubts on the safety of the old, broken stairway.

"Are you sure about this?" Pete asked.

"You're not afraid, are you?" Crane tried to sound confident but his voice cracked, foiling his attempt at suavity.

"It should be fine," Griffin replied. "Right Phineas?"

"Well I did scale it once years ago, though there were more steps at the time..."

"We'll follow you then since you have the experience," Griffin said.

He nodded and took a couple cautious steps up the stairs. Chip flew ahead of them to watch their progress from above.

"Don't put your full weight on anything until you've tested it. Better yet, try to only use the steps that I use."

Step by step, the group inched their way up the cliff side, jumping gaps and stepping on whatever looked stable. Penny lost her balance for a moment and teetered on the edge of a wobbly step. Chip swooped down and grabbed her arm, flapping his wings furiously till she regained control.

She took a deep breath and let it out slowly. "Whew, that was a close one. Thanks!"

After that the owl seemed to think it best to remain on her shoulder. He felt it was his duty to protect this fragile, pink, flightless creature. They soon came to their first real obstacle when they had gone up about a hundred feet. Twelve steps in a row were missing. It was too far for even the tallest of them to attempt a jump. Phineas crouched down and removed his backpack. He pulled out a sturdy rope attached to a homemade grappling hook. The hook had been crafted from the skeleton of an old umbrella that he had welded and reinforced. He swung the rope with expert hands and tossed the hook onto the rail of the stairs above them. It caught on the first throw. He gave it an experimental tug, then, without a word, swung across to a foothold on the other side. From there, he was able to hoist himself up to the steps above. He didn't ease up on the rope until he was sure the steps would hold his weight.

"Next," he called as he tossed the rope back across. One by one, they each swung across. It was Crane's turn now. He tried to make his knees stop shaking. He looked down, and regretted it right away. The ground seemed to be spinning. His stomach felt like it had a fish out of water flopping around inside.

"Heads up!" Griffin called as he sent the rope toward him. Crane's reaction time was dulled by his fear. He looked up in time to see the rope coming toward his face. It hit his lip, leaving a bright red welt. He fumbled for the rope as it began to swing back the other way. He lunged forward but his hands groped at the air.

"Crane, look out!" Penny warned, but it was too late. He was falling.

Chapter Twenty-One

Crane flailed his arms around. Memories of falling from the tree flooded his mind. He knew this had been a bad idea. Now there were no branches to slow his fall. His whole body tensed in anticipation of his eminent crash. He gasped as his body jerked to a halt. He looked under him in confusion, but he still couldn't tell what was holding him up.

"Don't worry, I've got you," he heard someone say. He looked up to see Phineas holding his fingers to his temple. His other arm was outstretched. Penny gazed in wonder as Phineas lifted Crane through the air with his mind and brought him to rest on the steps next to her. Chip, who had grabbed Crane's shirt and was flapping with all of his might, had thought he was the one responsible for his rescue. He seemed quite pleased with himself as he flew back to her. He thought he must be quite strong indeed. He puffed out his chest and let out a series of proud hoots. It was sure a good thing for these creatures that he was around.

"Brilliant!" Haldor exclaimed.

"Thanks," Phineas whispered, then collapsed. Griffin barely managed to catch his limp frame.

"I'm sorry." He gasped. "I guess I'm a bit out of practice. It's bound to happen after over a decade of not using my ability."

"No need to apologize..." Crane said, still in shock. "I'm just glad that you remembered at all!"

"It was instinct, I suppose," he replied. "I don't know if I could do it if I actually tried." Phineas began to rise, but then slumped back down. "Just a few more minutes and I'll be fine," he told them.

As they rested, Griffin looked toward Pete and Crane with curiosity.

"So I know that Penny is a Morphous, and Haldor is a Refiner, but what about you two? What can you guys do?"

"I'm a what?" Haldor scratched his head.

"It must be what they call people with your ability," Penny explained.

"Oh, I see. A Refiner? Interesting."

"I burn stuff," Pete said darkly. Griffin snapped his fingers.

"Oh, a Firebrander! I should have known."

"What do you mean by that?" Pete said, looking angry.

"I mean no offense," he countered. "You just happen to have a rather explosive demeanor."

"I do not!" he shouted. "I mean, I do not," he said in softer tone.

Griffin stifled a smile. He turned his attention to Crane now.

"I am a black belt," Crane said, jutting out his chin and trying to squint his eyes to look as menacing as possible. "That is the most powerful ability there is back home."

Griffin looked quite impressed.

"I didn't realize you had other abilities on Terra as well!"

Pete scoffed and opened his mouth to speak.

"We need to get going," Phineas cut in, interrupting whatever Pete was about to say. "We have already endangered ourselves enough by lingering on these unstable steps."

"Quite right," Griffin agreed and helped him stand up on his still wobbly legs.

The worst part of the climb was now behind them, but it still took a great amount of focus to keep from making a fatal mistake. Penny glanced down.

The sun glistened off the steps below them. It hurt her eyes to look at it.

"Almost there. Hurry up, lads!" Phineas yelled from above.

She thought about mentioning that she was not a lad, but she was already out of breath and couldn't be bothered. Once she reached the top, she looked over the edge to see how Crane was doing. He always tried to hide it, but she knew how much he hated heights. Ever since that silly tree incident. She felt a bit responsible for him falling. After all, she had been the one who said, "Step on the car, Crane-zilla! Squish it!" He had been more exuberant then she had anticipated.

"Doing all right down there?" she called down.

"Doing good," he huffed.

She sat down on the hard ground near Griffin who was resting against a rock. "So let me see if I have this right. A Morphous can shape-shift, a Firebrander can make fire, and a Refiner can manipulate metal. What's left?"

"The only other known race ability is what Crane just experienced," he answered. "Those that can control the air around us are called Mistrels. Phineas is a Mistral.

"But I didn't feel any wind," Crane said as he joined them.

"It doesn't necessarily have to do with wind flow, though some powerful ones are rumored to control winds. It is more about the hidden particles in the air. Each ability is considered to be linked to particles we call micronites. Penny, you use the hidden particles in moisture to manipulate liquids into solid matter, forming any shape. I'm sure you have noticed by now the fluidity you feel when shape-shifting."

She nodded, though she had never thought of it 'til now.

"And Pete," he continued, "you essentially use the fragments found in the static energy all around us to create fire.

"And I use the micronites found in metal?" Haldor asked.

"Exactly. Certain minerals that are found in most metals contain them."

"All right, let's keep moving," Phineas said once Pete had reached the top. Penny felt bad for Pete who hadn't gotten to sit at all, but for once, he didn't complain. As they continued, the rocky terrain around them gave way to smaller rocks and more frequent plants and trees.

Penny looked up at Chip who seemed to be sleeping on her shoulder. She was glad that he chose to stay with her. She had never owned a pet before. Well, except for a tree frog named Hopsy that she had found in her backyard when she was little. He hadn't lasted long. Her father accidentally stepped on him while she was trying to train the frog to fetch his slippers. She wondered where her parents were now. She sure hoped that they were safe.

Haldor, who had been mulling over the information that they had just heard, now picked up his pace so that he could walk beside Griffin.

"Theoretically, shouldn't we be able to control the micronite particles used in all four types of abilities?" he asked as they walked along.

"You would think so," Griffin answered, "but it doesn't seem to work that way. Each one is unique. There are legends however, that certain particularly-gifted individuals can learn to control each kind. I've never seen it though. Most of what we know is all speculation anyway—men trying to make sense of what they don't understand."

Haldor nodded. "I can identify with that."

"We're getting close to Hangman Hills," Phineas called back to them. "We may have to stop for the night."

"It's only just starting to get dark. Why are we talking about stopping already?" Penny asked. She felt like they were just now making progress after spending so much time climbing that cliff.

"Trust me, you don't want to cross Hangman Hills in the dark," Phineas replied. "There is dangerous night life."

"Why do they call it Hangman Hills?" she asked with a shudder.

Phineas removed his top hat and ran his fingers through his hair.

"Well, during the great war, Esmond made some enslaved builders create these horrible half-spider, half-machine beasts," he explained. "They shoot a kind of webbing from their front legs. They aim it at your neck, and then throw you over their back like some sort of prize. It works just like a noose. A single hangman spider could carry as many as twenty corpses around on its back."

"That is horrible." She gasped. "But none are still around, right?"

"Esmond didn't deem it necessary to remove them. And in his incredible wisdom, he had the beings built with the ability to have offspring. Luckily—or unluckily for us tonight—they seem to prefer to stay in the vicinity of Hangman Hills where they were originally dropped."

Haldor was intrigued. "A machine that can make more machines? Those builders are remarkable..."

They all seemed to be walking a bit slower. None of them were overly eager to arrive at Hangman Hills now that they knew what they were. Pete, who was near the back of the group, slowed to almost a halt.

"So, they are only in the hills?" Pete asked, his voice quivering.

"Yes, don't worry," Phineas shouted back over his shoulder. "We still have a mile to go till we arrive. They seldom stray far." Penny looked back toward Pete. He stood as still as a statue, gazing as if hypnotized at something off to the side of their path. She strained her eyes to see what he was looking at. Pete said something she couldn't understand.

"What did you say?"

He spoke again. Penny had to listen closely. His voice was just above a whisper. "I think I see one."

Quick as a bolt of lightning, a thread shot from the trees and wrapped around Pete's neck. Penny only had a moment to see the look of terror on his face before he was snapped into the woods by an unseen foe.

"Oh no," Phineas said in a low voice. Then yelled, "Everyone get down!" They dropped to the ground. Chip fell with a clunk from Penny's shoulder where he'd been dozing. He hovered above them and looked around, blinking his eyes in confusion. Haldor was so fascinated by what was going on that he still stood rooted to the spot, his wide eyes searching back and forth.

"Haldor, get down!" Penny shouted and pulled his feet out from under him just as a web shot over his head. She looked toward where the shot had come from and saw a glint of metal, then a rustling of leaves as if the creature were retreating. Griffin pulled his goggles down over his eyes and scanned the tree line.

"What do you see?" Phineas asked.

"It looks like two of them," he said. "They are both headed northeast."

"You three stay here," Phineas ordered. "Griffin, come with me."

"We want to help too!" Crane objected.

"You can help by staying down. They have a much harder time attacking you if you stay a small target."

Penny nodded and pulled Haldor, who was already starting to rise up again, back to the ground.

"Oh, and now would be a good time to take out your weapons. And guard your necks!" Phineas added before disappearing into the trees with Griffin. Penny removed her blade from its sheath and held it in front of her. All had gone quiet. They could barely hear the others moving through the forest. These woods seemed to act as a sound barrier, suffocating and killing any noise around them. A soft breeze blew, rustling the leaves.

"Do you think there are any more nearby?" Crane whispered.

She began to answer but stopped short. "Do you hear that?"

"Hear what?"

"It's like a clicking noise," she answered. Penny thought she saw something out of the corner of her eye. She turned slowly to look behind them and screamed. A six-foot-tall arachnid hovered over them. One of the creature's razor-sharp metal legs was raised to attack. The scream seemed to confuse it. It wasn't much of a window, but it was long enough. She rolled to the side just as the beast's leg smashed into the ground, leaving a deep hole behind. Crane turned to see what was happening. He let out a cry and fell back into Haldor.

"Guard your necks!" Penny shouted. A web shot out from another spider just behind the first, catching Crane around the ankle. It pulled him in faster than he could react. Another web shot toward Penny. She managed to deflect it with her sword. She could hear Chip hooting wildly from somewhere above, as if cheering them on.

"Haldor, these guys are metal, can't you do something?" she cried.

"I'm trying, but I have to get closer."

"Help!" Crane yelled from where he hung upside down from the spider's back. Haldor jumped to his feet and ran at them, swinging his spear around. He let out a gasp as a spindly leg knocked him to the ground. Another rose up to make the kill. Penny leapt forward and chopped the leg in two with her sword before it could connect.

The metal shrapnel scattered onto the ground. Haldor took that moment to drive his spear into the soft underbelly of the animal. It let out a horrible shriek but only seemed to be angered more. It came at him again, foam dripping from his fangs, his glass eyes gleaming red like a hundred tiny traffic lights. Haldor fell back, losing his grip on the spear. The spider lunged just as Penny attacked it from behind, stabbing her blade deep within his thorax. She then swung around, looking for the spider that held Crane. She could see it skittering toward the forest.

"Come on!" she yelled to Haldor who was wriggling out from under the spider corpse. She ran to the spot where she saw the creature enter as Haldor hurried to catch up. She scrambled through the brush until she came to a stream. There she saw the spider. He was across the water under a large tree.

Above him were several objects swinging in the breeze. It took her a moment to realize that they were rotting bodies strung up by their necks. Their unseeing eyes stared eerily into the darkness. Upon closer inspection, she saw that there were at least thirty of them. She retched silently as she tried to think of a way for Crane to not become one of them. The spider was already trying to wrap a strand of webbing around his neck. A thought occurred to her. An outrageous, outlandish thought. *I can do this,* she assured herself. She tried to picture every last detail of her slain foe—every creepy crawling, hairy, shiny detail.

Penny could feel the energy pulsing through her. Her hands were no longer her own. Her teeth had become fangs, and her eyes were the eyes of a killer.

Chapter Twenty-Two

Haldor, who had arrived just in time to see her transformation, clapped like a child.

"Shh." She tried to whisper, but all that came out was a low clicking sound. There was no time to lose—the spider had successfully gotten the webbing around Crane's neck and was about to hang him next to the others. Penny hurried out of the underbrush, stumbling on her new legs. The other spider turned toward her.

"S-s-sis-ster, we-e-e-e thoughts-s-s you-u wer-r-re deads-s-s," the spider clicked. She couldn't believe it. Somehow she could understand that horrible clicking! "You-u brought-s-s a sna-ack," it said upon seeing Haldor. Penny tried to motion with one of her legs for Haldor to help Crane while she distracted the spider, but she wasn't sure if he could tell what she meant. Oddly enough, he could. He nodded and stepped back to wait for his opportunity. She lunged forward with her fangs bared. The other spider dropped Crane and widened its many eyes as it leapt out of the way.

"S-s-sis-ster, hav-ve you-u gone mad-d-d? You-u hurts-s-s our-r fee-elings-s-s, now you-u die again-n-n!" the spider yelled, skittering toward her. The spider raised its front legs and stabbed them toward her in rapid succession. Penny retreated back, dodging and deflecting the blows as well as she was able. She realized that, to her dismay, this spider was much larger and more skilled than the other had been, and Penny was not used to her new body. She tried to co-ordinate her legs. Putting every ounce of strength she had into them, she sprung forward. She landed on

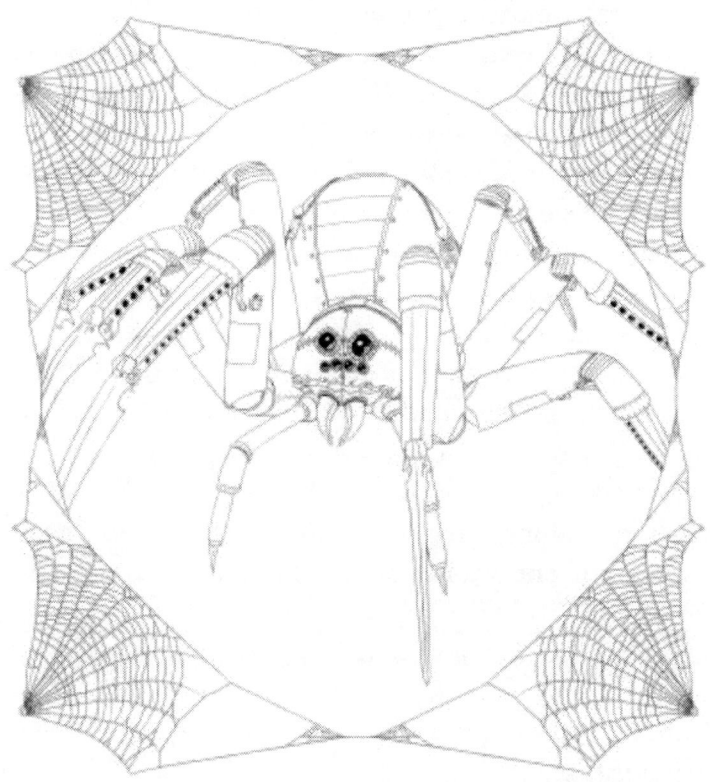

the other's back and began stabbing at it with her feet. The spider howled in rage and threw her to the ground. In a panic, Penny tried to use her webbing, shooting it at random. One shot hit the spider in the eyes. As it was pulling at the webs, Crane appeared and swung a well-aimed blow at the spider's neck, chopping its head clean off. She heaved a sigh of relief and collapsed on the ground.

Crane stood over the body. "I squish spiders for breakfast!" he shouted. "Wait no, let me try that again." He thought a moment. "Nope, that's all I've got."

Penny transformed back to herself, taking extra care to remember her clothing this time.

"Anyone know the way back to the clearing?" she asked.

Crane shrugged. "I was a bit preoccupied."

"Sorry, I got turned around as well," Haldor apologized. The sun had gone down, making it hard to see. She scanned the trees, looking for the direction they had come, but it was no use.

"Well, I think it was somewhere in this direction," she said, gesturing to the others to follow her lead. They walked on for a while, stopping every now and then to listen for the others with no luck. The terrain became quite uneven. They would climb a large hill, only to climb straight back down the other side.

Penny speculated that they had entered Hangman Hills by now. The sound of leaves crunching nearby made them all stand still. They ducked low behind some brush and waited. A large twig snapped close by. She stifled a scream as she saw the head of a large spider not five feet from where they hid. It paused as it walked by, as if it suspected they were near. Her heart beat so hard that she was sure it must be making a terrible racket. Fortunately, whatever had stopped the spider must have made it lose interest, for it continued on as if nothing had happened.

"Maybe we should go back," she whispered once the spider was out of sight. "This must not be the way to the clearing."

"But it could be the way out of here," argued Crane.

"He might be right," Haldor said. "Anyway, it's probably best to keep going in one direction. It will lead us out eventually."

"All right, if that's what you guys think."

After seeing the last spider, they trod more carefully. They saw a few more spiders as they walked along, but none of them noticed the small group. They all seemed distracted as if they were in a hurry to get somewhere.

"Where do you think they're all headed?" Crane asked in a whisper.

Haldor scratched his head. "It is quite curious."

As it turned out, they didn't have long till they saw for themselves. Ahead of them, they could hear a loud commotion. They peered through the leaves and were met with a terrifying sight. Dozens of spiders were converging onto a single spot. They skittered and leapt about. Some squealed in pain and fell back, while others clicked angrily and charged forward. Penny strained her eyes in the darkness to see what was causing all the commotion.

She gasped as she saw a familiar top hat. "It's them."

"Can you see Pete?" Haldor asked, searching for an opening in the mass of thoraxes and legs.

"I only saw Phineas's hat. We have to help them!"

"Any battle plan?"

She looked from Crane to Haldor. Both seemed to be waiting for her to make a plan of action. Penny racked her brain for some sort of solution. This looked to be a futile situation, but as she looked toward the mass of insects, a shred of an idea began to form.

"Haldor, their heads seem to be made primarily out of metal. If I could get you in the center of that crowd, could you literally, crush some skulls?" she asked.

Haldor's face brightened. "I'm willing to try."

Penny handed Chip over to Crane and concentrated. She tried to remember what it felt like to be the spider. It came easier to her this time. In a matter of seconds, she'd made a full transformation.

"No offense, but you're ugly," Crane whispered.

Penny clicked back a snippy response, but the interpretation was lost on him. She shot out a short length of thread and draped it around Haldor. She hung him carefully on her back so that he looked like a captive.

"Ready?" she clicked.

Haldor seemed to understand the question even if he couldn't make out the words. "I'm ready when you are."

Taking a deep breath, she crawled out into the clearing. Instantly, she was assaulted by the voices of the frenzied insects.

"Kill-l-ls-s-s them, Kills-s-s-s them-m!"

"Wee wants-s-s to eat-t-t the chubsy on-ne-e!"

As she walked forward, she could see Pete swinging his sword in every direction. He was covered in several strands of webbing, making it difficult for him to see. From the charred-looking remains of several arachnids nearby, she could tell that he had been using his ability. Phineas was deflecting blows with his staff and trying to push back the horde. A large mountain lion was standing beside him. To her surprise, the lion seemed to be helping them. It was grabbing the spiders in its massive teeth and lashing out with its razor-sharp claws.

That must be Griffin! she thought with a touch of awe. A good-sized pile of dead insects were piling up around the small group. They were looking tired though. Penny knew that they wouldn't be able to hold out much longer at this rate. Luckily, none of the spiders seemed to show any suspicion toward her or Haldor. They were far too preoccupied by the hunt. Penny stopped when she thought that she was about in the center.

Haldor noticed the pause and prepared himself. This was the most metal he had ever bent at once. This would certainly be a challenge. He assessed how many were in range and counted about seventeen that were near enough to be affected. Making a mental note of their locations, he closed his eyes. A horrible shrieking rang out all around him as he crushed them. The sound made him flinch, and he felt a wave of remorse for killing these amazing creatures, but he knew he must continue. He opened his eyes as Penny advanced, and he selected new targets, then closed them again, but not to concentrate. He squeezed them shut so he would not have to see these wonderful beings die.

Once the shrieking subsided, he opened his eyes with reluctance and looked around. The bodies of the slain lay in heaps and he could see the remaining spiders retreating back into the forest. Penny detached Haldor from her side and set him on the ground. He walked over to the nearest spider and knelt down, staring sadly at the crushed skull.

"It's a shame, isn't it?" Phineas patted him on the shoulder.

Haldor dropped his eyes to the ground. "Yes, they were such amazing creations."

"But you did save us," he reminded him.

Haldor sighed and nodded. Phineas walked over to Penny who had turned back into her normal self.

"Nice work. That was some advanced transformation."

"Yes, it was," agreed Griffin who had also taken on his usual form.

As they were talking, Penny noticed a few curious spiders lurking nearby. She knew they needed to get moving again. A sound from the brush made them all pause.

"There is no time to discuss this now," she said. "They could be coming back!"

They agreed and started to leave the clearing. "Wait, has anyone seen Chip?" Penny asked, her brows knit with concern. She had lost track of the owl during all the commotion and now he was nowhere to be seen.

"We can't wait here," Griffin said, eyeing the bushes.

"He'll catch up. I'm sure of it." Phineas assured her. Penny let out a loud whistle and looked around.

"Shh, you're going to make more show up, stupid!" Pete said.

Penny sighed and reluctantly left the clearing with the others. As they hurried to put as much distance between themselves and the spiders as possible, she kept looking over her shoulder. She couldn't help imagining Chip out there, scared and alone. What if he thought she had abandoned him, or what if...? Penny gulped. What if the spiders had caught him? She tried to push any negative thoughts aside, reminding herself that Chip had been on his own before he met them. He could take care of himself. At least, she fervently hoped so.

Their journey brought them up another large hill and then down into a valley. Thanks to the insects, they had gone much farther that night than they intended. After they felt like they had gone a safe enough distance from Hangman Hills, they began to look for a safe place to stay. The trees here were few and far between. It looked like they had entered a small farming community. They came upon an old, abandoned-looking barn that appeared to be a perfect place to stay for the evening. They all set up their bedding close to one another. No one wanted to be too far from the others tonight. Even Pete who usually stayed a little ways from everyone remained close. It was a pleasant little barn, and it provided a much appreciated shelter from the sharp, icy wind blowing around outside. When everyone was settled, Penny slipped outside and ventured a few long whistles into the sky. She scanned the horizon for any sign of Chip, but nothing appeared in the dark, freezing night sky. Not even the stars were visible through the thick clouds. She jumped as she felt something placed around her shoulders.

"Sorry," Crane apologized. "I just thought you might be cold."

She pulled the blanket around her. "Thanks."

"He's going to be fine. You'll see. He'll probably be here by morning."

Penny sighed. "I sure hope you're right."

"Do you want me to sit out here with you for a while?"

"No, we need our sleep. We still have a long journey ahead. You especially should rest. How is your side anyway?"

"It's doing pretty good. Whatever Clara put on it is working wonders."

"That's great! I'm so glad."

"You guys should come inside. It's not safe out here," Griffin said as he appeared at the barn door.

Crane seemed annoyed. "Yeah, yeah, we're coming. Shall we?" He reached for the door just as Penny was going through. His hand thudded into her backside, making his cheeks flush crimson.

"Sorry," he managed to squeak.

She laughed. "Did you just slap me?"

"No, I slipped. Honest!"

"Sure," Penny teased.

Crane smiled. "Don't flatter yourself, Gilbert."

The others were already lying down as they came in. Penny tried to settle down in the scratchy straw, but her mind refused to shut off. She looked over at Pete who was rubbing his neck where the web had been. He had been lucky. If he wasn't wearing that armor that partially covered his neck, he would have been a goner.

Rolling over, she gazed up at the rafters. Wherever Chip was, she sure hoped he was safe. She had become quite attached to the little guy, and the thought that he might be out there, scared or hurt, filled her heart with dread.

Penny also couldn't help wondering what dangers tomorrow might have in store for them. She shivered and wrapped her blanket tighter around her body, as if the woven fibers could somehow keep her safe.

Chapter Twenty-Three

Penny woke to find the barn was crawling with enormous spiders. Haldor and Pete were plastered to the wall. Their eyes cried out silently for help. She tried to stand, but was held fast by webbing around her body. As she thrashed around, trying to free her hand enough to reach her blade, a spider no larger than her hand landed on her chest. A scream burst from her lungs as it bit her neck.

Her hand managed to grip her knife, and she pulled it from its sheath. She cut the webbing holding her arms and stabbed at the spider who easily dodged. The spider was joined by several others. Soon they were covering her entire body and she couldn't move from the sheer weight of them pressing down on her. She opened her mouth to cry out, but her cry was muffled by another spider landing on her face. She couldn't move, couldn't see, couldn't breathe. This was the end.

Penny let out a blood-curling scream as she woke up, drenched in sweat. Her dream was so vivid that she was still shaking. Her blanket was wrapped so tight around her that it still felt like she was trapped in a web. As she threw her covers away from her, she tried to steady her breathing.

Crane came to her side. "What's going on? Are you all right?" They all stood over her now, looking quite concerned.

"I think so. I just had a horrible dream. Where's Pete?" she asked after a moment.

"Oh he's right..." Haldor's voice trailed off as he scanned the barn. "That's odd. I thought he was with me."

Movement from above caught Penny's eye. She looked up toward the ceiling and saw a young spider crouched in the corner of the room looking down at them. A large lump hung from the middle of the ceiling.

"Pete!" she cried as she recognized the shape swinging side to side. Griffin grabbed his crossbow, preparing to take aim at the creature, but it had already disappeared into the rafters above.

Crane took a step back. "Did you see how fast it moved?"

"*Mmmmrffff!*" The sound came from the lump on the ceiling.

Coming to their senses, they cut Pete down and removed the webs from around his face and body. Luckily, the spider was still young and inexperienced and had strung him up by his ankles instead of his neck.

Pete couldn't control his shaking. "Stupid spiders. I hate spiders. Keep them away. Keep them off me!" He wasn't the only one shaken. Everyone was on edge after the night's events. They decided to forgo sleep for the remainder of the night. There was no way any of them were going to get any sleep now. Penny looked back as they left the shelter of the barn with a pit in her stomach. How would Chip ever find them now?

"Only half a day's journey till we get to the port town of Pankor," Phineas announced after stopping for breakfast. Cheered by this news, the group felt more invigorated and motivated to continue. They hadn't been walking long 'til they came upon a dirt road. Soon they saw several cozy-looking homes. The houses here were quite different from the ones in the clockworks. Instead of being made of brick and iron, these homes were made of wood with thatched roofs.

"Just a couple more miles," Phineas announced.

"Have you ever been to Pankor?" Penny asked Griffin.

"I went there once with my uncle, but I was pretty young at the time so I don't remember much."

She hoped that they wouldn't see too many bishops in Pankor. She had seen enough of them to last her a lifetime. "Is it much like the clockworks?" she asked.

"It has some similarities if I remember right. I have heard that they are a bit more monitored by the bishops though."

"More monitored? How is that even possible?"

"Well they don't guard the entrance to the city, but unfortunately, since it's a port town, they keep a pretty close eye on all ships coming and going. That's why we need our travel documents. We should be fine as long as we have them."

Penny reached into her bag where she kept the papers, relieved to find they were still there. They went by a rundown house covered in moss that teetered to one side. A woman was standing nearby beating her rugs, and several children were outside playing in a large mud puddle.

"Good afternoon," Phineas said with a nod. The woman scowled and stopped her work. She looked them up and down, then turned and, without a word, went inside her little hovel.

"I must say, I remember them being friendlier."

The grubby little children watched them curiously as they passed by. Penny felt a pang of sympathy for them. It seemed as though they were often left to their own devices and she could relate. She smiled at a young girl of about six or seven with stringy hair. The girl smiled back and motioned for her to come closer.

"Hi there," Penny said as she drew close.

"Hi there," the girl mimicked in a singsong voice, before slinging a fistful of mud right in Penny's face. The girl tossed back her head and let out a howl of laughter. Her siblings joined in, pointing and jeering. Feeling a little less sympathetic, Penny wiped the mud from her face and rejoined the others.

"Nice kid," Crane remarked.

"Yes, lovely," she said, rolling her eyes.

As they grew closer to town, the homes and buildings changed. Penny guessed that there must be quite a class separation between the people in town and those on the outskirts. She mentioned this to Griffin, who confirmed it.

"Most of those who live in town are merchants that give a large portion from the profit of their goods to Lord Esmond. They are therefore afforded his protection against the elements and allowed to live in town. He couldn't care less about those outside the city that he can't profit from. Some people choose to live in the outskirts to be less under his thumb, but most would do just about anything to afford lodgings in town."

"Welcome to Pankor," Phineas called back to them.

Penny looked around. The town was quite impressive. The buildings were all cylindrical with metal-grated walkways wrapping around them and connecting them to each other. She looked down at the walkway beneath their feet and was startled. Below them lay nothing but clouds and empty sky. She hadn't realized that the town was built onto the side of a cliff. Now that she looked closer at the buildings, she could see they were held up by propellers underneath the structures. It looked like the whole city was getting ready to fly away.

"Amazing..." she breathed. They continued along the walkway, winding their way up higher. Crane tried his best not to think of how high they were. He looked a bit pale, but he pressed on with the others all the same. Because so many people passed through this port town, the people here were all so diverse. They passed by a woman who had so many tattoos, that not an inch of her skin color was visible. Another man who had a mechanical leg and an eye patch, smoked a pipe outside of a pub.

"Can ye spare a piece of silver for an old sailor?" he asked as they passed by. Without thinking, Penny dug into her pocket, pulled out a quarter, and gave it to the man.

"Hey, what's this?" he asked in confusion.

A sudden hand on her shoulder made her turn round. Several bishops stood behind her. The man with the vice grip on her arm narrowed his eyes. "Well, well, what have we got here?"

"That's her, that's the girl I told you about!" a woman cried, stepping out from behind the guard. She recognized her at once. It was the woman whom they had seen near the road.

"I told you it was her! See, look here!" she said, pulling out a paper from her robes. The slip she had in her hands appeared to be a wanted poster. A crude picture of Penny had been drawn on the front, with the words: "Wanted, Dead or Alive" printed in large letters.

"Now I'll get my reward, right? Finally, I'll get to live in the city!"

"Begone, woman!" one of the guards shouted, tossing a few coins in her direction. "We will take it from here. Your reward should be the satisfaction of knowing that you have done your duty by helping us apprehend a dangerous fugitive."

"But—" the woman began, but stopped short after a glare from the man. "Yes, my lord," she said as she backed away.

Crane stepped forward. "Now wait just a minute."

"Say," the guard said as he looked at him. "You look a bit familiar too." The man pulled out another paper with Crane's face plastered on it.

"Arrest them all."

The bishops surrounded them.

"Let's not get hasty," Phineas cut in.

"Give us any trouble, and we'll not hesitate to kill." The man waved his gun in the air as he spoke. "We can just as easily collect the reward if you're dead. In fact, I'll bet it would make things much easier," he said, putting his weapon to Penny's head.

She flinched away from the weapon. Things were happening so fast. There was no time to think. Just as she thought she was done for, the bishop dropped his gun and put his hands over his head. Penny looked up to see Chip dive-bombing the man. His metal talons were cutting into the guard's arms as he dove again and again. She felt a flood of relief wash over her seeing the little owl safe.

"Don't just stand there," the bishop cried out to the other guards. "Help me!" Forgetting their captives, the other men hurried to help their captain. Chip was like a whirlwind. Penny's relief soon gave way to admiration. She had never seen him like this before. Quick as lightning, he swooped down on the other guards. One of the men screamed as he was knocked off the walkway. Several other guards attempted to shoot Chip, but the bird was too fast. Their shots flew uselessly into the sky. The commotion was attracting a crowd from all over the city. The man she had given her quarter to had been watching the entire scene.

"Follow me," he said as he stood up. "Unless ye would like to be involved in a bloodbath," he added, seeing their trepidation.

"We have to help Chip," Penny cried. But the owl was already flying back to them, leaving the guards still stumbling around in confusion and waving their arms about madly.

"Get the demon bird away from me!" one of them shouted.

Penny held out her arm. Chip landed and climbed to his favorite spot on her left shoulder.

"Come on, while they still be distracted," the man urged. Knowing that the bishops would soon come to their senses, they relented and followed after the stranger. They followed him down a set of stairs and across a suspension bridge that was near the edge of town.

"Where are you taking us?" Phineas asked.

"To me ship of course," he said, urging them to go faster. They soon reached the end of town. There were many ships coming and going. Some of them were like the great steel ones they had seen earlier, but most of them were smaller, more modest ships. They looked almost like the old pirate ships that sailed the ocean long ago. Only instead of sailing the sea, these ships sailed the air. Where the sails would normally go, the ships had giant hot air balloons. And instead of a small rudder, the ships had large rudders to catch the wind, and propellers to move it through the sky.

The man turned down the dock, walked past an old ship that looked like it was falling apart, and stopped in front of a wonderfully elegant ship. It was huge! The wood had been polished 'til it gleamed, and the balloons overhead were a bright white.

"Is this your ship?" Penny asked in disbelief.

"Er, no... This one is," he said, pointing to the ship that was falling apart.

"Oh."

The air boat looked like it had been constructed out of various other ships and whatever scraps happened to be lying around. The balloons were well worn and had several patches on them.

"I made it me-self," the man announced with a smile as he directed them onboard. "Hurry now, we must be gettin' along." This vessel wouldn't have been their first choice for a charter, but, under the circumstances, they had no other option.

Once they were all aboard, the man directed them to a hole beneath the floor of the ship and told them to hide. He then released the ropes holding them to the dock and set sail. A small guard ship approached him at the edge of the docks. Penny could hear the murmur of conversation from where they hid. Chip was so happy to see them all that he kept making soft, almost-purring sounds in the back of his throat.

"Shh, I'm happy to see you too," she whispered, stroking the bird behind his ear, "but right now, we need to be quiet."

She listened again. She couldn't make out what they were saying, but it seemed pleasant enough. The voices went on for a bit longer and then stopped. She exhaled sharply as she felt the ship moving forward again. Wanting to be safe, they waited below for several more minutes. The time seemed to be moving in slow motion.

"You can come up now," they heard the captain yell. They slowly climbed out of the hole, looking around. Penny could see the city shrinking in the distance behind them. Soon the whole city was obscured by clouds. She walked to the edge and ventured a peek over the side. She could see nothing but sky and clouds. The puffs of clouds rolled under the ship like smoke, making it hard to see very far below them. Crane came and stood next to her.

"I can't believe we're in a floating pirate ship!"

"I ain't no pirate," the captain insisted. "Who have ye been talking to? I may or may not do a bit of smuggling, but I ain't no dirty, stinkin' pirate!"

"Sorry. A flying, smuggling ship then."

"Alleged smuggling ship," the captain corrected. "They can't prove nothing, and they never will neither!" he finished with a crazy peal of laughter, his good eye bulging. His laughter stopped as suddenly as it began.

Penny glanced at Crane. "Cra-zy," he mouthed.

Phineas strode forward and offered his hand, introducing each person in turn. The captain shook his hand roughly.

"I be Captain Griswold Hawthorne, and you be aboard the Soaring Manatee."

"Thank you so much for coming to our aid."

"Aye, twasn't any bother. To tell the truth, the idea of smuggling live cargo, be a might exciting to me. I love a good adventure!" he exclaimed.

"Well we're prepared to pay you for your services," Phineas said as he pulled a leather pouch out of his coat and began counting out the coins.

"Adventure be the best payment of all."

"That's generous of you." Phineas opened the pouch again to put the money away.

"Although I don't want to be causing offense," Griswold said, scooping up the coins before they could be returned. "So where ye be headed?"

"To Lord Esmond's fortress on The Dark Isle," Griffin said soberly. "We have...business with him.

Chapter Twenty-Four

They had been sailing for hours, and Penny was enjoying every moment of it. She was so excited to be sailing through the beautiful sky and so happy to have Chip back. She almost forgot their dire situation as she gazed through the sky from atop the crow's nest. It was so beautiful. Clouds appeared in front of the ship through the blue sky like great waves. The ship cut through them like whipped cream. It was such a smooth ride. The wind hardly affected the stalwart vessel at all. She held out her hand and let the wind flow through her fingers. Crane sat beside her, looking at the horizon.

"You're looking a little green," she said. "Do you need to get down?"

"I'm fine. Just a little seasick, or rather airsick in this case."

The wind picked up speed, making Penny shiver.

Crane wrapped his coat around her shoulders. "So, I guess we're wanted people now. Weird, eh?"

"Yes, they must have gotten our descriptions from the men on Esmond's ship."

"Hey, Penny?" he said after a moment.

"Yes?"

"About this Griffin fellow..."

"What about him?"

"Well I was just wondering..."

"Wondering what?"

His face turned from green to red in a matter of seconds. He cleared his throat before going on. "Well, do you...do you like him?"

"Sure, he seems like a nice guy." She didn't like where this conversation was headed, and didn't want

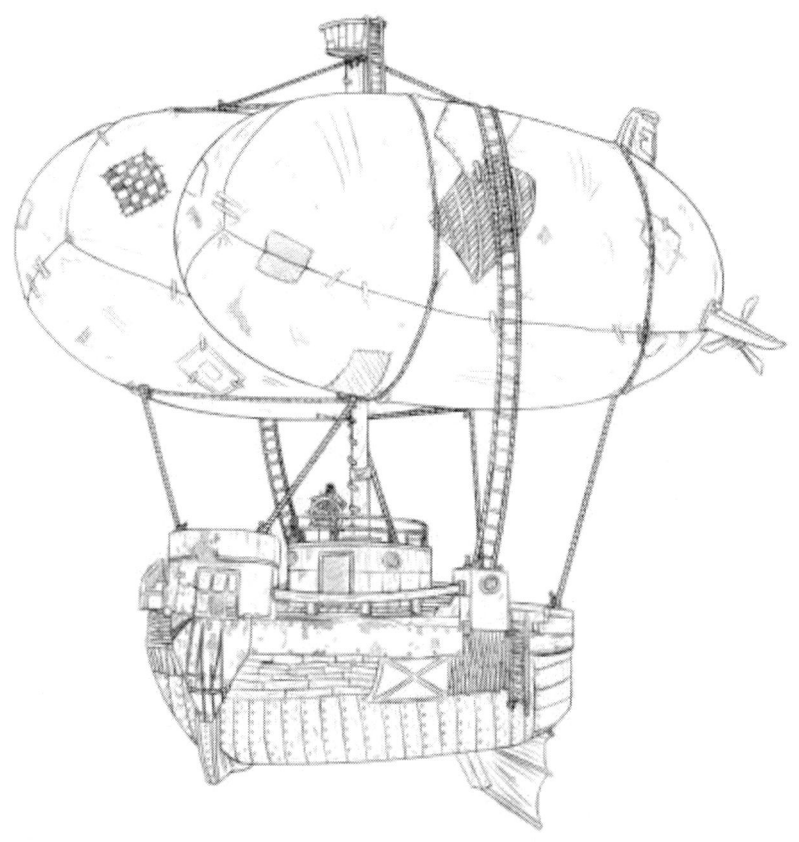

to hurt his feelings. "Say, maybe we should head back down. It's getting awfully windy up here."

He didn't seem to hear. "I was just wondering because—"

"Hey guys," Griffin interrupted as his head popped into view over the side. "The captain told me to come and get you. There is a storm on the way, and a big one by the looks of it."

"Fine, fine." Crane waved his hand. That guy always seemed to be cramping his style. Penny was relieved and all too happy to climb down. As they neared the bottom, Griffin offered his arm to help her the rest of the way down. She noted to her satisfaction, how hard and muscular his arm felt as she lowered herself to the deck.

"Thanks, pal," Crane said, grabbing Griffin's arm before he could let it down. He pushed down with the majority of his weight as he dropped to the floor. He landed with a *thud* onto Griffin's foot. Griffin flinched, but retained his composure.

"No problem," he said through tight lips.

Griswold hadn't been kidding about the windstorm. They had gotten down just in time. The wind was now swirling around them, and big puffs of clouds were cascading over the sides of the ship. A crash of thunder made Penny jump. She looked up at the ominous clouds above them just as the rain began to fall. The rain felt like icy needles against her face. Not wanting Chip to get blown away, she tucked him inside of the coat she had borrowed from Crane and held him close against her body.

"You best be getting below deck with the others," Captain Griswold shouted from the wheelhouse.

"Is there anything we can do to help?" Griffin called back to him. Before he could answer, a huge gust of wind came upon them, striking the ship, and sending them hurtling toward the rail. Penny let out a moan as her rib cage struck the wood.

Crane helped her to her feet. "Are you all right?"

"I think so." She checked to make sure Chip hadn't gotten crushed. He seemed to be fine. Just a bit shaken.

"Get below," the captain said again. This time it was an order, and they didn't hesitate. On unsteady legs they made their way down the stairs. They were all holding onto the beams for dear life. Pete had a large bruise forming under his eye from not holding on tight enough during the last gust. Penny held her body tight against the beam just as another large gust shook the room.

"Someone should be helping the captain," Phineas said. "I am going to see if there is anything I can do."

"Be careful," Penny called after him.

Once on deck, he strained his eyes to see through the storm. He could see the wheelhouse, but the captain was nowhere in sight.

"Captain Griswold!" he yelled above the sound of the wind and rain. "Where are you, Captain?" He heard a muffled cry coming from the side of the ship. He carefully made his way to the back, clinging to the rail. The sound seemed to be coming from below the ship. He looked over the side. Griswold was clinging to the porthole on the side of the vessel. His face looked pale, yet determined.

"Stand aside, I'll be back up in three wags of a pig's tail!" he yelled up to him.

"Don't be absurd. Grab my hand!" he shouted, reaching toward him. The captain hesitated a moment. A crash of thunder shook the vessel and lightning lit the sky. Seeming to make up his mind, Griswold grabbed hold of his outstretched hand, and Phineas hoisted him aboard.

"Thank ye for your assistance, but for the record, I was in full control of the situation," the captain said, straightening his coat.

"Of course you were, Captain. Now let's get you back to the wheel." The two men put their heads down and walked back to the wheelhouse. This time, Griswold took a few moments to lash himself to the wheel.

"Is there somewhere nearby, where we could wait out this storm?" Phineas asked.

"Aye," the captain said, looking down at his compass. "Cape Achilles lies just ahead. We can wait it out there." He gave the wheel a sharp turn to the right, and pressed forward. Cape Achilles was gradually coming into view through the clouds. A flash of lightning lit up the sky again, this time striking one of the balloons. The rain put out the fire, but the ship was rapidly losing altitude. Captain Griswold steered the ship toward the land, praying they wouldn't sink too fast. He aimed for a smooth spot on the ground, and held his breath. The bottom of the boat just missed a large tree and came to rest with a *thud* on top of a mud bank.

"Ha, ha, nothin' to it. A slice of pie!" he exclaimed happily.

"Right, I-I knew you could do it," Phineas stuttered, looking faint.

Penny opened the door and peeked outside. "What happened?"

"Well, we was sailing by good ol' Cape Achilles, and Phineas and I decided to stop in and rest a bit," Captain Griswold announced. "Oh, and the pesky lightning went and blew a hole in one of me balloons," he added as an afterthought.

"We kind of crash landed," Phineas said as he removed his hat and mopped his brow with his handkerchief. "We were lucky we were so close to an island."

"Yes well, I suppose that were a bit of luck now that ye mention it," Captain Griswold admitted.

"What would have happened to us if we fell?" Penny asked, although she was afraid to know the answer.

"I've never tried it me-self, but the winds that surround Azure would most likely tear ye apart," said the captain almost joyously. "And what was left of ye, would drift down to the mythical land of Terra!" he said with a laugh.

"I fail to see the humor of the situation," Haldor whispered to Crane. "Am I missing something?"

"No, Haldor, for once you aren't."

"Don't worry though," the captain went on. "If we ever needed to abandon the poor old girl, we could always use the life raft. I suppose I shoulda mentioned that before the storm. No matter! I'm off to find material to be repairing the balloon. I'll be back faster than a kitten tickling a rooster." With that, Griswold dropped a rope ladder from the rail of the boat and disappeared over the side.

"I had better go with," Phineas said and climbed down after him. Griswold could be heard humming a jaunty tune as the two of them made their way across the field and into town.

"What an unusual guy," Crane said, shaking his head. "I think I like him."

Penny went below deck and changed into dry clothing. When she returned, Griffin and Crane both greeted her.

"I am going to take a walk into town," Griffin said. "Would you like to come?"

"Sure. Oh, but wait. I'm on wanted posters now."

"No problem." He handed her a hat and scarf. Penny put the items on and then looked at him doubtfully.

"Are you sure I look different enough?"

"You'll be fine. Besides, this is a small island and Esmond doesn't have much jurisdiction here. He usually just pays attention to the more profitable areas. Shall we go?" He offered his arm.

Crane stepped between the two, while pretending to be oblivious to Griffin's intentions. "Yes, let's. Anyone else want to come? Haldor? Pete?"

Pete yawned. "Not me, I am going to take a nap."

"And I think I'll stay here and study the map," Haldor answered.

"I guess it's just the three of us then. You don't mind me coming, right?"

Penny shook her head. "Of course not. Why would we mind?"

"Yes, why would we mind?" Griffin echoed with a tight smile.

This town was much different from the one they left. Everything was made of weathered-looking wood, and the streets were made of dirt. It reminded Penny of a ghost town she had visited once on a field trip. Music and laughter could be heard drifting out of an old tavern which seemed to be the central meeting place in town.

"Let's step in here just for a moment to see if we can gather any new information," Griffin suggested.

They stepped inside and were instantly assaulted by billows of smoke. A couple of men playing cards looked up at them as they walked in.

Penny coughed on the foul-smelling vapors, as she tried in vain to wave them away. She looked around the dingy room. There were wooden tables set up all around. One table had several men seated at it that looked to be playing some sort of dice game.

Crane stood at her side. "Wow, this feels just like the Old West."

"I know, right?" She coughed again. The smoke was getting to her. It was even making her eyes water.

"Griffin, is that you?" asked a man seated at the bar.

"Silas! How have you been?" Griffin walked over and shook hands with the man. "These are my friends, Penny and Crane. And this is my friend, Silas. We go way back."

"Indeed, we do! Why I could tell you such stories about when this boy was a tyke," he exclaimed.

Griffin blushed. "Yes well, we need not go into that now."

"Stories! Stories!" Crane chanted.

"Well, once when Griffin was eight—"

"They don't want to hear about that right now," Griffin cut in sheepishly. "Besides, there is a business matter I'd like to discuss with you."

"Business, eh? All right, but let's get a corner booth," he said, noticing a man leaning toward them.

Griffin nodded, and they followed Silas to a table that was tucked into the corner of the room. They slid into the booth across from Silas. Griffin looked over his shoulder to make sure that no one was nearby.

"I am looking for some information."

Silas frowned and nodded toward Penny and Crane.

"Oh, they're with me. It's all right."

"Well my underground connections are not as strong as they once were, but I'll see what I can do. What do you want to know?"

"Have you heard anything about a large transport of prisoners being moved by Esmond's men recently?"

"There have been rumors..."

"What kind of rumors?"

Silas took a large swig from his tankard. "Well, I heard from my contact, Johnston, the stable hand, who heard from Helga, the housemaid, who heard from Hargrim, one of the enslaved builders that lives in Esmond's fortress, that he's making them work on some sort of project. A project that involves draining the abilities of Pythians in order to harness their power."

"Draining abilities? Can that be done?"

"According to Hargrim it can. He said that a large group of Pythians were captured for that very purpose. But all of us are in hiding, so I don't know how he would gather so many in such a short amount of time. I haven't heard of anyone going missing either."

"He got them from Terra," Griffin whispered.

The man leaned back, laughing. "Terra? That is an old wives' tale."

"I don't have time to go into how I know, but trust me, Terra is real, and these prisoners are the children who were sent away during the war."

The man's face went pale. "If what you say is true, then this is a tragic twist of events. To survive all this time only to be sacrificed would be a calamity."

"Sacrificed?" Griffin asked in alarm. "Does draining their powers kill them?"

"Yes, I heard that it extracts their life essence."

Griffin sat back against the bench, trying to process all this new information.

"Thank you, Silas, you have been a big help. I have just one more question. An important question. Do you know where the prisoners are being held?"

"If Johnston's information is correct, they are being held in a secret facility just west of the Island of Stones. The building is essentially a floating prison that was made for this purpose. It is hard to find if you don't know where to look, because it has been shrouded in clouds."

Penny looked at Griffin. "Then that's where we need to go."

Silas grunted. "Even if you do find it, it's protected by some kind of sky creatures. Trying to go there would be a fool's errand."

They stood up. Penny's head swam with the new knowledge.

"Then I guess we're fools," she said.

Chapter Twenty-Five

Rainey studied the dirty, downtrodden faces of the people around her. They looked miserable. They looked tired. And most of all, they looked defeated. She had no way of knowing how long they had been in captivity, but it felt like an eternity. When they had seen Penny and her friends, she had felt a surge of hope. But now Penny was long gone, and probably had no idea where Rainey and the other captives were.

Rainey didn't know where they were being held either. They had been transferred from the prison ship into another equally uncomfortable cell. At least there was a bit more room to move around now that they had separated the girls from the boys, but it was also harder to plan their next move. *Next move... Who am I kidding?* She gazed out of the tiny window in their cell, but all she could see were clouds and sky. That's all she could ever see. She was glad for some sort of view though; at least it was a pretty one.

"I'm hungry," said a voice belonging to a girl named Greta, one of the youngest girls in the group.

"I know. We all are. They should be bringing our supper soon though." Rainey tried to sound upbeat, but her voice came out hollow and thin. With hope of rescue now gone, it was hard for her to maintain an enthusiastic demeanor. Her head ached as well. She blamed the dirty drinking water for that one.

"What is going to happen to us?" Greta asked as she sat down next to the other girl's feet.

Rainey lowered herself to the floor and put her arm around the sullen figure. "I don't know," she replied honestly.

"They are going to chop us up into little bits, that's what," said a girl with black hair. Greta squealed and buried her face against Rainey.

"Don't say that," Rainey scolded. "I'm sure everything is going to be okay. This all has to be some sort of mistake. You'll see. They can't keep us here when we haven't done anything wrong."

"Apparently they can," the black-haired girl retorted.

She opened her mouth to argue, but no words came. What could she say to that? The girl was right.

"This can't be the end," she said, as if to herself. Rainey could feel her anger boiling within her. What right did these people have to keep them caged like animals? She stood and looked out the window again. The clouds were swirling about like tufts of cotton. It made her think of all the cottonwood trees near one of the foster homes she had lived in. She used to walk through them in the spring. She longed to see them again. "I will see them again," she said with sudden determination.

"You will see what again?" Greta asked from where she sat on the floor.

"Everybody listen up," Rainey said as she turned around. "We have been going about this whole thing the wrong way."

The girls in the room all stopped talking and instead turned their attention to her.

"We can't keep waiting to be rescued," she went on. "Frankly, the possibility that we will be saved is wishful thinking. From now on, we need to think of a plan to rescue ourselves. We need to join together to get out of this wretched place and back to where we belong!"

"But how are we supposed to do that?" Greta asked.

"Yes, how?" the others echoed.

"I'm sure that you have all heard the saying that the best defense is a good offense?" Several of the girls nodded. "Well," she went on, "I think it's about time we went on the offensive."

❦

Penny and the boys returned to the ship to find Captain Griswold at the top of the mast, struggling to repair the damaged balloon. He was singing casually even though his footing looked extremely precarious.

The words he sang drifted down. "Oh I never met a lass that I didn't prefer. I'll buy her diamonds and fluffy white fur. Her beauty is unchallenged and I think you'll agree, with the exception of my pet monkey."

Phineas stood on the deck of the ship, looking quite nervous. He subconsciously held out one of his hands as if to break the captain's fall as he gazed upward.

"Careful!"

"Wha' was that?" Griswold flung his body back to get a view of the deck, putting himself in an even more precarious position.

"Nothing, never mind!" Phineas shouted. To the others, he mumbled, "I could swear that this man has a death wish. So, where have you all been?"

"In town," Penny replied. "We've discovered something important. Let's gather everyone together."

The singing above them ended abruptly. They looked up in time to see Captain Griswold sliding down the mast. He landed with a *thunk* beside them.

"Good as new!" he bellowed with pride.

It wasn't long till they were all gathered on deck.

Pete felt quite cranky from being woken prematurely. "Well, get on with it."

Griffin nodded and as they all listened intently, he related what they had learned from Silas.

Griswold was the first to speak. "Blimey, what 'ave ye got me into?"

"We would understand if you want us to get another ship," Phineas said.

"Are ye kidding? I wouldn't think of missing out on the adventure! I'll start making preparations to leave at first light," the captain said and hurried off.

Haldor scratched his head. "So, let me see if I have this right. He can somehow harness their power?"

Griffin nodded. "That's what it sounds like."

"But why?"

"Because he is power hungry," Phineas cut in. "He's always been jealous of people with abilities. If he were to get his hands on this kind of power and be able to wield it, there is no telling what he could do. None could stand against him, and all hope of overturning his kingdom would be lost."

Penny leaned forward. "Well, then we will just have to prevent that from happening."

"Right you are," Phineas agreed and unrolled the map onto the deck. "Now, where did he say the floating prison was located?"

Griffin knelt down and smoothed out the map with his hands.

"According to Silas, it should lie just west of the Island of Stones. So right about here," he said, pointing to an empty spot on the map.

"How long will it take us to get there from here?" Penny asked.

Phineas sat back on his heels and adjusted his hat. "If the wind is with us, I think we could make it in two days. If the wind doesn't cooperate, it could take up to five."

"Well, I'll be sleeping the whole way," Pete said with a yawn.

"There won't be much time for sleeping though," Penny said, "We need to train."

"Train?" Pete guffawed. "Like we stand a chance against an army of guards."

"We'll stand a whole lot better chance if we hone our abilities and skills."

"She's right," Phineas agreed. "I know that if I am to be useful, I can't be fainting every time I levitate a feather."

"But will two to five days of training be enough time to make a significant difference?" Haldor asked.

"Maybe not, but it could give us the edge we need," she answered, setting her jaw with determination. "Griffin, maybe you could show me some of your shape-shifting techniques."

"I would be happy to!" he answered with a smile.

Crane felt distressed. What good was he going to be if it came down to a fight? He wished that he could train like everyone else. If only he still had that lightning gun. Then he could at least be of some use.

While the others discussed the various training methods they might employ, he slipped off to be alone. He came upon the captain who was checking ropes and tying knots.

"Ahoy!" he called as he approached. "Exciting journey ahead, eh?"

"Yes, exciting," Crane mumbled without enthusiasm.

Griswold didn't seem to notice his lack of zeal however.

"Here, hold this," he instructed, handing him a rope. "Some of these confounded lines and connections were damaged in the storm. Best get 'em fixed up for tomorrow."

Crane held the line while the captain continued to work.

"Say, Griswold?"

"Aye?"

"What kind of abilities do you have? I'll bet you can bend metal. Am I right?"

"Nay, I don't need all that newfangled magic. Why I once single-handedly took out an entire ship of pirates who was trying to take me cargo."

"How did you do that?"

"It twer twenty-percent luck, eighty-percent brains, and one-hundred-percent skill with me sword. The poor pirates didn't stand a chance against me and old Bessie."

"Bessie?"

"Aye!" The captain pulled his sword from his sheath and waved it around. "Bessie and me go way back, we do. And she has a mighty appetite for pirate blood."

"Do you think you could teach me?" Crane asked, hopeful.

"Maybe." Griswold looked Crane up and down. "First, let's see your weapon."

Crane drew his blades and held them out in front of him.

"Well, they ain't Bessie, but they'll do." He sniffed. "What be their names?"

"Their names? Well I hadn't really thought about it."

"They gotta 'ave names. A good weapon is like a friend. After all, what man simply calls his friend, 'person?' Would that make the friend feel good? Nay. Weapons perform better if ye take the time to learn their names."

"Um, I suppose I could name them, Stabby and Stabert."

"Why, ye didn't even ask them their proper names! Ye have to listen closely," Griswold said, holding his sword close to Crane's ear. "Hear that? My sword says, 'Bessie' as clear as a bell." Crane heard nothing of the sort, but he nodded his head anyway.

"Um, what are your names?" he asked, holding up the blades on either side of his head. He paused for a moment, pretending to listen. "I think they said Jack and Jill," he said finally.

"Ba-ha-ha, ye must be a might crazy," the captain howled. "Swords don't talk!" he exclaimed holding his belly.

"But you said—"

"Ah, ye are a funny lad. Jack and Jill sound like good names though." He wiped a tear from his eye. "First thing tomorrow, we will begin training." He finished tying the last knot and slapped Crane on the shoulder, still grinning. "Phineas, the lad thinks that his swords are talking to him," he said as he walked down the steps.

Crane leaned over the rail and gazed at the sky. He took a deep breath, enjoying the fresh air that filled his lungs. Maybe he could be of some use after all.

That night, they dined on potatoes and dried beef. Everyone was in high spirits. Even Crane, who had seemed a bit down earlier that day was looking more optimistic. Penny couldn't explain the sudden boost in the atmosphere. Perhaps it was because they felt better now that they had a clear goal. Or perhaps it was on account of the warm meal. In any case, it was nice to feel something other than the frantic fear that had settled in the pit of her stomach since this whole thing had begun. She crossed her arms and leaned back in her chair. They were all listening to Captain Griswold recount a heroic battle between himself and a sky creature with ten limbs.

"And that was how I lost me leg!" he finished with a flourish.

Crane whistled. "Wow, that was brilliant! Do you have any more stories?"

"Aye, but maybe they should be saved for another night." The captain yawned. "After all, ye have a big day of training with Jack and Jill tomorrow." He winked in Crane's direction. Griswold rose with another yawn and shuffled off to his quarters. "The ship sails at sunrise," he called over his shoulder.

Penny hesitated. She still had so many questions that were unanswered. One in particular was weighing on her mind. "Before we head to bed, I was wondering something. If we do manage to pull this off and rescue everyone, what will we do then? How will we take them home if we can't return to Terra? We can't navigate through the strong winds, can we?"

"I have been pondering this same question," Phineas admitted. "Only the elders from the race of builders knew the location of the passage through the wind, and they were all killed by Esmond."

"Well somehow Esmond must have discovered the passage through the wind," Haldor chimed in.

"Yes, he must have if he was able to leave. If he does know of the passage, then I'll wager he has it guarded by now," Phineas said.

Penny rested her chin in her hands. "Isn't there any other way back?"

"No, it's the only way we know of."

"There might be one other way," Griffin offered. "Old Lady Johnson told me about it."

"Widow Johnson has many strange ideas," Phineas said. "She was the lady at the meeting who was going on about the 'Chosen One' who will save us all with great power." Penny remembered her well. Her wild eyes had been haunting her dreams.

"What did she say?" she asked.

Griffin leaned forward in his chair. "Well, there were once two portals created by the ancient builders. The knowledge to create more has since been lost. You could step through one and be sent to the other. One of the portals became damaged beyond repair during a fire. The other one went missing long ago."

"Well, what good does that do us?" Pete wanted to know.

"When the children were sent to Terra, two of the most skilled builders went with them to try to build a new portal from the remnants of the old one, while the builders here searched for the one that was lost. They wanted to have an escape plan in place in case Esmond were to ever invade their sanctuary and they should need to relocate. No one knows if they ever found it though, or if the other one was repaired."

"It is just one of the many fantastic rumors that have circulated about the war," Phineas said. "Desperate parents will cling onto almost anything. I should know."

"Many people thought Terra was a rumor too though," Penny reminded him.

"That's true," he admitted. "But finding the portal means finding the builders. In any case, we are going to need their help. First things first though," he said with a yawn. "We need to get some sleep."

As they walked across the deck from the galley, Penny glanced up at the sky. The stars seemed so much closer and brighter here. She almost felt as if she could reach up and snatch one out of the sky. She paused at the rail to take it in for a few moments. As she gazed up at the expanse, her mind wandered to thoughts of lying on her roof back home with Crane. The two of them used to climb out of her window on clear nights and look for shooting stars. Crane always seemed to see one right as she would look away. She half-suspected that he made them up just to drive her crazy. How long ago that seemed.

"Your shoe is untied," Crane said as he sidled up beside her. She glanced down at her feet.

"There! Did you see that one?" he asked as she was looking at her boots. "Oh, you missed it. What a shame."

Penny gave him a playful shove. "Sure I did." She rolled her eyes. *Same old Crane.* They stood in silence for a couple minutes, each lost in their own thoughts.

Crane cleared his throat. "So...feeling nervous?"

"About the rescue? Strangely I'm not. Not right now anyway. You?"

"Are you kidding? Super Crane never gets nervous."

"That's good to know. I'll keep that in mind the next time a spider needs squishing."

He wrinkled his nose. "Spiders are different, and you know it."

She chuckled. "Right. How silly of me. Anyway, we should get some rest."

Crane nodded and they turned from the railing. Before they got to the door, he cleared his throat. "Hey, Penny?"

"Yes?"

"Um..." He seemed to flounder for a moment, as if trying to decide how to word what he was going to say. "Goodnight," he mumbled and slugged her arm before hurrying through the door.

"Goodnight," she said, though there was no one to hear her. She rubbed her sore arm. She wasn't sure what had gotten into Crane lately. He was acting even stranger than usual.

Chapter Twenty-Six

"The machine is almos-s-st ready, my lord," hissed the snake-like voice belonging to Francine Snyder.

"That is what you told us two weeks ago," Esmond said. His voice had a dangerous edge to it. "Perhaps you are not motivating them properly." As he spoke, he gazed from his open window, watching several sparrows flit from branch to branch on a tree that grew near the fortress.

"But this time, the builders have assured me that they will be done in no more than three days' time."

"For your sake, we hope so. We wouldn't want you to end up like poor Henderson. He was a nice man, and we hated to see him leave us, but it couldn't be helped. Although, he did make a nice addition to our little collection," he said, extending his gaze past the tree and onto several dozen pikes. Each spike was barren, with the exception of a single human head stabbed up through the skull.

"N-no, master," she stuttered. "Don't worry, sir. It will be finished."

"Good. As you know, we are quite patient." He sprinkled a few bread crumbs on the windowsill as he spoke.

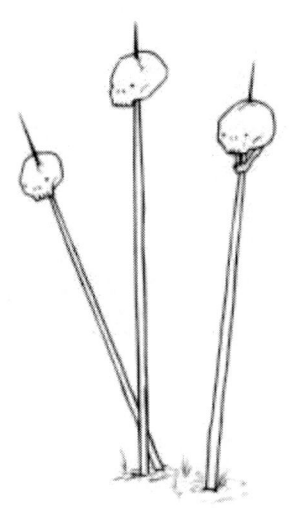

"Yes, of course you are, my lord," she agreed with haste.

Esmond watched with hungry eyes as one of the birds ventured onto the edge of the window.

"But even tolerance has its limits," he said in a voice just above a whisper.

The sparrow hopped closer to the bread crumbs, viewing Esmond with caution.

"Thank you for your gracious understanding," Snyder replied, backing toward the door. The bird took another tentative leap forward. Esmond smiled, exposing his pearly white teeth that had been chiseled to points. The sparrow, who seemed to sense no immediate danger, began to peck at the crumbs. Before the bird could react, Esmond sprung forward and scooped it up in one nimble motion. Snyder jumped as she was taken off guard. He brought the sparrow close to his face. He could feel the bird's heart beating like the ticking of a clock.

"Remember, you are nothing more than a sparrow to us, and just as easily broken." As he spoke, he began to squeeze the trembling bird. A small chirp passed through the bird's beak as it struggled to squirm free from his tightening grasp.

"Excuse the intrusion, my lord," a man said as he burst through the doors.

"What is it?" he shouted, lessening his grip on the sparrow. The little bird took advantage of this momentary lapse and managed to wriggle free. Flapping its wings frantically, it fluttered out the window.

"This had better be important," he spat out.

"It is, sir. It's about the children who escaped."

"Oh?" Esmond's ears perked up at the mention of this. "Out with it," he demanded.

"They were spotted in the harbor town of Pankor. The girl and one of the boys were positively identified."

"Well, where are they now? Have you brought them here?" He looked toward the door.

"Er, no. They managed to escape. However," he added, seeing the murderous look on Lord Esmond's face, "a woman reported seeing them get on a ship headed east."

"Well, what are you waiting for? Dispatch vessels to search the skies of Azure from the Port of Pankor, to the eastern border. Do not return without them."

"Yes, my lord," the guard replied and marched from the room.

"But, sir, surely these young people provide no threat to your plans," Snyder said with a laugh.

"Anyone who defies me, must be made an example of. We will find this ship yet. And when we do, they will be far less fortunate than that sparrow."

A hooded figure stood on the other side of the room. Penny didn't want to go any closer, but something compelled her to move forward. The dark form seemed to be muttering something to itself. The figure's cloak swayed from side to side as if blown by a breeze, though the air was still. As she drew near, she could almost make out a few of the words uttered.

She was within reaching distance now. The voice sounded hoarse and urgent. Without wanting to, she reached for the hood of the cloak. Before she could pull back the material, a claw-like hand shot out from beneath the cloak, gripping Penny's wrist. She gasped as familiar eyes bore into hers. It was the wrinkled face of Widow Johnson, the woman from the underground meeting.

"When that which was lost is returned, the Chosen One will liberate us with great power!" The old woman was practically yelling at her. Spiders crawled in the woman's now vacant eye sockets. Penny recoiled and jerked her arm away. She fell backward, her heart in her throat. But instead of hitting the ground, she continued to fall. She gasped, and tried to scream, but her voice sounded far away and not her own. She braced herself for the inevitable impact. Every muscle in her body tensed.

She sat upright, gasping. It took her a moment to remember where she was. She had been jostled awake by the motion on the ship.

What a horrible, vivid dream.

It still felt early. The four lumps in the beds nearby told her the others weren't up yet. Even Chip was still resting on his perch. She rolled out of her hammock and crossed the cold floorboards to the porthole. Peering outside, she could just see a bit of light amid the clouds. When Captain Griswold said they were to leave at first light, he meant it. She shivered and rubbed her arms, trying to warm them in vain. Teeth chattering, she dove back into her hammock. She pulled the covers over her head, hoping for a few more minutes of rest. A few more seconds was all she managed. She could hear the others stirring now.

A loud *thunk* could be heard as Crane fell to the floor. "Sorry," he whispered from where he lay tangled in his blankets.

She could soon hear the others getting ready in the dimly-lit room, and she gathered by their whispers that they were trying to be quiet. By now, Penny was wide awake and found it impossible to fall back asleep. Reluctantly, she swept back the covers and swung her legs to the floor. Everyone had left the room with the exception of Chip and Pete who was still snoring away in his bunk. They were all so eager to begin training, that by the time she dressed and roused Chip, they had already finished eating. Penny gulped down a quick breakfast of toast and jam and hurried to join them on deck.

"Now, step back on yer left foot, and parry with Jill," Griswold was saying. The captain had rigged the wheel to stay straight using a sturdy rope. This left his hands free to oversee Crane's training.

"Like this?" Crane stepped forward and slashed out with his blade.

"No, no. I said to parry with Jill, not thrust with Jack."

"Who's Perry?"

The captain shook his head and groaned. Penny turned to see what the other two were up to. Phineas stood in front of a bucket. A look of pain mixed with concentration was on his face. Using his levitation ability, he lifted one object after another off the deck and into the pail. Haldor sat on a crate cheering him on while casually bending a nail into a pretzel. Phineas paused to lean against the railing after moving a hammer. He mopped his brow and took a deep breath as he surveyed his progress.

"Don't push yourself too hard," Griffin cautioned him.

"Nonsense. I need to push myself. I should never have let myself get out of practice like this." He puffed.

"Good morning!" Griffin called, seeing her approach. "Are you ready?"

Penny nodded but felt hesitant. What if she wasn't any good? Worse yet, what if she forgot her clothes again? Her cheeks colored at the thought. Griffin looked at her, his brows knit in concern.

"Are you all right?" he asked.

"Oh, yes. I'm fine."

"Well then, let's get started!" Penny followed him to the far end of the deck, away from everyone else. "So that we can concentrate," he explained. "You seem pretty far advanced already. What transformations have you done so far?"

"Well, the stapler was my first accidental transformation. A stapler is a tool that attaches paper together," she explained when she saw him looking perplexed. He nodded.

"Got it. Go on," he urged.

"After that I turned into my teacher, a couple different guards, the chair, and the spider. I think that's all so far."

"That is quite a list of accomplishments. Usually someone doesn't transform into an inanimate object by accident. That takes great concentration and full intent."

"Well... I did," she said with a shrug. "Hey, so I have been wondering something."

"I'll answer if I can."

"Well, when we were fighting the spiders in the forest the other day, how did you turn into a lion? I can only transform into things that I've recently seen. Did you see a lion in those woods?"

Griffin pulled a brown leather book from his pocket.

"I didn't see one that night, but I did see one in the past." As he spoke, he flipped through the pages of the small book. "Here we go," he said, turning it toward her. Drawn in neat precise lines was the image of a lion. Various numbers and notes that Penny didn't understand surrounded the drawing.

"What is this for?" she asked.

"For reference. After growing frustrated at the limitation of only turning into something that I had just seen, I began to experiment. It took me many months to perfect the lion's shape. These measurements and notes make it easier by helping me recall specific details. Plus, the more you transform into something and the more familiar you become with it, the easier it is next time." He reached into his pocket again, producing an identical book. "For you," he offered.

"Thank you," she said with a shy smile.

A loud explosion in the sky made them both jump.

"Pirates off the port side!" yelled Griswold. The sound had been cannon fire. They were being fired upon by a ship in the distance. Any further training would have to wait. They both hurried to join the captain at the bridge. The others were already there.

"What's going on?" Pete asked, rubbing the sleep from his eyes.

"We be under attack from them scurvy pirates, that's what," Griswold spat. "They be wanting the cargo."

Crane lowered his swords. "But, I thought we were your cargo."

"Aye, but they don't be knowing that."

"But if they break any of our balloons, we'll crash and they won't get anything," Penny said.

"That's why they don't be aiming to make us sink, they be aiming to intimidate. Besides, ye can cause a lot of damage without putting holes in the balloons," the captain said darkly. "Why do ye think my ship is in the shape it is? But they have never gotten me cargo yet, and I don't be aiming to let them have it today. Stand aside." He strode down the steps and rolled an old rusty cannon to the railing.

Griffin put his hand on the cannon. "I can help with that."

"Aye, you get her ready while I get up alongside." The captain returned to the wheelhouse and gave it a sharp tug. A loud crash shook the boat as a cannonball struck their vessel, sending Penny toppling to the ground. Chip fell from her shoulder. Feeling rather ruffled, he decided to fly up to the crow's nest and observe. The ship was getting dangerously close. As Crane helped her to her feet, she could see the leering faces of the crew staring back at them.

"Surrender!" one of them shouted.

"Not on yer putrid excuse for a face!" Griswold shouted back. "Fire now," he ordered. Griffin obeyed. The cannonball hit its mark, leaving a giant hole on the hull.

"If ye won't surrender, then prepare to go down!" yelled the captain of the other ship.

"We'll never surrender!" Griswold yelled back. The pirates rolled several other cannons to the rail, preparing to open fire.

"This be your last chance!"

"Maybe we should listen to them," Phineas urged.

"Nonsense, the Soaring Manatee still has a trick or two up her sleeve." Captain Griswold stomped twice on the deck, causing a panel full of buttons to appear. "Let's see how they be liking these oranges," he said, flipping a couple toggles then pressing a bright red button. They could feel the ship rumbling beneath them.

Penny felt a sinking sensation. In every movie she had seen, the red button was some sort of self-destruct command. But the captain wouldn't do that...would he? As she looked into his insane-looking eyes and grin of anticipation, she wasn't so sure.

"Fire!" the pirate captain shouted. The boom of several cannons could be heard just as the ship rose at a rapid rate. The cannon balls missed the ship's hull by mere inches as they lifted into the sky.

Thrown off balance by the sudden motion, she grasped the rail for support. "Ha! Me patented jet thrusters gets 'em every time," Griswold cried gleefully. Their ship was now hovering just over the pirate's vessel.

"Lower the anchor!" he shouted. Pete lifted the heavy anchor at his feet and tossed it over the side. They could hear it hit the ship below with a clunk.

"Take the wheel," Griswold ordered. Placing a knife between his teeth, the captain climbed over the rail and shimmied down the anchor chain. He stopped once he reached the top of the pirate ship. "Ye best be getting to land. It looks like ye have a nasty hole in yer balloon!" he called down to them. Before they could react, Griswold had slashed a good-sized hole in the canvas.

"Kill him!" yelled the pirate captain. But Griswold was already shimmying back up the anchor. Their weapons bounced off the bow.

"I'll get 'em, Captain," one of the men said, firing his blunderbuss.

"No!" the pirate captain shouted. But it was too late. The shot missed Griswold entirely and instead riddled the already damaged balloon with holes. Griffin and Crane hurried to hoist an out of breath Captain Griswold back on board.

"Are they going to sink into the Azure winds?" Penny asked.

"Maybe not, if they hurry to land," Griswold said with a laugh. "That will teach them to be messin' with the Manatee."

Chapter Twenty-Seven

This was going to work. It had to. Rainey had overheard the guards talking. Something big was going to happen tonight, and she was certain that it wasn't going to be good. They had to escape before something called, "the extraction," took place. Last time she got something extracted was at the dentist's office, and that was horrible. She could only imagine what they might have in store for them.

She wasn't sure how much time they had left, so she had to work fast. Rainey called a meeting, leaving one girl to guard the door. They all gathered around the small vent in the corner of the room. They had found that by boosting one of the girls up to the vent, they could communicate with the boys in their cell. Greta, who was the smallest, was selected to be the one to go up. She gave three sharp raps to the grate, which were quickly returned.

"They are ready," she whispered down.

"Okay, listen up, everyone," Rainey said. "They have kept us alive this long, so they must need us to be in one piece. If our safety is threatened, they would have no choice but to come inside, right?" The girls nodded, while Greta relayed the message to the boys.

"So, do we pretend that one of us is sick?" a tall girl asked.

"I'm not sure if they would risk coming in for one sick person. It's not urgent enough. No, what I would like to do is stage a fight. I think it would be best if it were between several of the boys. Then when the guards come in to intervene, boys hidden near the door can jump them and take their weapons and keys. Then they can come release us."

"It will never work," one of the older girls piped in. "We're all too weak. I think we should just wait and see what they want from us. Maybe someone is paying our ransom or something and they are going to let us go." Hearing this, several of the other girls looked hopeful.

"There is no ransom," Rainey replied. "You heard the men speaking. Tonight is the night of the extraction. That can't be a good thing."

"I still think it's no use," the girl mumbled.

Rainey ignored her and instead turned her attention to Greta.

"What do the boys think?" she asked.

Greta put her ear to the vent and listened for a moment.

"They think that a fight is a good idea. They say they're ready."

"Good. Tell them to wait till the guards are sure to hear them. They should be checking on us in an hour. They should do it then."

On the other side of the vent, the cell was buzzing with anticipation as the boys prepared themselves. They were all eager to participate in the fake fight. After days of doing nothing but waiting, they were all excited to be doing something useful.

"We are going to need people to jump them from behind too," Rainey's brother Derrick said. Several hands went up right away.

"I can't wait to get my hands on those guys," a large boy said, cracking his knuckles. His statement was met with murmurs of assent. Derrick looked around the room, deep in thought. He wanted to take every precaution. He ordered the boys to gather the bedding and rig a makeshift net to drop on the guards. Meanwhile, he set to work making a lever that would drop down and prevent the door from closing once opened.

"Only an hour left to go," he said to no one in particular. "An hour 'til freedom."

They were all still a bit shaken from the run in with the pirates yesterday, but that didn't stop them from continuing on. If anything, they felt invigorated. They had been sailing all night and afternoon. The winds had been with them and Griswold thought they were getting close. Penny had been training with Griffin for several hours, but it was slow going. She had been fortunate enough to see a sparrow on the ship that morning, and was trying to replicate it, using the notes she had jotted down in her book.

She was able to turn into the bird that morning after seeing it, but now her memory of it was fading and the notes didn't seem to help. Griffin stood nearby, offering words of encouragement while petting Chip who was hooting appreciatively.

"Remember, you aren't trying to look like just any bird, you are trying to become that bird. Feel the micronites in the water all around us. Let them flow into you."

Penny just couldn't try anymore. She was exhausted. She tossed the book aside in frustration and slumped against the mast.

"No worries. It took me months, remember? I had to study that same lion on numerous occasions. Looking back, I realize that I should have chosen something less dangerous," he said, raising his sleeve to reveal several large gashes.

"Are those scars from the lion?" she asked in awe.

"Kind of. They are from when I fell on some rocks while trying to sneak closer to his cave. Let's take a break and work on sword training again with Crane and Griswold."

She agreed and together they walked toward the wheelhouse. Pete, who had been asked to stop training after starting a small fire on deck, was sword fighting with them.

"Mind if we join in?" Penny asked.

"Sure, grab yer weapons," Griswold replied. As clumsy as she felt at transformation, here she felt even clumsier. Pete lunged forward, and she nearly toppled to the ground. She took a deep breath and steadied herself, then swung toward him. Her blade met with his and let out a satisfying *clang*. She had to admit, she was at least doing better than yesterday. Griswold had helped her with her footing.

She wasn't doing nearly as well as Crane though. He seemed to be a natural. The fluidity of his movements had taken her by surprise. She had never seen him do anything so smooth. She had never seen him try so hard at anything before. He didn't take things seriously enough to try, but the look in his eyes told her he was serious this time. He was taking on both Griffin and Griswold at the same time now. Penny paused to watch and nearly got her arm lopped off.

"Hey, pay attention! I almost cut off your arm," Pete cried.

"Sorry," she mumbled, continuing to watch Crane. He was backed up against a barrel now. It looked like they had him pinned. They were both advancing. Just when it looked like they had him for sure, he leaned back and, using the barrel to support his back, shot out both legs. His feet connected with their chests, causing them to fall back. Both of their swords clattered to the deck on impact. Before they could even sit up, Crane was standing over them with a blade pointed at each of their throats.

"Nice one," Griffin conceded.

"What do ye mean by tossing an old sailor on his back?" Griswold sputtered as Crane helped him to his feet.

"I'm sorry. I was just—"

"Just yankin' yer anchor," Griswold laughed. "Good job, lad. Now, let's see how ye fare with this," he said, tossing him a knife.

"A knife fight?"

"Not exactly. You see, I'll still be using me sword."

A frantic hooting sound coming from the crow's nest caught Penny's attention. She looked up from the practice session to see what was wrong. Chip, who had been sunning himself, seemed bothered by something.

"What is it, Chip?"

The little bird flew down to her shoulder. He ruffled his wings, still seeming alarmed. She looked toward the sky and noticed for the first time that the clouds around them had been increasing. They were now completely surrounded by the white fog.

"Um, guys?"

But the others had noticed too. Griswold untied the wheel and stood at the alert, his eyes searching the skies.

A soft whooshing noise made Penny's eyes dart to the left. "Did you hear that?"

Before anyone could answer, the whooshing sound came again. This time louder and on the other side of the ship. They all spun around, looking for the source of the noise.

"There!" Crane cried, pointing. "I saw something through the clouds. It looked like some sort of tail."

"Did it have red underneath and thick-looking iron plates?" Griswold asked.

"Yes, I think it did. Do you know what it is?"

"Aye. It be a leviathan," the captain said, his eyes opened wide in awe.

"A leviathan? What's that?" Penny asked. But Griswold seemed too lost in thought to answer.

Phineas, who had stopped his training with Haldor to join them, replied instead. "They are creatures Lord Esmond had built for the war," he said. "I've heard stories of their existence, but I've never seen one myself. They are extremely dangerous. They had entire villages running in fear."

"Sounds fascinating," Haldor said, stepping closer to the rail.

The sound was growing louder and more frequent now. It seemed to be coming from both sides at once.

Pete's eyes grew wide with terror. "What do we do?"

"Duck!" Captain Griswold yelled just in time. A wave of flames danced over their prostrated figures, singeing their clothes. They stood and hurried to put out the flames that had sprung up above the captain's quarters. The deck was now charred in a few places and several of the ropes had snapped from the heat.

"How can we fight what we can't see?" Griffin wondered aloud.

"We can't," Griswold hollered. "But perhaps we can outmaneuver it. Everybody hang on," he said as he pushed a lever forward. Penny gasped as the ship took a sharp dive down, then up again. The noise of the leviathan did not diminish, however. Griswold next took them through a series of turns and maneuvers. His flying managed to disorient all on board but failed to shake the beast who didn't seem to have any trouble seeing through the clouds.

"I think it's toying with us," Haldor said. "For now, he seems to be curious."

Penny took a deep breath. "Yes but for how long?"

Just as she finished speaking, the entire ship shook violently. Something had rammed against the side.

"I'll wager his curiosity is wearing out." Penny peered over the side. She could see nothing but a blanket of white.

"The old girl can't hold together much longer!" the captain shouted down. The ship shook again, this time knocking Penny to the floor. There must be something they could do with their abilities against these things, she thought to herself. If only they could see them through all the cloud cover. Suddenly, she had an idea. Standing up on wobbly legs, she approached Pete.

"Listen, do you think you could send some fire off the bow?"

"I guess so. But—"

"And Phineas," she continued, "could you direct the flames and heat around the outside of the ship?"

"Well I've never tried to move fire before, but I could certainly try."

"What are you planning to do?" Griffin asked.

"Ever used a blow dryer to defog a mirror?"

"A what?"

"A blow dryer. Oh, well I suppose you wouldn't have. Just trust me," she assured him. "Ready?" she asked Pete and Phineas.

They nodded and took their positions near the bow.

"Now!" she shouted.

Taking care not to burn the ship, Pete shot out a large flame in front of them. The clouds evaporated wherever the heat of the flame touched. Concentrating with all his might, Phineas spread his arms to the sides of his body. The flames responded, licking all around the hull of the ship. Penny felt the intense heat all over, making her face feel like a tight mask. She hoped this wasn't a horrible mistake. Pete and Phineas did have the most volatile and unpredictable abilities among them. But to her relief, her plan seemed to be working. The clouds all around them were burning off, leaving a wide chasm of clear sky surrounding their vessel.

"Brilliant idea," Haldor said. "I should have thought of it myself."

Now that the clouds around them had been cleared, the sky had become eerily quiet.

"Where did it go?" Crane asked, standing ready with his sword.

"There!" Penny cried as a glint in the clouds caught her eye. They stood gazing at the spot, waiting for the thing to reappear, when without warning, a long body burst through the clouds behind them. Penny spun around, looking directly into the creature's eyes. They burned like red-hot coals piercing into her. She wanted to look away, but stood as if in a trance. His sharp metal teeth glistened like razor blades as he flew closer. His entire body radiated strength and power. His metal scales encircled him like armor, protecting his mighty body. She watched in horror as the leviathan drew back his head, preparing to spew fire. There was nowhere to run.

This was the end.

Chapter Twenty-Eight

She felt the heat before the flames even came close. Heat so intense, it made her feel lightheaded. She turned away, but she knew it was no use. There was no escaping this blast. She squeezed her eyes shut and waited for the imminent pain, but it didn't come. Opening her eyes, she looked around. Phineas had stopped directing Pete's flame and was now standing in front of her, arms extended. The creature's fire looked like it was being held back by some sort of invisible force field just inches from Phineas's hands. The leviathan roared and let out a second blast, but Phineas held his ground. Penny recoiled as she realized the sizzling sound she heard was coming from Phineas's burning hands.

Griffin fired a crossbow shot toward the monster, which bounced harmlessly off his scales. The bolt did succeed in distracting it. The creature ceased firing and turned with a snarl toward Griffin. Phineas dropped to his knees and cradled his hands. The beast dove toward where the others stood, jaws snapping. Crane spun to the side, lashing out with his sword. The sword struck the metal scales on the creature's neck, making a loud *clang*. The blow didn't even leave a dent in the creature's armor, but it seemed to confuse him.

The beast changed direction and let out a roar of rage before diving back into the clouds. The air around them became silent.

"Do you think he's gone?" Penny asked.

"Shh." Griswold held out his arm for silence. After a moment he said in a low voice, "It don't be the way of a leviathan to give up that easily." They all stood gazing at the spot he had disappeared into.

"Let's get out of here before that thing comes back," Crane whispered.

"Too late!" Griswold pointed behind them.

The creature let out a roar as he appeared from the cloud cover. A river of flames leapt from the mouth of the leviathan, catching the deck on fire. Pete yelled as the flames leapt upon him, engulfing

his leg.

Penny threw her cloak over Pete as the others tried to put out the fire on deck. "Are you okay?" She pulled back the cloak, bracing herself for the gruesome sight of Pete's burned leg. Pete's right pant leg was burned clean away, all right. The edges were blackened and still smoking, but Pete's skin underneath looked pink and unscathed. "How did you...? Pete, how are you not burned?"

But there was no time for further discussion. They leapt to the side as another volley of flames enveloped the ship.

"If that fire gets to our balloons, we'll be going down for sure!" Griswold shouted.

"Haldor, can't you do something?" Penny asked.

"I'm trying, but he only gets close enough while he's breathing fire!"

"Get behind me," Pete ordered Haldor.

"Why, what are you going to do?"

"Remember the lasers?" Pete asked.

Haldor thought a moment, then nodded as if something dawned on him.

"Then get behind me."

Haldor obeyed and crouched behind him.

Pete stood up straight and held his arms in the air. "Hey, you old tin can, come and get me!" The beast turned and looked toward Pete, his big, red eyes gleaming.

"Pete, what are you thinking?" Crane asked, thoroughly bewildered.

"Stay back, moron."

"But—"

Penny grabbed his shoulder. "It's okay, he knows what he's doing."

The creature snapped his jaws then let out a low rumbling growl. The ship shook with the sound.

"That's right, you sorry excuse for a trash bin! Come and get me. I dare you."

The beast hurled himself at the ship, his tail twitching from side to side.

"Here he comes," Pete said to himself.

The creature arched his back, then let out a huge blast directly at him.

"Pete, no!" Crane yelled. The fire engulfed his body, but he managed to somehow hold his ground. The smell of the burning fabric filled the air as Pete's clothes sizzled. Frustrated, the leviathan flew in closer, breathing a steady flame in Pete's direction. Haldor crouched low behind him. He was breathing raggedly and was slumped over like he was about to pass out from the heat.

"Now!" Pete yelled as the creature stopped to draw in another breath. Haldor leaned out just enough to see. Before the flying beast could release another flame, Haldor struck. The metal on the leviathan's metal belly made a horrible racket as it bent and collapsed inward. It roared and twisted, striking the rail of the ship as it fell. The impact knocked Pete to the deck. Penny ran to extinguish the flames before more of the ship could catch fire. Griffin stood at the edge of the ship and watched the Leviathan fall until it disappeared below the clouds. Pete stood up and looked down at his clothes. They were tattered and burned. Just a few scraps of material remained, but he, as before, had somehow remained whole.

"What happened?" Crane asked. "How is Pete not dead?"

"I had heard some Firebranders have the ability to withstand flame," Griffin said. "I guess it's true after all!"

"No time to talk now," Griswold piped up. "Sometimes they be hunting in pairs. We best move on."

Penny looked at Phineas. "Do you feel well enough to help us through the clouds?"

He was pale as a ghost but he managed to murmur a faint, "Yes."

Crane and Griffin helped him to his feet and he took his place by Pete. As the others made sure every flame on the now blackened ship had been put out, Pete sent out fire, and Phineas directed it forward, clearing the clouds ahead and allowing them to see where they were going. Soon they saw it. Looming in front of them like something from a gothic movie was their destination. The floating prison looked like a sinister castle in the clouds. Penny couldn't quite tell what was holding it up. Such a massive building must weigh a ton. As they approached the structure, everything was quiet. The clouds seemed to block out every sound except their own breathing.

"Spooky, eh?" Crane whispered to her. She nodded, daring not to speak. They approached the prison from the back, so as not to be seen.

"I can let ye off here," Griswold said, indicating a strip of land. "The clouds should keep the ship hidden from view 'til ye be coming back."

Penny searched the sky. "What about the leviathans? There could be more."

"I can stay here and help him," Haldor offered.

She nodded. "Chip should stay aboard too. He can be your lookout. You should stay behind too, Phineas. You need to at least bandage your hands."

"Nonsense, I feel fine." He slapped the railing for emphasis as he spoke and stifled a cry.

"She's right, you need to stay here," Griffin agreed.

"All right, I guess Griswold might need me anyway. He allowed himself to sit down on a crate.

"Oh, and Phineas," Penny called as they exited the vessel. "Thanks."

He gave her a nod as the ship drifted into the fog.

As they stood on the bank watching the ship disappear, her heart began to race. This was it, this was why they had come all this way. Succeed or fail, it had all come down to this moment.

❦

Inside their cell, Derrick and the other boys were ready to put their plan into action. The traps were set and the volunteers were in place, ready for action. Derrick took one last look around the room. Satisfied, he sat down to wait. But the guards didn't come. Something was wrong. They always dropped the food through the slot at the same time each day. When the sun had just gone down, that was the proper time. Now it was beginning to grow dark.

"I think we should talk to the girls and regroup," he said, after the waiting became too much.

"Wait, I hear something!" said a boy with his ear to the door. He jumped back with a start as the slot in the door slid open. Dark eyes peered through the hole.

"Change of plans, boys," the man said in a gruff voice. "There will be no dinner tonight. Consider yourselves lucky, you get to meet Lord Esmond." The man laughed with a deep, throaty chuckle. "Now, step away from the door and line up. Come out one at a time with your hands behind your head. Anyone who makes a wrong move gets it," he said, holding up the dreaded electric prongs. The man slid the slot back into place and unbolted the door. Panicked whispers could be heard throughout the cell.

"What do we do now?"

"How can we escape?"

"Shh." Derrick silenced them as the door clanged open. The guards didn't set foot inside. Instead, they grabbed the boy standing nearest to the door and ordered the rest to follow. Taken off guard, the boys began to revert to following orders from the guards. Several others had already gone through the door. Derrick knew that he had to do something.

"Get your smelly face out of my way," snapped a boy named Matthew who stood behind him. Derrick was confused for a moment. Matthew had always been so mild tempered and easy to get along with. "I said move it, smelly face!"

"Hey, break it up in there!" yelled one of the guards.

Then he remembered. "Your face is far smellier than mine," Derrick shot back. It wasn't the best comeback. "What I meant to say," he tried again, "is, step off, you stupid oaf. I could beat up horses like you when I am hungry for dinner."

"You're so lame you don't even make sense," joined in another boy.

"Your mom is the lame one," he returned. Derrick wasn't sure who threw the first punch, but soon fists were flying, and no one seemed to know how to be gentle. He had received an elbow to the eye, a fist to the nose and a knee to the stomach before the guards finally stepped in to break up the fight.

"Now!" Derrick shouted. Spinning around, they took the guards by surprise. They turned to go out the door, but found themselves covered in the make-shift nets.

"Close the door!" one of the guards yelled to the one who had remained outside. But thanks to Derrick's invention, the door refused to shut. Several of the boys ran out to subdue the man in the hall.

"Take this," cried a boy who had wrestled away one of the electric prongs. With a loud zap, it connected with one of the guards who collapsed. Derrick found a set of keys attached to a man's belt, which he removed.

"Let's go," he ordered.

They all filed out, shutting the cell door with the guards inside. Moving down the hall, they soon came to another locked door. Using the keys found on the guard, Derrick opened it. The girls cried out in relief, seeing them standing in the doorway.

"You did it!" Rainey exclaimed.

"See what happens when you actually involve me in your harebrained schemes?"

Rainey shrugged. "Yeah, well—"

"I'm just giving you a hard time. It was a good plan."

"Thanks, but we still have a long way to go. Are you guys ready?"

Her question was met with shouts of enthusiasm. They couldn't wait to get away from that wretched room. Once outside, Derrick urged them all to keep quiet as they crept down the hall. They climbed a set of stairs and came to a large iron door. It swung open easily. Standing on the other side of the door in a large courtyard, stood a bewildered-looking guard. Before anyone could stop him, he began to yell.

"The prisoners are escaping! The prisoners are— *ahhg!*" he yelped as he was silenced by a prong. But the damage was already done. An alarm was sounding all around them. Several dozen guards appeared from all sides.

"We are surrounded," Derrick cried. Several of the children raised their arms as if to surrender. Rainey looked around at the terrified faces. She couldn't let it end like this.

"I don't know about the rest of you," she cried, "but I'm not going down without a fight!" One by one they lowered their hands. With sullen determination, they all readied themselves and prepared to battle for their lives.

Penny and the others had climbed up the bank to the front gate. They paused, not knowing how to proceed. A sound from behind made them seek a hiding spot. From their position in the ditch, they watched. The sound was getting closer. What started as a soft whirring noise was now a dull roar. As they watched, a large vessel appeared from the fog and came to a halt at the edge of the island. It looked similar to the ship they had stowed away in back on Terra, only this ship was smaller and more elegant.

"It's Lord Esmond's ship," Griffin whispered.

Penny's hands shook. She wasn't anxious to meet this Esmond guy.

Some men jumped out and tied the ship to a post. They shrank back deeper into the shadows as the doors opened, and a walkway was lowered down. A tall, thin man stepped out, gracefully descending from the ship. He wore a long coat and carried a cane. The hand gripping the cane looked machine-like. His metal fingers glistened in the moonlight. Despite the cane, there was nothing feeble about this man. He had a robust stride and a powerful presence about him. His face looked pale in the moonlight. Almost ghostly. The dim lighting hitting his brow cast shadows across his face and created dark caverns around his eyes. She was struck by how much the man resembled a skeleton.

As he walked closer, followed on either side by a bishop, she noticed how young he was. He couldn't have been over thirty-five. His hair had gone prematurely grey, but what color was left was jet black. The years had not been kind to him. His face bore a scar reaching from his hairline, all the way to his pointed chin. His face looked tired and worn out. His eyes, however, were a different story.

His eyes made her shiver though the evening was warm. She could see them well even from where they hid and couldn't help but think that she was looking into the calculating eyes of a psychopath. They were black and gleaming with malice and excitement. Penny held her breath as he walked across the bridge to the door. She heard a series of clicks before the door swung open. For a moment she panicked, thinking that the light streaming from the door would surely reveal them. They must have been hidden better than she thought. Esmond's eyes flicked across where they hunched.

"Leave the door unbolted," his singsong voice ordered. "We have many guests arriving tonight."

"Yes, my lord," the guard answered and pulled the door closed behind them.

"Come on," Penny whispered. "We have to hurry before any other ships arrive."

Crane nodded, drawing his swords. "All right, let's go."

After making sure no one else was around, they left their hiding spot and opened the door. The entrance appeared to be empty. The room they were standing in had several doors branching off in every direction.

Crane sighed. "How will we ever find them?"

"Well I didn't want to risk splitting up again, but it might be our best option," Penny said. "In any case, we need to get away from this doorway. Which way do you think seems best?"

But before anyone could answer, they heard a terrible commotion.

Pete pointed to a door. "I think it came from this way."

They pushed through the door and found themselves standing atop a balcony. The sight that met them below was one of chaos. There was a battle going on between the prisoners and the guards. From the look of things, the prisoners had managed to hold their own for a while. Several bishops lay on the ground, but many more were still coming at them. Unless they intervened, the prisoners would soon be over taken. Their rescue had just gotten much more complicated.

Chapter Twenty-Nine

Penny drew her sword from its sheath. "Come on!"

While Griffin fired shots from above using his crossbow, the others raced down the steps. Crane was the first to engage the enemy. The man he attacked was taken off guard and defeated easily. Pete, meanwhile, expelled fire at all who were in range. Penny lunged forward and attacked another who had turned around to face them.

He dodged her blade, causing her to lose her balance. The man was armed with a prong. He jabbed it toward her prostrate figure. She rolled to the side. The prong struck the ground with a *clang*. Putting her weight on her hands, she kicked his weapon with her foot, knocking it back into his leg. The prong's electric shock made him fall to the ground. As she stood to face another opponent, she realized how futile their battle was. Several doors had slid open around them, and new bishops and officials were pouring in to subdue the crowd. She knew she had to do something. Crane was surrounded, and Pete was already lying unconscious on the floor.

She jumped as something landed nearby. It was Griffin in his lion form running into the fray to help Crane. He took down a couple guards with sweeping blows from his claws, but more guards took their place. They were all in big trouble. Penny saw an empty room nearby. If she could only get to it, they might all stand a chance. She dodged a man coming at her by sidestepping behind another guard. The men collided. It was just the distraction she needed. Staying low to the ground, she slipped into the dark room. If ever there was a time she needed to be accurate with her transformation, this was it. She closed her eyes and waited for the familiar dizzy sensation to come over her. Once she was satisfied all had gone well, she stepped out of the room.

"Stop!" she commanded in the most authoritative voice she could muster, but no one seemed to notice her presence. Walking over to the stairs, she strode to the top and addressed the room again.

"I said stop!" she commanded again.

"It's Lord Esmond!" she heard someone say. Soon she had the attention of the entire room. She cleared her throat before going on.

"What do you think you're doing?" she shouted down, trying to sound irritated. "Do you want to damage my specimens?"

"But sir," said a bishop stepping forward, "the prisoners were trying to escape."

"Don't argue with the great and powerful Esmond!" she shouted, making the man shrink away. "Leave the room immediately, all of you. I can handle these children."

"But—" the man ventured again.

"Do you doubt my power?" she said with a scowl. "Off with his head!" A couple guards nearby seized the confused man and drug him away. Perhaps she had gotten a bit carried away. She didn't want to be responsible for sending this man to his doom. "I changed my mind. Send him to the dungeon," she corrected. "I will, uh...take care of him later myself," she said, trying to smile menacingly but looking deranged instead.

"Does anyone else doubt my abilities?" Her question was met with silence. "Then leave, or face my wrath," she told them. Quicker than she would have thought possible, the uniformed guards cleared the room, leaving the group of prisoners standing quite perplexed in the center.

"Don't worry, it's me, Penny," she cried with jubilation after she was sure they had gone. Her scarred face looked down at them from the balcony, her smile looking quite unnatural on Esmond's pallid face.

Crane clapped his hands. "Great thinking, Gilbert!"

"Yes, good job," came a voice from behind her. "What shall we do next?"

Penny whirled around, coming face to face with Lord Esmond himself. She only glimpsed his crooked smile for a moment before she felt herself being hurled from the balcony. She hit the ground hard. She gasped for breath as she struggled to sit up. Crane and Griffin both rushed to her side. Her ribs felt like they were on fire. She wondered if they could be broken.

"I'm fine, really I am," she mumbled in a voice just above a whisper. "Tell the others to find a way out of here while I hold him off."

"You're not thinking straight," Crane objected. "I'm not going anywhere. You can barely stand on your own."

And it was true. She was swaying back and forth as she held her side.

"I'm not going anywhere either," Griffin chimed in.

Pete narrowed his eyes. "We can take this skinny nerd."

As they spoke, Esmond wound his way down the steps, humming to himself.

Crane looked at Derrick. "Get everyone out of here while we stall him."

He nodded and directed the others out the far exit.

"My, my, how touching and noble. What a shame. We hate touching moments," Esmond said, finally reaching the lower level. "They will never escape that way, you know. It's a veritable labyrinth of passageways with no exit except the one behind us. It is where we bury the bodies of expired prisoners. It is where you will end up." His eyes gleamed in excitement as he gazed at the four of them. "We shall rather enjoy killing you. It's been far too long since blood stained these hands." He laughed, looking down. "Oh, my mistake," he corrected, licking his long fingers. "We still have some from this morning. Our breakfast was cold, you know," he said, as if this somehow explained things.

Penny, who had turned back into herself once more, stood glaring up at him. "There are three of us, and one of you."

"Yes," Crane chimed in, "and we hear you have the ability of a one-legged dog."

Esmond's eyes flashed for a moment before he regained his composure.

"I'm afraid you were misinformed."

While he spoke, his hands began to rotate as if forming a ball. As they watched, a glowing sphere started to materialize in his hands. A buzzing, electric energy seemed to emanate from the sphere. An instant later, the sphere was hurtling toward them. They barely managed to jump out of the way. The energy ball hit a pillar, exploding on impact. A shock wave shook the building as it struck. Bits of stone rained down on them, covering them with dust.

Penny winced as she stood up again. The pain in her ribs was excruciating. Every breath caused a sharp, stabbing sensation to radiate through her body. She tried to cover up the pain she was sure must be showing on her face, by staring up at Esmond defiantly.

"Is that all you got?"

Esmond laughed and brushed off the bits of dust that had fallen on his shoulders.

"I'll wager that you're wondering—along with whether coming here was the biggest mistake of your lives—how I came to wield such great power."

Griffin and Pete fired upon him at the same time. Esmond held out his hands and casually stopped the arrow and fire in mid-flight, suspending them in the air.

"How deliciously quaint," he said with a smile then hurtled the objects back toward them. They both hit their targets. Griffin cried out as the bolt pierced his calf, and Pete flailed his arm, forgetting that the fire couldn't hurt him, as his already burnt sleeve danced with flames.

"I will answer both of your questions," Esmond went on as if nothing had happened. As all quite mad dictators were, Esmond was thrilled to share his brilliant plans with anyone who would listen.

"We managed to hunt down a few of your kind and use them in our magnificent machine. By infusing ourselves with certain particles in their blood, their nitrite energy then became ours. Unfortunately the machine overloaded after a couple uses. No matter though. It has now been repaired and improved, and your youthful energy is much more potent than my former patients. Soon you and all your friends will be ours. And to answer your first question, yes, coming here was the biggest mistake of your lives," he said, his voice growing higher with excitement.

🐿

Rainey, Derrick, and the others were hopelessly lost. Each corridor they walked down looked the same as the one before. Rainey stopped and leaned against the wall, trying to get their bearings, but it was no use. They had been in such a hurry to flee, that they hadn't paid any attention to where they were going.

"I don't think there is a way out this direction," Derrick began. "We should turn back."

"But even if that were true and we wanted to go back, I don't think we could," she said, pounding her fist against the wall. "Everything looks the same."

"We are going to starve to death!" a tall girl cried.

"No we're not," Rainey said. "We just need some sort of system. What if we only took right turns from here on? That can work right?" she asked.

Derrick shrugged. "It's worth a try anyway."

They set off again, this time using their new system. Every time they had to turn, they chose right. If there was no right turn available, they stayed straight.

"I lost my bracelet," a young girl whined after they had been walking for a bit.

Rainey ignored her and pressed on. She was sure they were making progress now. They had to be.

"Found it!" The girl exclaimed a few minutes later. "It was right here on the floor."

Rainey moaned aloud. That must mean they were still going in circles.

"You will never get out if you continue on like that," came a soft voice in the darkness. They all jumped and looked around. Rainey looked at Derrick. He shrugged. A couple of the younger children grabbed Rainey's arm for comfort.

"I can show you the way out," came the voice again.

"Who are you?" Derrick asked. "Show yourself."

A figure in tattered clothes dropped down in front of them. His eyes gleamed in the dark passageway.

As he took a step closer, they could see that this was no ordinary man. His pointed nose and bushy eyebrows took up most of his long face. His unkempt, white hair stuck up at odd angles above his prominent forehead. What struck them the most unusual, however, was that the man was only about half their size.

"I am Hargrim," he said. "Follow me." Without another word, the man turned and began walking swiftly down the corridor.

"How can we trust him?" Derrick questioned. The man was almost out of sight. They had to decide. Rainey shrugged. Not having a better alternative, Rainey started after the strange little man. They soon caught up. He stopped in front of a dead end, rubbing his large nose in thought.

"I don't think he knows where he is going," whispered Derrick.

"Shh," Rainey put her finger to her lips.

"Aha!" Hargrim proclaimed. He reached above his head and pressed a brick on the wall. The wall swung inward, revealing a hidden passage.

"This way," he said, continuing forward. They followed him through several more turns and finally climbed up through a trapdoor under the bridge that was in front of the main gate. They breathed in the cool evening air. It felt great to be outside. At one time or another, they had all questioned whether they would ever see the outside of a cell again.

"No time to waste—they will come looking for you all soon," Hargrim said. They scrambled up the bank after him and took a look around. Walking to the edge of the prison wall, Rainey was dismayed to discover that they were trapped. Below them, she could see only darkness.

"Can we climb down?" she asked Hargrim.

"Nay, the only way off this island is to fly, and to do that, we need a ship."

"You mean like one of those," Derrick said, pointing to several ships docked on the island.

"Perfect!" Hargrim exclaimed. "They must be here for the, uh, 'festivities' tonight."

They selected the nearest one and climbed the gangplank. The ship appeared to be completely empty.

"All aboard?" Hargrim called.

"Wait," Rainey said, "we can't leave without the others."

"Others?"

"Yes, they were fighting some crazy-looking guy. I think I heard them call him Esmond."

"If they are up against Esmond, then I'm sorry, but they are as good as dead. There is no hope for them now."

Chapter Thirty

Penny, who still held her side, tried to suppress the blood that came from a large cut on her forehead. The others were all in just as bad if not worse shape. Each time they tried to attack, Esmond would use their own ability against them somehow. When they weren't attacking, they were trying to dodge the endless array of energy spheres being hurled at them.

"Who is a weakling now? Who is powerless now?" Esmond said with a delirious laugh. "They said we were crazy! Well, now they are dead and we are in charge!"

She knew that their only chance to survive was to escape, but every time they approached a doorway, Esmond would strike the wall above the door sending debris showering down.

"We have to get out of here before he brings the whole place down on top of us," she said to Griffin who had just dodged a volley of his own arrows.

"Yes, but how? He's too strong."

"Maybe we could—" Penny stopped short as a blast above caused a large piece of debris to come tumbling down. She cried out as the rubble knocked her to the ground. She tried to stand, but found her legs pinned beneath the heavy stone.

"Well, this has been fun," he said with a yawn, "but we think it's time for us to be going. We know we should save you all for our machine, but killing you seems more delightful, and we have many more brats running around that we can pick up at our leisure." Esmond's eyes gleamed, and he raised his arms, preparing to strike her while she was down.

"Over here, you buffoon!" Crane shouted, trying to draw his attention. Esmond didn't seem to notice. He saw Penny's weakness, and he was ready to pounce. Crane tried again. "Hey, I'm talking to you. You...you weakling!" Esmond stopped and turned his head.

"What did you call us?"

Griffin seized this opportunity to lift some of the rubble from Penny's body.

"You heard me. Your powers are pathetic! You're nothing but a wannabe. If it weren't for you stealing power from little kids you would have nothing!"

Sweat glistened on Esmond's brow and his hands trembled with rage. When he spoke however, his voice was deadly calm. "We will catch you and skin you alive while your friends watch. Then we will see who is pathetic."

Esmond thrust his hand forward, pinning Crane to the wall with an unseen force. As Crane struggled to free himself from the wall, Esmond pulled a long, thin dagger from his cloak and began to descend the stairwell.

"My lord?" came a voice from above.

"What is it?" Esmond snapped as he turned to see the source of disruption. A guard stood at the door looking apologetic.

"Forgive me for interrupting, my lord, but we have a situation with the children from the cell."

Esmond waved him away. "Yes, yes, we know all about that. They are wandering the tombs. They won't escape."

"But, sir," the guard went on, "they have escaped, and they have taken one of our ships!"

"What? Why didn't you say so? Don't just stand there. Send out the warships and retrieve them!"

"Yes, my lord."

Esmond began to climb the stairs again, then stopped. "We will be along after we finish here."

The guard bowed and hurried down the hall. Penny was now able to stand, though her legs still felt wobbly. She leaned against Griffin for support.

Esmond turned his attention back toward Crane who was still struggling to free himself from the wall. "Sorry to cut this short. Don't worry though, it will still be plenty painful." Esmond rotated his hands in front of him creating a huge ball of energy. Satisfied that it was large enough to do the job, he sent the sphere hurtling at Crane.

Penny tried to run toward Crane, but she stumbled and fell. "No!" she cried, not even noticing her own pain as her ribs struck the floor.

Crane gritted his teeth and prepared himself for the blast. A horrible sizzling sound echoed throughout the room as the glowing object struck flesh. He gasped aloud and clapped his hands to his chest.

Expecting there to be more pain, he ventured to open his eyes and saw Pete lying on the ground in front of him, blood gushing from his side. Had he purposefully stepped in front of him to absorb the blow?

"Pete!" Penny shouted. She and Griffin rushed over to kneel by his side. Crane fell to his knees, the unseen force no longer holding him in place.

Crane sobbed. "Oh, Pete, why did you do it?"

Pete coughed violently before responding. "Because..." He paused to cough again. "I knew you were too much of a weakling to take it." Pete grimaced in pain then looked off into the distance. He gave a scream of agony before his head fell back and his eyes closed.

"No-o-o-o!" Crane charged at Esmond who was watching the scene with amused curiosity.

"Temper, temper," he chided, deflecting Crane's blow and tossing him aside. "Now, where were we? Oh yes, one down, three to go. We think we will just take care of you all at once. We are growing weary."

As Esmond spoke, he began to rise into the air as if lifted by an invisible puppet master. Penny froze, still hunched over Pete's mangled body. She couldn't think straight. Couldn't breathe. She didn't know what was coming, but she could feel the electric energy in the room.

"Prepare yourselves," Esmond cackled.

She felt herself being lifted to her feet. Crane and Griffin stood on either side of her, grasping her hands in theirs. Crane's hand was shaking, but his voice was steady.

"I'm sorry I couldn't protect you."

She gave his hand a squeeze. "I'm sorry I dragged you into this."

Crash!

Rubble fell all around them as a thunderous noise shook the room. Penny looked up, expecting the worst. Instead she was confused. Where Esmond had been standing laid a large ship. It had left a gaping hole in the wall where it had crashed through. A panel slid upward from the side of the vessel, and Rainey's head appeared from the opening.

"Need a ride?" she asked.

Penny didn't realize she'd been holding her breath. She let it out with a relieved sigh and fell to her knees, unable to stand anymore. Griffin bent down, scooped her into his arms, and ran toward the ship. Crane hesitated.

"What about Pete? We can't leave him behind." He grabbed Pete's arm and tried to drag him. "Somebody, help me!"

Rainey leaned forward, grabbed Penny's hand and helped pull her into the ship. "Look!" She motioned toward the place where Esmond had disappeared. Esmond's long, thin fingers were emerging from under the rubble. They could hear him breathing threats and curses as the debris began to fall away from his body.

Griffin looked back at Crane. "Come on! Pete died saving us. Don't let his death be in vain."

Crane paused for a moment in indecision. "Thanks, buddy," he said softly before releasing Pete's limp frame and racing to join the others. The ship was already rising as Crane approached. He jumped from atop a pile of debris and grabbed hold of Griffin's outstretched arms.

"We will destroy you all!" Esmond shouted after them, sending a blast toward the ship. The energy ball grazed the tail and sent them spinning. Penny held on to the side, trying to keep her balance. Esmond sent a few more blasts, but they were out of range now. The ship soon stabilized, and she collapsed into the nearest seat.

Her breaths came in ragged gasps. She felt numb to her injuries. Even her bruised ribs caused only a slight pang of discomfort. Her shoulders slumped as if a heavy burden had been placed upon them. She held her head in her hands as she tried to wrap her mind around what had just happened. She couldn't stop thinking of Pete. Crane couldn't either. He sat on one of the benches, rocking back and forth. Penny glanced out the window next to her. This time, the thick clouds were in their favor. With any luck, Esmond's men wouldn't be able locate them.

She stood up and hobbled over to Crane and sat beside him with a sigh. "It's not your fault, you know."

"I know. It's just that...well, he shouldn't have done it, that's all. It should have been me."

She tried to think of something comforting to say, but nothing came to mind. "Well I'm glad it wasn't," was all she managed. She hoped that was an appropriate thing to say. Now she was worried it sounded callous.

But Crane didn't seem to think so. He gave her a weak smile. "Thanks, I guess."

She gave his arm a squeeze.

Griffin approached them. "Sorry to interrupt, but we need to decide where to go."

Penny tried to push aside the tears she could feel welling up by focusing on what Griffin said, but his voice sounded like he was under water.

"Did you hear me? I was saying that Hargrim knows of a safe place he can take us among his people."

She tried to keep her voice even. "Who is Hargrim?"

"He helped us escape," Rainey explained from the seat ahead of them. "I think he's some kind of gnome," she added with a whisper.

"He is a builder," Griffin corrected.

"A what?"

Derrick appeared from the front of the cabin, looking alarmed. "There's a ship dead ahead, and it looks like it could be trouble."

Griffin sprang up and looked out the window. His look of trepidation soon gave way to a wide grin. "It's the Manatee! But they look like they are about to fire on us with the cannons."

❦

Onboard the Soaring Manatee, Captain Griswold was indeed getting ready to fire.

"The ship is in range, captain," Haldor announced.

"Good," Griswold said with a gleam in his eye. "I've been saving this round for a special occasion. It should be knocking them right out of the sky! Get ready to fire on me mark. Ready, aim—"

"Wait!" Phineas shouted from the crow's nest. "They are raising a white flag."

"I'm sure it be a trick," Griswold huffed.

Phineas squinted through the spyglass as he tried to get a better view. "They are opening the door now," he said.

"It's a trap. I'm sure of it," the captain cried. "Prepare to fire."

"Why, it's Penny!" Phineas called down. "Don't shoot. They have Penny aboard. I also see Crane and Griffin," Phineas said in surprise. "They appear to be waving. Well I'll be! I think they've commandeered the vessel."

Griswold steered the ship alongside them, and Penny, Crane, and Griffin boarded the Manatee.

"We will follow you," Penny called to them. "Tell Hargrim to lead the way."

"A builder is aboard," Griffin explained to Phineas. "He's one of the contacts on the inside we've had all these years. He says he knows of a safe place with his kind."

"Sanctuary?" Phineas shook his head. "No non-builder has ever been there."

Griffin shrugged. "Well then we will be the first."

"Anywhere sounds good as long as it be away from here," Griswold replied. "We need to be getting out of this place. Esmond is sure to be hunting us down soon."

"What's next?" Phineas asked. "The builders won't want us to invade Sanctuary. They chose to live apart for a reason. Many of them despise humans. They might even try to kill us themselves."

Griffin shook his head. "I guess we will have to trust Hargrim."

"If they do let us in, I guess we will find out once and for all if the portal to Terra exists," Penny said.

"The portal that supposedly leads to Terra?" Phineas shook his head. "Don't get your hopes up about that. Even if it does exist, we don't know if the builders who went to Terra were able to get the other one working again."

"I believe it," Griffin said. "We just have to have a little faith. The builders will help, and we will get everyone home."

"Where is Pete?" Phineas asked, looking toward the other ship. Crane looked down at his feet.

"He, um…"

"He is a hero," Penny interjected. "He died protecting us."

Haldor's face went pale.

"He's gone?" Haldor looked as if he were about to be sick. Phineas clapped his hand on his shoulder, wincing because of his still burnt hands.

"No better death than going in the line of duty," Captain Griswold said, staring into the distance.

"I think I need to go lie down," Haldor said, excusing himself and leaving the others to stand in silence. The only sound that could be heard was the mast flapping rhythmically in the wind. Crane broke the silence. His voice was flat but resolute.

"Esmond needs to die. I don't know how, but I'll kill him for what he did to Pete."

Chapter Thirty-One

They traveled all night and day, coming to rest behind a mountain range on a large island. The ships were lashed together, allowing the occupants to go from one vessel to the other. That night a large feast was held to celebrate their escape. Penny excused herself from the festivities and wandered out onto the main deck of the Manatee.

So much had happened in the last few days that it was just now sinking in. Their capture, their escape from the van, leaving her parents behind, Pete's death, the rescue. It was all too much. She wondered where her parents were now. Were they safe? Would she ever see them again? And now that they had rescued everyone, she had no idea what to do next. So many emotions that she had been holding back now bubbled to the surface. Her shoulders shook with a sob as tears began streaming down her face. Chip nuzzled her face with concern, and she held him close appreciatively, then gave an involuntary start as she felt a hand on her arm.

Crane let his hand fall. "Sorry, didn't mean to scare you."

Penny wiped the tears hastily from her face. "Oh, that's okay."

"Are you all right?"

"I'm fine. I mean, we won, right?" She tried to sound enthusiastic. He was silent, waiting for her to volunteer more. Penny shuffled her feet and picked at a frayed rope. "It just seems so hopeless though, you know?" she went on. "Trying to get our lives back to normal, I mean. It seems hopeless."

"But is that what you want? Normal?" He cocked his eyebrow. "Look at us. We're on a flying ship in another world! It's the biggest adventure of our lives. Besides, you're the incredible, amazing Penelope Gilbert. You got this."

Penny bumped him with her hip. "Thanks, I just wish I knew everything was going to be all right."

"Don't worry. Everything is going to turn out just fine. You'll see. Remember the time you almost drowned when you fell in the river and got pulled under that log?"

"Yeah, I remember."

"That seemed pretty hopeless, right? Well what happened?"

"You saw me fall in as you were walking by and you pulled me out," she said with a smile. "You saved me. I'll never forget that day. If you hadn't been there, I would have drowned for sure."

"Well I'm here now," he said softly.

Esmond brushed the dust from his hair. He shouted from one guard to another, a froth forming on the corners of his mouth. "How could you have let them all escape?"

"I'm sorry, sir, but you told us to leave the room. You were quite explicit, my lord.

"That wasn't us, you imbeciles! It was a poor imitation done by a raggedy, little girl. How could you mistake a gutter-crawling cur like her, for us?"

"Well she did look a lot like you."

"Silence," he shouted, running the man through with a jagged piece of stone. The guard gasped and fell backward.

"Anyone else have something intelligent to say?" The question hung in the air. Nobody dared speak. "We thought not."

"Sir," a man ventured after a moment.

"What is it?"

"This one still seems to be alive."

"Not for long," Esmond spat, striding over to where he lay. He stooped down and picked up a large stone. Raising it over his head, he prepared to bring it crashing down on the unconscious person's head. He started to swing the stone, but then stopped himself. "What is that you say?" Esmond muttered to himself. "Why yes, yes we could. What a good idea, my lord."

"Thank you," he replied to himself, quite overcome by his ingenuity. "We have always been resourceful."

He bent down to look at the figure. "Poor fellow, not a friend in the world," he said to the still knocked-out figure. "Your comrades seem to have abandoned you. And after you tried so hard to protect them. Don't worry, we can be your friends now. We wouldn't abandon you. We believe your name was Pete, wasn't it?"

End of Book One

About the Author

Emily A. Steward spent the better part of her childhood dressed as a ninja and trying to convince others to call her 'Ace.' When she wasn't saving the world from evil samurai, she could usually be found in the branches of a tree reading a good book. She now lives in the Pacific Northwest with her husband, three daughters, and dog Bentley. Though she seldom dresses as a ninja now, her adventurous spirit remains as does her love of tree climbing and reading good books.

About the Illustrator

Chad Steward is an elementary school teacher with a passion for art. He has been drawing most of his life, and dabbled in many different types of mediums. In his teen years, he became really angsty and only drew anime characters with cool-guy poses. In his later years, he diversified and began developing his talent as a graphic artist. Chad also loves llamas and alpacas. When he is not drawing, he's dreaming of petting their delightful fur.

CPSIA information can be obtained
at www.ICGtesting.com
Printed in the USA
FSOW02n0012221016
26360FS